God Bless the Child

by

Merilyn Howton Marriott

FIREFLY
SOUTHERN FICTION
LIGHTHOUSE PUBLISHING OF THE CAROLINAS

GOD BLESS THE CHILD BY MERILYN HOWTON MARRIOTT
Published by Firefly Southern Fiction
an imprint of Lighthouse Publishing of the Carolinas
2333 Barton Oakes Dr., Raleigh, NC 27614

ISBN: 978-1-946016-87-4
Copyright © 2019 by Merilyn Howton Marriott
Cover design by Elaina Lee
Interior design by Karthick Srinivasan

Available in print from your local bookstore, online, or from the publisher at:
ShopLPC.com

For more information on this book and the author,
visit: https://merilynhowtonmarriott.com/

Brought to you by the creative team at Lighthouse Publishing of the Carolinas
(LPCBooks.com): Eva Marie Everson, Yolanda Smith, Kay Coulter, Sue Fairchild,
and Evelyn Miracle

Library of Congress Cataloging-in-Publication Data
Marriott, Merilyn Howton
God Bless the Child / Merilyn Howton Marriott, 1st ed.

Printed in the United States of America

PRAISE FOR *GOD BLESS THE CHILD*

Often, the author writes, "I hate my job. I love my job." That's how I felt when reading this novel. I hate the brokenness of people. But then, the author assuages that by writing, "Their brokenness—unnoticed by a therapist or another loving, caring person who might have been able to reach them—left their lives spinning forever out of control." As I read *God Bless the Child*, I began to pray, "God bless the therapists." They are in a group to be appreciated, like those who spend their lives as public servants, caring for our physical and spiritual needs. The author has written an important novel, revealing that in the mental illness and emotion of brokenness there is treatment and hope.

~**Yvonne Lehman**
Author of 59 novels, 14 nonfiction books, and co-director
of Writing Right-A Mentoring Service

God Bless This Child is an intimate glimpse into a therapist's world of intense emotion, heartache, and heartwarming victories interwoven with faith. The beautifully written story, which continues the saga begun in The Children of Main Street, captured me from the beginning and held me captive until the end.

~**Pat Nichols**
Author of *The Secret of Willow Inn*, The Willow Falls series

The shingle reads, Catherine Collier: Licensed Professional Counselor. Katie, as she is known to her clients, offers us a glimpse into the uncertainties and sadness behind her profession through their stories. But, *God Bless the Child* also, along with Katie's expertise in bringing relief to desperate children and parents, portrays God's loving care for the details of our lives. Katie's solid faith and her prayers for wisdom in handling the depths of despair bring solutions and hope. Poignant sessions in Katie Collier's antique house in the small town of Port Arthur, Texas with its colorful flowers evoke a relaxed atmosphere yet with enough mystery, tension, and resolution to create a good read. Katie shows us how to reach out with our own gifts and callings to show others what a life with Jesus as its focus can be. Read *God Bless the Child* to understand how one person can make a difference in the community around her and yet be teachable herself.

~**Marlene Houk**
Author of *Hidden in a List: secrets from Bible women*

In God Bless the Child, Merilyn Howton Marriott's beautifully lyrical writing style is put on display showcasing her vast understanding of the human mind. The poignant stories of the children portrayed in the book will shatter your heart while her depiction of the Father's love will piece it back together again.

~Annette O'Hare
Author of *The Bolivar Point Lighthouse Series*

Merilyn Howton Marriott's book, *God Bless the Child*, engages the heart, mind, and gut as stories of children are told from the perspective of Katie (Kat) Collier, a clinical psychologist who analyzes terrible happenings to children and must make life and death decisions to seek best solutions. The first book in the series, *The Children of Main Street,* was irresistible. Merilyn Marriott may be creating a new phenomenon of readers who are co-dependent on her continuation of these lovable characters and their heart-wrenching and gut-punching stories. This is one book you will want to hug close and read again.

~Janice Garey
Book reviewer, a writer of short stories, poetry, and articles

ACKNOWLEDGMENTS

No one writes a novel alone. It takes a dedicated team and I'm grateful for mine. I would like to acknowledge my parents, Lewis and Marie Howton, who are gone but planted a deep love of God and His faithfulness in my heart. Watching their love of helping others led me into the professional counseling field.

Thank you to my sister, Patsy, who is my biggest fan other than my husband, Rick. Your endless willingness to read this novel over and over to help shape it is what being part of a large family is about.

To my daughter, Dana, my sweet girl and idea generator. When I'm stuck, you always think of something that pushes me onward.

Thanks to my sons, Jimmy and Michael, who believe I write well and tell me often.

To Ramona Robinson, my best friend in the world, you cheer me on. You pray when I'm discouraged, and make me laugh when I hear your voice. You are an ardent fan and a dedicated member of my launch team.

To my wonderful editor, Yolanda Smith. Working with you was a pleasure. You embraced this project, and the book is better because you touched it. Your hand print is indelible. You and I became great friends during this process and for that friendship I am grateful.

To my mentor and managing editor, Eva Marie Everson, my undying admiration and love. You take my calls even when you don't have time. You tell me everything will be okay when I can't see through fog. When I lose my way, you point the right direction. I owe my writing career to you.

To Eddie Jones at Lighthouse Publishing of the Carolinas, you took a chance by publishing my first novel, and now my second. I will forever be thankful.

To my agent, Linda Glaz, you go to bat for me every time I need you. Thanks.

To many other friends who believe in me and read my books. You know who you are and I love you. You guys are ever eager launch-team members.

DEDICATION

*To my husband, Rick, my partner, friend, and compass. You respect my
writing time and always believe in the words I put to paper. Your feedback
is always honest and inspirational. You pray for me, you encourage me,
but most of all, you love me. Your life gives mine meaning and purpose.
There is no Merilyn without Rick.*

Chapter 1

"He's how old?"

"Three."

I felt my brows lift. "In dog years?"

"No. He's a toddler."

"And he's been kicked out of day care and can never return?"

My assistant stood in my treatment room wearing her hard-to-resist begging face. Alicia always pled the cases of new clients I didn't have time to see. She wore fresh scrubs, dark blue pants with a white stripe racing down the leg, and a round-neck checkered top in a lighter shade of blue. She weighed less than a hundred pounds, and, despite her age, resembled one of the children for whom she petitioned. Concern dug fine lines around her mouth.

I waited for additional information.

"Katie, we got an urgent call from his mother, a gal who works at the college—"

I taught psychology classes at the university Tuesdays and Thursdays so I'd acquainted myself with most of the faculty and staff. "Who?"

"Marianne Miller." Alicia reached for the tiny silver cross dangling from her necklace.

I shook my head. "I don't know her." We walked into the hallway, halting for refreshments where I poured a cup of herbal tea and squeezed in a dollop of honey from the bear-shaped bottle on the counter.

"She's new in Student Affairs." Alicia glanced at her notepad. "She knows you … or about you. You've seen her ex-mother-in-law."

"I have seen—"

"Everybody's ex-mother-in-law," we chorused together.

"She wants to come on her lunch break."

"Ali, it looks like we'll both retire before we eat lunch again."

"Just you." She tucked straight chin-length hair behind her right ear. "I'm hitting a drive-thru for some grease when I run to the post office." She shrugged. "I'd bring you something, but you won't eat fast food."

"The phone call," I reminded her. "It was … Marianne?" I savored the aroma and flavor of my tea. "Wants advice concerning the child?"

"Not exactly." Dark brown hair slipped from behind her ear again. "The deal is, well, it's not Marianne seeking advice. She's bringing ..."

"Her *kid*," we said together.

Scary. I'd lost the ability to speak independently of Alicia. "Are you serious about him being three years old?"

"Terribly." She didn't scan her notepad this time, but tucked it under her arm. She possessed near-total recall when a child was in distress. "Day care called Marianne and said she has one hour to pick him up along with termination papers."

"Wow." I rattled through the drawer, fished out a spoon, stirred my tea, and stared at her. "Wasn't I supposed to start seeing more adults and fewer children?"

"Yes, and you will. But he's a baby. And this is his seventh day care." She stared at me, pitiful, pleading. "I didn't know there was a black list for toddlers, but there is, and he's on it." She made her signature side-to-side head wag while hunching her shoulders near her ears with arms still crossed. "No day care facility in this area will take him. If you don't see him, Marianne will have to quit her job."

"If I don't accept him ... and his name is? I gripped the curled cup handle and gestured widely. "Then—"

"Alexander."

"Thank you. Okay then, if I don't see Alexander, Marianne—whom I don't know but have seen her mother-in-law—will lose her job."

"Miller. Marianne and Alexander Miller, and yes," she said, falling into the familiar habit of nodding her head while sliding her cross. "That's pretty much it." Her deep brown eyes begged when she needed them to.

"Marianne is a single mom. It's just the two of them."

"Grab the phone book, girlfriend." I set my cup on the counter. "Check the yellow pages under psychologists to see—"

"If there is only one name listed." She finished my sentence again, leaving me with my mouth open.

"Tell her okay."

She grinned and shrugged again, "They're on their way." She tossed a "Ya know I love ya," as she headed down the hallway toward her desk.

Alicia was a divorced single mom. She'd dumped her near-useless husband, but then he'd stepped up as a reliable babysitter. Time and again she toggled between filing charges against him for nonpayment of child support and being grateful he was always home to manage their kids.

She would forever be a soft touch for other single mothers and youngsters.

2

I watched as she hacked her way through the jungle of child-rearing without a husband to help wield the machete. She navigated, along with twenty percent of America's population, the ins and outs of aloneness in a world where she'd expected and sought to walk as half of a greater whole. God love my Alicia.

A new client's arrival five minutes after the hour meant no time to fill out forms before I talked to the child. A door slammed in the driveway. They'd arrived.

#

Marianne Miller opened the front door of my clinic for her son. She appeared stomped down, and overwhelmed.

I walked into the foyer that doubled as a waiting room and stood observing, diagnosing.

"Alexander," Marianne said, "please walk through the door for Mommy."

He remained inert beside her. "Duht," he said, pointing to the front door.

"No, sweetheart." His mom touched the antique wooden door. "It's not dirt. See?" She held her fingers in front of him. "It's clean. The dark stains are part of the wood grain. Just the way this wood looks, baby."

The youngster strolled through the door like a placated barracks inspector. He posed tiny, his furtive detective eyes casing the joint. He exuded a fascinating su-casa-es-mi-casa sort of awareness. I knew instinctively that doctors' offices—probably including counselors' offices—were familiar territory for him.

His mom rushed in behind him effusing thanks that I would see him on short notice. Closing the door, she said "Hi, I'm Marianne Miller, and this is my son, Alexander."

The boy, a wiry little turkey, patrolled the foyer. His short blond hair spiked on top, held with stiff gel. His T-shirt was tucked into belted jeans and his shoes shined ready for military inspection. He inched close to chairs, tables, the antique dresser where a brown earthenware bowl full of peppermints sat on top. The wee fellow backed away from the counter surveying the pen and standing holder nestled beside the sign-in book. He peered at everything and noticeably touched nothing. Clear gray eyes scrutinized, while he kept his arms protected at his sides.

I pulled my eyes from Alexander to focus on his mother. "Hi, Marianne. I'm Katie Collier."

She propped against the closed door. "I'm grateful to finally meet you." She turned to watch me observe her son. "Thank you so much. Alexander's mee-maw said you could help him." Marianne searched my face. She needed me to nod, or say yes, or anything that would give her hope she could get her son back in the most recent day care he'd been kicked out of. "He's active," she said, "but he's adorable." She paused, struggling to say what came next. "He's odd. Kids don't like him."

I held up my hand to stop her, but she didn't—or couldn't—notice.

"Parents don't want their kids to play with my baby." The dam inside this mom—the one that had held back hundreds of words—crumbled.

"He's really a wonderful kid. His dad left because he couldn't handle the energy it took to be around him and I'm desperate. I mean not desperate ... but ... okay, I'm desperate. I love him so much. The thing is, I have to work.

"Friends told me before he walked he seemed different. I wasn't sure. He's my only child. I didn't know how a boy should behave. I only had sisters. We—"

"Marianne," I said firmly, "we're still in the foyer."

"Oh gosh," she said, bringing both hands to her flushed face. "I'm embarrassed."

"Don't be. It's best if you not say things in the foyer," I nodded toward Alexander without taking my eyes from hers, "that you might feel badly about later." I pointed to a chair. "I don't have lots of time, so I want to use the first few minutes with the little one."

She managed a shy smile and sat.

"Relax a few moments. Take a couple deep breaths, then fill out the paperwork." I gently touched the arm of this beautiful, blond-haired mother, who owned a pair of clear gray eyes—Alexander's eyes. "Really. Breathe. I'll chat with your boy, then I'll come get you."

Alicia, my long-time assistant whom I loved like a member of my own family, attempted to guide Alexander into the playroom while I calmed Marianne. I gazed, fascinated, when he refused to open the door for himself. "Jums," he said to Alicia, "I not touchin' that doah."

"Sweetheart," Alicia said to him, "this door was painted last week and cleaned this morning."

He scowled at her. "I not you sweethea't."

"Okay, I'll call you Alexander."

"You bettah 'membah."

"Promise." Alicia allowed him to stroll into the room without assistance.

Marianne glanced at me. "Are you sure you don't want me to come in with you?" Her eyes rounded and she bit her lip. "Alexander can be difficult." Her face held no color, and it appeared more than a lack of makeup. Marianne's lovely features had resigned to ashen.

"Not yet, but in a bit." I tried to calm her with my voice. "I need to see what he's like away from you. Your presence will change the way he interacts with me." At the playroom door I turned to Marianne again. She bordered the edge of despair. "You okay?"

She nodded.

"Alexander is adorable," I said.

"If you say that on your way out, I will fall at your feet."

"I bet I will." I turned and hurried into the playroom.

As Alicia exited the room, she read the message in my eyes: keep an eye on the mother, I'm worried about her.

"Alexander Miller." I scrutinized my little drill sergeant. "What a fine substantial name. I like it. I'm Miss Katie." He presented in an unusual manner. His movements measured. His appearance a bit too perfect. The way he stared at everything in the foyer but showed curiosity toward none. Correcting adults in a manner suggesting he stood in charge of all things. Something, or maybe everything, appeared all wrong.

He poised with his weight evenly distributed and hands plugged deep into both pockets. "Gimme some gwubs," he ordered.

"What?"

"Some gwubs. Gimme some fwikin' gwubs." He pulled his hands from his pockets and turned them palms up.

"Are you saying gloves?" I asked, unsure.

"Yeah." He shook his palms. "I want gwubs." He then spewed four-letter words I'd rarely heard from adults I knew.

I hadn't realized until that day such language could come through the lips of a three-year-old. "So, Alexander Miller with the good substantial name, you like to cuss."

He bobbed his blond head. "I say words I wike. I say—"

His list floored me. After I found my breath I said, "I think I got it."

He stared a hole right through me cussing like a foul-mouthed grown man in movies I don't watch.

"If you don't give gwubs, I'm leabin'." With palpable anxiety, he surveyed the room. He wandered to the shelves, but finding nothing of interest, continued to circle. He halted in front of the small child-level sink that had been installed when my daughter Bailey had spent hours in this room being tutored.

I pointed Alexander toward the Fisher Price table. "Will you sit?"

"Not till I hab gwubs."

"What would you do with gloves if I gave them to you?"

"Git me the fwikin' thangs and I show ya." He edged away from the sink and inched closer to the door.

Get a plan, girlfriend. I picked up my trusty little this-has-never-failed-me suction-cup ball, a favorite of kids from three to ten. I sailed it hard past his right ear, straight to its mark. It slammed onto the Plexiglas window behind his head. Melded to the window, the ball dangled impressively.

"That ain't gwubs," he said, turning up his nose and shaking his head.

"I don't have gloves."

"Is this a doctah's oppis or not?"

"Yes."

"Ah you the doctah?"

"Yes."

"Then you have gwubs." He extended both hands like he intended to prep for surgery.

"What do you like besides gloves?" My chance to engage Alexander grew tenuous.

"Hand over gwubs, and I tell ya."

"I don't give gloves."

"Then you ain't no doctah." He inched closer to the door, "and I leabin'."

"Hey, give a gloveless doc a break, will you? Do you like snow cones?" I wheedled.

"No." But he stopped and spun back to face me.

"What, then? You like *something*, Alexander Miller."

His eyes showed a glimmer of interest. "Umbwewwas, and bacuum cleanahs, and Pledge with a scent 'a wemon." Mercy, this child was adorable.

But he was also extremely ill.

Chapter 2

"Do you wear gloves when you vacuum?"

"Ah course. I ain't gittin duht on my hands. Hey, whewe my gwubs?" He examined his hands for an emergency dirt inspection.

I contemplated a pair of latex gloves stowed under the sink. That little turkey had been on to something when he'd stopped in front of it. I could get the gloves and pacify him for a moment but decided against it. It would be a short-term fix. Rewarding his symptoms would make him happy, but this kid needed to learn to live in the dirty world of day care with the rest of creation.

His eyes roamed.

"Do you like Mickey Mouse?" Please say yes.

"No, that Mickey stuff is fah sissies." His eyes jerked.

His anxiety held us both spellbound.

"Why don't you like school?"

"It stinks." He crinkled his nose. "And they take my cweanin' suppwies, and wock up the bacuum cweanahs."

"They lock up the vacuum cleaners?" I blatantly stalled for time.

"They do." He strung curse words together with abandon. "So, I poke 'em with my umbwewwas." His right fist jabbed at the air.

"Did you poke someone with an umbrella today?"

"Yeah." He assumed a full action-figure stance and stabbed again.

So far I knew what he felt obsessed to collect and what his favorite words were. Oh, and I knew he wanted to leave the premises. "Who did you poke?"

"Two sissies and a teachah."

"Two sissies and a teacher, what?"

"I fwikin' told you." He glared at me. "I poked two sissies and a teachah with a umbwewwa. Okay, thwee sissies," he self-corrected.

"I see."

He startled and scrutinized his feet. "This cahpet is duhty."

"I'll vacuum if you won't poke me with an umbrella."

"I wike to bacuum." He brightened. "Let me see you bacuum cweanah." He glanced at his hands. Then his eyes grabbed mine. He opened his palms and made a circling motion. He squinted. "Mothah—"

"Alexander," I said before he could speak the expletive.

"I can't hep. You don't have gwubs."

"It'll have to wait. You're right, I don't."

"Well, you can't bacuum without fwikin' gwubs." He shook his head. "Othah people touched it."

Oh, Lord, heal this beautiful child. "What kind of gloves do you like?" We hadn't moved from the middle of the playroom.

"Watex, gahden, bwown ones and long wubbah ones. I wike watex best. A doctah bwows em up and pwetends it's a animal … like a woostah or tuhkey."

"Why have you visited so many doctors?"

"Fwikin' ear infwections." He stared toward the door. "Whewe's my mom? She knows how to tie the gwubs."

"Into animals?"

"Yeah." He pulled his lips into an Elvis curl and raised his right brow.

"Does your mom have a boyfriend?"

"Hundweds."

Maybe, baby boy, but I don't think so. I suspect that Ms. Marianne has her hands full taking care of you. My teeth brushed my bottom lip. "Anyone special?"

"I hate em with my umbwewwas."

I tilted my head and leaned in closer. "You hate them, or you hit them?"

"Yeah. And I'm leabin'." He then turned on scuffless heels and closed the gap between himself and the door.

I dashed to catch him and opened it myself. "Please stay," I said while reaching for him.

He stepped away from my touch, back inside the playroom.

I eased into the foyer feeling humbled. "Marianne, I need you to come in after all."

I could tell she'd expected me. She hugged the edge of her seat, but rose and walked into the playroom. "You're probably going to need these," she said, pulling a pair of latex gloves from her purse. Her gray eyes searched for her boy.

He wasn't hard to find. Still stood dead center in the room.

I reached toward the gloves and passed them to Alexander. "Here you go."

He perceptibly calmed. "Thanks." He clutched them to his chest.

"What an adorable children's space," Marianne said advancing toward her son and laying a gentle hand on top of his head. "He didn't pay a lick of attention to it, did he?"

"No, sweetheart, he didn't."

Together we talked Alexander into sitting at the small play table after I cleaned and disinfected it. He wanted to help but I didn't have his special cleaners. He insisted I wrap the soiled paper towels in Saran Wrap. I complied—having the plastic stowed under the sink—mostly to assess the extent of his obsessions.

"Did you give him latex gloves?"

"No. I needed to see what happened when I withheld them."

She pulled additional paper towels from the roll and fed them into my still-damp hands. "He has two hundred and ten pair, folded and stacked in see-through sealed containers. They are sorted by fabric and color—most are latex gloves."

"I hab eben moah when I leabe here."

"No, you won't," she said. "We have a three-year supply at home."

After Alexander seated himself at the colorful table, I set a box of crayons and a large sheet of paper in front of him. He picked through the box finding a few that were unbroken and appeared new. His mom and I sat near him, facing each other in two antique rockers upholstered in pink and white plaid.

For the most part he sat quietly, drawing. He didn't look at us, but listened and corrected his mother over any disparate detail.

Marianne described life with her son. There were not hundreds of boyfriends. There were none. No second dates with the mother of Alexander Miller.

"His room contains a bed and a table. No lamp. He owns twenty-seven flashlights in assorted sizes."

"No, I do not." Turning to face us, he said, "I hab twenty-eight of those fwikers and you know it." Bristling, he turned his face away again.

Marianne raised her right hand in courtroom solemnity. "God, as my witness, Katie, he did not learn that language from me."

"It's indirectly part of his disorder."

"No, it's not Tourette's syndrome," she insisted. "I've already asked his pediatrician about that."

"No, it is not Tourette's. That's why I said the cuss words are indirectly part of the disorder."

She leaned toward me as though desperate for information.

"The words don't spew involuntarily as in Tourette's. It's his anxiety level that's near debilitating. He feels a loss of control due to his obsessive thinking. The first time he heard a cuss word he repeated it like any two- or three-year-old."

Marianne's eyes glued to mine.

"When he got a reaction, whether adults laughed or were shocked, he felt empowered, leaving him to focus on reactions instead of his ever-present, free-floating anxiety. My guess is he uses these words like weapons. They have become tools in his arsenal to stave off out-of-control feelings."

Marianne stared, blinking. "Tell me more about him ... the way you see him." She gazed at her son, then at me.

"I will. But it's okay," I said. "He's okay right now."

Marianne pulled a calming breath.

I reached across and squeezed her hand, then nodded, encouraging her to talk.

"He has no toys. None. He helps with cleaning chores under tight conditions, using his own supplies, his vacuum cleaner ... cleaners. He has," she stopped for a minute and counted on her fingers, "seven. And nine dust busters." She glanced at Alexander to assure her count was accurate.

The emperor nodded.

"His only other interest is umbrellas. His collection sports nineteen." She peeked his way.

Again, he bobbed his head.

Marianne continued. "He seems to use the pointed end of his umbrellas as weapons to defend himself from demons and to disassemble furniture he doesn't want in his room."

"Okay."

"There are hundreds of holes in his sheetrock walls, and my final attempt to place a chest-of-drawers in his room granted him access to the ceiling." She blew upward, dancing her bangs. "Fourteen holes were umbrella-punched before the chest could be removed." She sighed. "Alexander runs the house with an iron fist sheathed in a spot-free white glove."

Rearing her son had reduced Marianne to a white-socketed, tight-fisted bundle of exposed nerves.

"I have to work. I need the money for flashlight batteries alone." Her chin quivered as she attempted a smile.

I grabbed more tissues. "How much sleep does he require?"

"I hate sweep."

Fresh drops crawled toward Marianne's mouth. "Twenty minutes ... spread over the last three years."

"Marianne, I'm glad you're here."

She glanced up, face lit. "Really? Almost no one has been glad to see me since Alexander turned two." Tears flowed unchecked.

I handed her the whole box of tissues. "Marianne, I can help you but not enough. He needs a psychiatrist. He's too young to be diagnosed, but he is textbook classic obsessive-compulsive and his disorder will require medication."

"I know." She bobbed her head and dabbed at her eyes. "He's bad. I'm a bad mom."

"He's not bad. He's ill. And bad moms don't ask to bring in their kids. Courts order them here."

"His mee-maw said to bring him here because you wouldn't put him on medicine." She turned and lobbed wet tissues into a nearby trashcan. "I don't want to drug my kid. I want him to behave." She pressed her fingertips into both temples.

She dropped her hands back into her lap. "I want him to go to day care and get along. He needs to let me put sheets and a pillow on his bed, and for goodness' sake, I wish he would wear pajamas instead of his father's worn-out T-shirt. I want him to sleep, for crying out loud."

"He can't."

"I want his father to take some responsibility."

"Me too."

"I want us to have a life together, and for him to let me have friends. I'd like for him to stay with my mom sometimes."

"I know."

"I want him to be happy."

"He can't be."

"What *can* he do? What can *you* do?" She pointed a trembling finger.

"Get him to a child psychiatrist today for an evaluation and medication."

"No, you can't. I've tried them all. No one can see him till September. This is May. Did you know this is May? How long until fall?"

"Yes, I know it's May." I looked into the face of this worn-out mother and longed to tuck her into bed and read her a story. "I am aware that September is months away ... and how endless those many weeks feel. But I have a few connections and yes, I can get him seen today."

She shook her head.

But I nodded. "That's my part. Unless the doctor I call is out of the country—and if she is, I'll call someone who isn't—your son will be seen today."

She reached up and pressed her temples again, massaging them with circling fingertips. She looked at her son. "I'm willing to do anything to make him better."

"Sit right here." I stood and laid gentle hands on her shoulders. "Marianne, Alexander is adorable." I smiled down at her. "I'll grab Alicia to make the call."

The little turkey stowed his gloves behind his back. "And get me some gwubs," he demanded, extending naked hands.

Marianne laid her face in her hands and wept.

"Stop it, Mothah," Alexander said. "Stop that cwyin'."

She didn't stop.

Chapter 3

I ushered them out the door, and toward a waiting psychiatrist, without Alexander touching any unclean thing. From Ali's desk I heard my finally-failed-me ball lose suction and drop to the floor. I stepped back into the playroom and scooped it up as exhaustion attacked me like a linebacker.

Returning, I tossed the useless ball into Alicia's waiting hands.

"Wow," she said, catching the ball. "How sad was that?"

My clinical work is confidential, but the early portion of this child's session played itself out in the foyer while Alicia had attempted the art of invisibility.

"On a scale of one to ten, I'd give it a nine." I leaned over the sign-in counter to chat with her. "Thanks for working your magic with the doctor's office."

"It's my contribution. It's the small part I can do." She smiled, looking shy.

Alicia was a conundrum of hard-to-sort-out characteristics. She spoke her mind in a rambling, meandering trail of words, oblivious to others who might want to speak. However, when praise of any sort bestowed itself upon her she turned into an embarrassed, self-conscious gal with pink crawling up her neck. Her incessant chattering notwithstanding, she overflowed with kindness and goodness.

"It's not small."

"So, will he be all right?"

"It's a hard one. Marianne is in this alone, as you heard. It's part of the mystery of the universe that some parents divorce their children. Marianne didn't have time to both make another appointment with me and get to the psychiatrist on time. Follow up hard on this one. I want to see this kid get better."

Alicia smiled. "Don't I always?"

"Yes."

She tossed my ball back. "Kat, I hate when fathers walk."

"Me too."

Her brows arched. "We both practically live here, but what do we really accomplish concerning dead-beat dads?"

"Pick up behind them, one child at a time."

"That's not enough." Sad drew itself on her face.

I walked around the counter and planted a small kiss on top of her head while hugging her shoulders. "How right you are. But try putting it up against doing nothing, and it gives us a reason to come to work every day." I waited until she smiled again. "Don't forget about Alexander."

"Yeah." She gave her characteristic shrug. "Couldn't you tell, I'll forget about him every day for months? Maybe even forget about him every day for years."

She dropped her head and scanned insurance claims.

#

Later that afternoon, Alicia reported that Marianne called. The psychiatrist's visit had been a success. Too early to diagnose, but absolutely OCD. He started medication that day. The doctor expected Marianne to see immediate improvement in his behavior. Her mother became willing to keep him on a short-term basis if he took his medicine, and a new local day care—where Alicia knew the owner and had placed a call—offered to take him for a probationary period. Marianne scheduled several weeks in advance to bring him back to me.

Sometimes I loved my job.

Chapter 4

The clinic on Main Street nestled beneath giant gnarl-limbed oaks and magnolias with shiny emerald-green leaves and huge white blossoms that perfumed the spring air—a symbol of the south and reminiscent of my Alabama childhood. A fence of red tips stood sentinel around the perimeter of the spacious backyard and fragrant gardenias bloomed alongside lantana overflowing well-tended beds. Huge concrete pots of petunias and begonias bookended both the front and side porch steps. Yellow hibiscus stood in tall urns smack dab in the middle of the large front porch. Ivy grew in abundance in the backyard beds, spilled onto the edge of the rear veranda, crawled to the railing beside the back steps then curled its way up and around the wrought iron. Beautiful weather had finally arrived in Port Arthur, erasing the memory of January's unprecedented ice storm. The clinic looked beautiful wearing its spring dress.

I loved this property and had planted most of the potted flowers myself when we'd remodeled the building—an old house jacked up on cement blocks. The trees had been growing for generations. Cypress swings and matching rocking chairs—painted white to compliment the cast-iron columns that flanked both porticos—created a glorious focal point for the entrance and posterior of the building. The piazza greeting the clients served as an overflow waiting room during the few beautiful days of spring and fall that southeast Texas offered while the back porch served as an extra treatment room—a favorite for kids.

My shingle hung outside the clinic's old oak door: Catherine Collier, Licensed Professional Counselor. Other names on additional shingles hung beneath mine. We'd recently hired a social worker and two counseling interns.

#

Clients filled my thoughts as I drove my car—a black convertible with the top down—toward the clinic. Wind and hair swirled around me creating one of those carefree moments I savored. I loved owning a practice where hurting people came for help and hope.

My heart soared because it was Friday. One of my favorite patients waited for me at 10:00. At 9:50 I turned into the driveway, parked beneath the tin-roofed carport, then entered through the back door. Before I reached the front desk to check on Alicia and scope out my schedule, Billy Martin ran down the hallway and jumped into both my arms.

I belly laughed. I'd loved that kid from the first day he'd trekked into my office wearing cowboy boots and a jacket during the stifling heat of a Texas July. He'd slapped me across the face at session's end on his first visit. His mother brought him, seeking relief for herself through medication she'd anticipated I would give him. But I don't drug kids for being kids. Instead, I'd taught him rules and boundaries, what behaviors I would and would not tolerate. Within a short intervention period he proved to be a great little boy.

Billy slipped both arms around my neck.

"You little turkey," I said, "you're squeezing my head off."

"Cuz I luv you and I miss you." He leaned back in my arms so he could peer into my face. "Why can't I come here ever' day?"

I beamed but an aching sadness slipped into place. "You come every Friday."

"This here looks like your house, so why can't I live in it?"

"Want to come home with me for dinner?"

"Yes. Yes. Yes." He squeezed harder.

"'Kay. 'Kay. 'Kay." I kissed his cheek. "I'll have Alicia phone your mom and if it's okay with her, it's great with me." His mother, Cindy, always gave permission when Billy wanted to go home with me. She would probably like it if he "lived" with me.

"Let's say hello to Miss Alicia before we start our session."

"I already said hello." He scrunched his nose. "She comed to school with a note and gotted me."

"Well, I still want to let her know I'm here." I let Billy slide down my hip, took his hand, and we walked to the front. "Good morning, Ali." I walked behind her desk and hugged her from the side.

She peered up, smiling. "Being a mother looks wonderful on you, Kat ... not to mention you glow." She turned her chair to face me. "Sometimes dreams have a way of coming true. Your hair looks good today."

I winked.

"Did you eat breakfast? I have fresh fruit in the fridge and brewed your tea all ready." She retrieved a pen rolling off her desk. "How did class go last night? Did I mention you look great?"

"Thank you. I ate but I'll grab a tea. And thank God, dreams and miracles have flooded my home." I held onto Billy's hand. "I'm both humbled and grateful." Jordan and I had waited fourteen years for a baby before God blessed us with our seven-year-old daughter, Bailey. Jordan and I had separated last year—before we adopted our little girl—but with God's help and changes in my attitude and work habits all things were new again between us.

"We have a full house today, so you'd better get started," Ali said.

Billy pulled at my hand. "Don't ferget 'bout me." He'd been my client for a year and had just turned five. He flourished with an adult who cared for him and made decisions with his best interests in mind. With me, he was well mannered and eager to learn. He loved being hugged and basked in the smile of someone's approval. He would jump through hoops to earn the joy of an "atta boy."

"I'd never forget about you. You're my favorite part of today's full house."

His brows knit. "'Kay."

My heart swelled as we entered the kids' room.

#

During Billy's first months as my patient, I'd hoped I could bring some order to his household. Though not a social worker, I made several trips to his home. I thought by going, I might teach his mom basic parenting skills. I attempted to explain a few housekeeping tricks so Billy would have a safe place to grow, but it didn't happen. Cindy showed interest in computer games, chat rooms, cigarettes, and whining about her children.

I discovered during my house calls that neither Billy nor his baby sister, Sara Beth, owned a bedroom. Or a bed. Both slept on the living room sofa. The family's only television stood in the same room. According to Cindy it entertained the family every evening until midnight or 1:00 a.m. If the volume I heard upon entering their home indicated its normal setting, that left Billy and Sara Beth to either stay awake until the wee hours or give up early and pass out. Billy always seemed tired. His teacher had mentioned his exhaustion when Alicia had driven to school to retrieve him. The teacher still harbored hope I could influence Billy's mother. Months earlier my optimism had seeped, then rushed as water from a colander.

At the clinic Billy learned to finish his puzzles in the allotted time and draw his way out of any maze. Unlike what his mother reported when she'd first brought Billy, he was not attention deficit—or hyperactive. He proved to be a delightful and smart little boy who just needed the right kind of attention. There were no outbursts from him ever … well, after the initial slap, and everyone at the clinic loved when he called Fridays, "Miss Katie Day." We were all glad to see him. With the addition of our social worker, Angie, and interns, Olivia and Ron, I was no longer the only counselor at the practice. This was part of my change in attitude.

At the end of his session I rewarded Billy with three one-dollar bills for work well done. He smoothed the cash in his hand and a sly look tugged the corners of his eyes. "Miss Katie, let's go next door and spend it all for candy."

"No, let's not." I laughed. "You don't need that much sugar. Take the money home and put it in your piggy bank."

"What's a piggy blank?"

"Silly goose, you know what a piggy bank is. A safe place to keep your money until you save enough to buy something special."

His eyes registered confusion.

"You mean for cigarettes?"

"What?" Bitter bile pushed its way to my throat. I tried with everything in my power to help the kids who came here. I did not need their parents working against me.

"Ever' time you give me money my mom buys cigarettes."

"Billy," I said through clenched teeth, "let's go next door and spend this money for candy."

And we did.

With his hand clutched in mine, and his other grasping a good-sized bag of candy, we walked from the store and back through the front door. "Buddy, Alicia will call your mom, and I'll swing by your house after work and take you home with me for dinner. But I'll take you back after we eat. Got it?"

"I tol' you I want to live with you."

I straightened his shirt. "Sweetheart, if you're gonna cry when it's time to leave, I can't pick you up. Your mom doesn't like it when you return crying."

He dragged the toe of his sneaker—that my husband Jordan and I'd bought him for Christmas—across the carpeted floor. He pouted then thinking better of it said, "I'll be s-o-o-o sweet."

I hugged Billy again before handing him over to Alicia. "She'll call your mom and tell her what time I'll be at your house."

"Okay, Miss Katie. I want peppermints too."

"Sure." I pressed palm to forehead as he dug his hand as far as he could into the bowl, causing excess candy to rain from the jar. He scarfed those up also.

He left happy as they walked toward Alicia's car. Candy dripped down his chin.

I opened the small window in the antique door that had once been a mail drop and watched as he trotted down the front steps. Enough couldn't be poured into Billy's life in fifty minutes a week and I hated when he left.

Still holding Alicia's hand, he stalled on the bottom step and turned around. "Miss Katie, did I forgotted to say I luv you?"

I opened the door and stepped onto the porch. "You didn't forget. I love you too."

He tossed one last baby-toothed grin.

Oh, my heart.

He climbed into her car, strapped himself into his car seat and waved through the back window until they drove from sight.

Standing, waving, a chill flooded my body in ninety-degree heat. What? It was more than a lack of beds or a mother whom I believed would allow Billy to live with me. Raw fear for the two youngest Martin kids caused my heart to drum and thud. Strange.

Chapter 5

A police officer in full uniform walked through the front door as Alicia and Billy drove away.

I extended my hand. "Hi, I'm Catherine Collier."

He reached his right hand for mine, taking it with a firm grip. "I'm Stephen Giovanni and I have an appointment with you at eleven o'clock." He released my hand and glanced at the watch circling his left arm. "Now."

He stood average height, broad shoulders, athletic build, coal-black hair, and intense dark eyes. Maybe thirty, thirty-two. Good looking, and when he smiled his eyes lost a bit of their intensity.

"My assistant stepped out for a minute, so let me find the paperwork I need you to fill out." I peered over the counter and spotted the form on a clipboard where Ali had left it. A yellow sticky-note with his name clung to the front page.

He reached for it before I could and lifted it over the counter.

"I'll need you to fill in these forms then attach your driver's license and insurance information to the top. Can I pour you a coffee while you complete this?"

"Yes, thanks, and black, please."

I pointed. "I'll be right down this hallway at the refreshment bar. Let me know when you're finished or just lay the papers over the counter and walk down the hall. My office is the last one on your left." I poured a hot caffeine pick up for Officer Giovanni and a mug of Red Zinger with honey for myself. Just as I'd filled both our containers, he walked toward me.

I handed over his drink and stepped behind him into the treatment room. "Have a seat." I signaled toward the over-stuffed sofa and the large comfy chair.

"Seeing a therapist is not exactly my style," he said as he seated himself. His gun squeaked against its leather holster, so he re-adjusted the weapon.

"I figured." I sat in my green recliner. "Do you have the completed forms?"

"No. I'm sorry. I dropped them on the desk where I found them." He stood. "Shall I grab them right quick?"

"I'll scan them later." I fetched a notepad and pen from the drawer inside the table by my chair, and wrote his full name, date, and time. "We'll do this informally."

"Nice." His eyes roamed my room. "I expected the pictures. Is that your family?"

"Yes. That's my husband, Jordan, and our daughter, Bailey." I smiled again, trying to put him at ease, hoping to make talking easier for him.

"I didn't expect a sink and folded towels to be in here." He chuckled.

"I know. But on occasion a client gets sick in here. A couple people have passed out and I needed to assist them." I felt his discomfort mount. Men hate asking for help. And this man was a police officer, accustomed to giving, not receiving it. "How can I assist you, Officer Giovanni?"

"Call me Steve. I won't be passing out."

"Call me Katie. I won't be wiping your face."

We both laughed.

"My wife and I are building a new home."

"Congratulations. That's an exciting time."

"I thought it would be. It should be."

"Problems?"

"The house is coming along. I think it's beautiful."

"I can imagine."

"My wife obsesses over each tiny detail in every room."

"Women do that sometimes."

"I started out excited about the house." He sipped his dark brew and nodded his approval. "But nothing about it is good enough for her. Every morning she presents a list of things she expects me to confront the contractor over." He placed his mug on the side table. "Me, mind you. She feels no need to challenge anyone."

"Not anyone?"

"Well, she has no problem opposing me." Black brows arched. "I don't see anything wrong with the house. I like it."

"Building a new home can be stressful."

"Stressful? Have you ever had a couple divorce while building?"

"Not any of my clients but statistics report many couples don't make it through construction to move in together."

"I'm sure." He looked again at the family pictures I'd showcased on a shelf over the sink and on a four-tier corner bracket to his left. He stared for a long time. "There may be an unrelated reason I'm experiencing so much anxiety just trying to get a residence built."

"Huh." I'd felt like something else lurked in Steve's mind. Some men would come to see me about problems related to building a house, but he didn't seem the type.

"I've been a police officer a long time." His fingers found the sharp crease in his gray pants. "I entered the academy the minute I turned twenty-one. After high school, I kicked around a couple odd jobs and took some classes at the university but hungered for the birthday that would grant me academy access."

"A man who pursued what he wanted. Do you enjoy your job, officer?"

"Steve, remember?" He gazed at me. "Most of the time. I started out loving it, couldn't imagine doing anything else … but horrible things happen, and sometimes to the best people."

"That would be difficult."

"I know I came to talk about a house … and my wife, but the pictures of your little girl distracted me."

I nearly pitched forward from my chair. "My daughter?"

"Yeah."

I don't know why the mention of my daughter made me so antsy. "Do you want to talk about it?" I shifted in my chair. "Do you have a child?"

"No. And don't intend to."

"There must be something about a child."

"I have seen many terrible things. Picked up bodies off the highway. Walked into houses never knowing what I'd find."

"We appreciate your work to keep us safe. Thank you." I reached for my mug. "But I'm not sure I could do your job."

"I couldn't do yours either."

We both paused, but his eyes grew more intense, turning an impossible shade of black.

"Your work must have involved children."

He didn't answer but studied the pictures of Bailey.

"Is there a little girl you need to talk about?" I returned my refreshment to the table.

"I'm not sure if I can. A house is easier."

"Steve, did you come here about the house?"

"I thought so." He coughed. "Now, I'm not certain."

"Let me freshen your cup of joe." I stood and reached for his empty mug and grabbed mine by the handle with the same hand. "While I step out, decide what you want to talk about. Whatever that turns out to be is okay." I opened the door and stepped toward the refreshment area.

His eyes glistened with unshed tears when I walked back in and handed him fresh coffee.

"Steve?" I nudged the door closed with my heel, placed my mug on the side table, then settled back into my chair.

"Some things involved in police work are harder than others."

"I'll bet." I pushed my foot against green carpet, setting my chair in motion, then sipped the warm flavor of summer.

"Wow. I don't know if I'm prepared to discuss this."

"We don't have to discuss anything until you're ready." I waited. Primed to listen.

His eyes locked on Bailey's picture. "She reminds me of the hardest case I ever handled." He squinted at her photo. "Almost haunting in its familiarity."

"In what way?"

"I took a domestic disturbance call in Nederland about a year ago." He coughed.

"May I get you a glass of water?"

"Please."

I slipped from my chair, grabbed an Evian from the fridge, then re-entered the room and handed it to him.

He swigged it gratefully. "Thanks."

"A domestic disturbance ..." I said, tracking him.

"Yeah." He set the bottle on the sofa table, careful to place it on waiting coasters.

"It's been about a year now."

"Yes, you mentioned that."

"About the same time since I've slept through the night."

"I'm sorry. It must've been bad. Do you want to tell me what happened?"

"I took the call when it came to the station. I grabbed my gun and badge, informed my partner, and we took off." He sniffed.

I sipped my steaming Zinger.

"While en route, we received another call from the chief apprising us of gunshots fired at the same address."

"Okay."

"I've told no one except the captain about this."

"That's all right."

"I try to keep my work at work. Too many divorces at the department."

"I understand."

"So many domestic disputes are just that ... disputes. But they can be the worst calls we receive. Someone had fired a gun. Still, it could've been an accidental discharge."

I cupped my chin with my hand and listened to his pain.

"It wasn't."

"I gathered."

"We drove to the address, an apartment building. Neighbors waited for us, pointing toward a flat on the first floor." He blinked, his troubled eyes the deepest black.

"From the fear plastered on the faces of neighbors, we were certain this call would not be typical. We drew our guns as we neared the door, standing ajar. We announced ourselves as the police and asked that everyone drop their weapons and come out with their hands in the air."

I realized I'd been holding my breath. "And?"

"And nothing. No one came out. Not one sound from inside the apartment."

"Okay."

"As we approached and tried to enter, two people ... bodies ... lay in the doorway." His head shook back and forth.

Trauma drew fine lines on his face.

"A woman, face down on bottom with a man sprawled on top of her. I felt for a pulse just in case, but sure enough they were both dead. We stepped over them to enter the apartment. We had no clue who else might be in there." He stood and walked to the window, staring into the back yard.

"Was there ... anyone else?"

"No, but we couldn't be certain. As we moved deeper inside, we found all kinds of toys ... toys that belonged to a little girl."

This story sounded a bit too familiar. My brain sought to flee the room. A drummer invaded my temples, and something vacuumed the air from my lungs. Coincidence. *Please God.*

"We looked for a tiny body, scared to death we would find one."

"Did you ... find one?"

He kept staring outside. "No. Thank God. No." His deep breath was an obvious attempt to regain composure.

"After we walked through the apartment, we moved back outside to look around and ask about a child. I saw a little blonde-haired girl who cried and struggled to break free, while a lady—who turned out to be the neighbor who'd called—held her back. The child tugged against the woman in an attempt to run toward the apartment we'd just secured."

Ropes looped themselves around my middle and pulled tight. I needed to make a response. I had a job to do. When I was able I said, "Was she the child who lived in the apartment?" As if I didn't know. That child was my daughter. I'd taken her home with me after this murder he described.

"Yes. She and her mom—the female victim—lived there. The male had been her mother's boyfriend. According to the neighbor, the child's mother had left the boyfriend and moved into the apartment two weeks prior. She had become afraid of him after he'd threatened both her and the little girl. The lady reported that her new neighbor, Sue Russell, had asked her to keep the child in the playground after the unexpected arrival of her friend." He shrugged. "When the neighbor—a Mrs. Hernandez—heard the shots, she called 911 and held onto the child. She saw Sue come to the door screaming but then watched her fall in the doorway. She said all she knew to do after she made the call was to keep the little girl safe."

Steve turned to look at me through haunted eyes and returned to his chair. Anguish painted his face with a wide brush.

The walls crowded me. A gray fog swamped the room. It could be another little girl. No, it could not. Bailey's last name had been Russell. Still, Russell was a common enough name. *God, please help me. And hurry.*

Steve peered at me expecting me to say something … something consoling … like I had said a thousand other times to a thousand other hurting people.

"I'm so sorry." Did I feel most sorry for him or for myself or for my sweet Bailey?

"I've been on tragic calls before, of course, so I'm not sure if the reason I can't get past this one is because the lady came so close to getting away, or if it was the little girl crying— although I've never been so glad to hear a child cry in my life—or the cruel nature of evil men in general, or the fact that the female victim had punched 911 into her phone but never had time to hit send … or just everything. Absolutely everything."

"My guess is everything," I managed to whisper. "What happened next?"

"Well, we were there a long time. I phoned the coroner and the neighbor took the child inside her apartment and told us where to find her."

"Okay."

"After we secured the scene, we knocked on the neighbor's door and asked about other relatives of the child. The little girl was six and knew her father's name. The neighbor wrote it on a scrap of paper, then handed the paper and the child over to us. I took her by the hand and could have sworn I had control of her. But in an instant, she jerked her hand free and ran toward her apartment— by then a crime scene." He reached for a towel and wiped his brow. "I darted behind her but she was frightened and ran like the wind. By the time we caught her—thank God, the coroner had removed the bodies—she was inside her home. We bolted after her, but she circled like a wounded animal inside the apartment. My partner and I ran in two different directions so we could rescue her. We did," he wiped his brow again, "but she had blood all over her. The bottoms of her tiny feet tracked bloody footprints everywhere. Putting that grief-stricken child in the squad car stands among the hardest things I've done. A patrol unit is no place for a six-year-old."

"It couldn't possibly be." The treatment room swelled with heat. Sweat dripped from every part of me. Taking notes would mean hanging onto a pen, but my fingers were slippery and perspiration dotted my forehead.

"You seem warm."

"Me?" I wiped my face on a tissue that peeked from a box on the chairside table. "No, no, I'm fine," I lied.

"You're probably not used to hearing stories this graphic," he said, "I'm sorry if this one upsets you."

"I have listened to more heartbreaking stories than I can count." Just not about my beautiful child. A lot of this I knew. Some of it, I didn't. I tried to keep my composure.

"Maybe if I can get this out of my head, I'll sleep." He shrugged. "I might even manage to get a house built and stay married while doing it."

"What happened after you put the child in your car?"

"The little girl?"

"Yes, her."

"Carried her to the station and handed her with care to the chief. We had radioed ahead and given him the child's father's name. He'd located the name and address. The captain called the house but no one answered. He drove to their home and a neighbor told him they were at their lake house and found a cell number to give him." Steve shook his head. "My partner and I took another call. When we returned to the station the captain and his secretary were entertaining the little one. I believe her name was Hailey ... or something close. She waited for her father. The lake house turned out to be on Cook's Lake."

"I see."

"She was still there when my shift ended."

"Sad."

"Yeah. I couldn't sleep that night. I asked the captain about the little girl the next morning. He didn't say much but seemed troubled by her stepmother's attitude when they arrived to collect the child." He rubbed his hand across his forehead. "The captain's secretary seemed to be in a snarky mood too. I didn't press the issue. My stomach felt queasy from the day before. It still bothers me."

I knew all about Bailey's father's wife, Jillian. Jillian Reynolds Russell. "I can tell. Our time's up for today, but I hope you'll come back."

"I will. I'm surprised myself, but I intend to come again."

We both stood. He pointed toward a picture of Jordan. "Did I tell you that Dr. Collier is my thesis chairman?"

"You didn't."

"Great professor."

"And husband." I smiled, glad to stand on solid ground again.

"And father," he said.

"What?"

"The pictures. He looks like he adores both of you."

"Yes, he does."

"Darn. Your daughter looks familiar."

"Perhaps you've run into them at the grocery store."

"Probably. I'll book another session."

"Alicia will be back at her desk now. She'll take care of you."

I shook his hand. Held my breath.

He walked through the door and down the hall.

I stumbled into the ladies' room spewing stomach contents into the commode. Would this story ever stop hurting? The additional details given by Steve Giovanni plucked my nerves and splintered my heart again for my child. Ten minutes later when Alicia wandered down the hall, footsteps echoing like she peeked into my room, I hung limp as a ragdoll over the toilet bowl.

Chapter 6

Though Alicia expressed concern about whatever had caused me to be sick, she appeared preoccupied. Different from the familiar and predictable Alicia with whom I'd greeted and exchanged playful banter earlier that morning. Not the same gal who'd left the building laughing with Billy.

She dampened a towel and fed it into my hands. Asked about anything further she could do for me. Was I sure about picking up Billy if I didn't feel well? She did everything right. But the surrounding atmosphere was charged with something discordant ... something I wasn't well enough to pull into focus. Alicia hurried away.

Gaining strength, and having brushed my hair and teeth, I walked down front and leaned over her desk. "Got something on your mind, girlfriend?"

"Did you say something, Kat?"

"Yes. I asked if you have something on your mind."

"I have to finish filing before I start billing."

"That's not what I meant."

"What did you mean?"

"Earth to Alicia ... what is troubling you?"

"I'm not sure what you're getting at."

"How's Kylie?"

"Who?"

"Your *child* ... Kylie."

"Kylie? Why do you ask?"

"I asked because you mentioned recently—while Jordan and I were still separated—that you were having serious issues with her."

"No, I didn't."

"Ali. Yes. You did."

Eyes, blank and empty, stared up at me.

"The day you stood on the back porch and confronted me about Jordan not living at home at that time."

"But Jordan is home and things are fine. Right?"

"Ali, where did you go? What is going on with you?" My brain struggled to wrap around what she said. "Will you say something? Anything that tells me what's wrong."

"I phoned Cindy. She's expecting you to pick up Billy at 5:15."

What? "Okay."

"I have work to do." She buried herself waist up in the file cabinet.

I stared at her back.

"Did you need something further?"

"Nothing. Not one thing." I walked down the hall and into my treatment room to prepare for my next client, all the while aware something had changed while she'd been gone that she didn't want to discuss, and Alicia always wanted to discuss everything.

Alicia, my office wonder, my partner in caring for people—especially the kids—who were patients at the clinic. My best friend. My confidant. The person who helped look after Bailey at the office before Jordan and I adopted her. A woman of God and devoted prayer warrior. The person who helped me face the heartbreak that daily walked through the clinic door. One of the best people I knew. And something was eating her up. I couldn't grasp what but determined to find out.

Her unprecedented behavior cleared the session with Stephen Giovanni from my brain.

That proved to be best for the moment because when I arrived at Billy's house, I needed to be his Miss Katie. Even at five, he would realize if something seemed wrong. Not to mention my husband and daughter waited for me.

#

When I entered my home that evening, holding Billy by the hand, peals of laughter and fragrant smells of dinner greeted us. Jordan cooked spaghetti or lasagna. Bailey—most always in the kitchen with Jordan when he played chef—busied herself setting the table. She looked up, spotted us, then stopped in the middle of laying out flatware and ran to hug me.

"Mama, Mama, you're home." She smiled. "Hey, Billy."

"Yes, I am home." I kissed the top of her blond head. I was still acclimating to the thrill of being loved by my own child.

Releasing Billy's hand, I trekked into the kitchen to find Jordan. "Hey you."

"Hey you too. Wait, is it Friday? I'd lost track of days but thought I heard Billy's voice in the foyer." He smiled and slipped both arms around my waist. "Your daughter has been waiting for you to come home and see her school work. You have no idea how much she talks about the clinic when you're working late."

Bailey had gone with me to the clinic each day the summer before, after her mom was murdered, while she lived with us but before we'd adopted her. "Bailey's had more than her share of adjustments. She loves being with you after school, but she misses everyone at the office." Hard for her. "I've been missing you guys too." Slipping both arms around his neck, I kissed him. "And it sounds like good news from school if she's anxious to show me her homework."

A smile broke across his handsome face. "Great news. But I'll wait for her to give you details."

Billy eyed us. He'd stopped beside the table when I'd let go of his hand. I turned around and lifted him into my arms, mussing his hair.

Bailey laid the last fork beside the plates, then asked, "Billy's only here for dinner, you said. Right?"

Ouch. Her lingering insecurities peeked around the corner of her attitude. She'd lost one mom to the murder Steve Giovanni had described—in devastating detail—at my office earlier.

She was growing heavier, but I leaned and lifted her into my other arm. "Yes, he's having dinner with us and afterward I'll take him home."

She whispered, "Okay."

"Time to eat," Jordan called as he set a bowl of spaghetti sauce and another of pasta on the white-washed pine table. I let both kids slide to the floor, washed and dried my hands at the kitchen faucet, foot pushed a step stool before the sink so the kids could wash theirs, then grabbed the salad and French bread and placed them beside the steaming spaghetti.

Bailey climbed in her chair—a green stool with wide steps she loved using as a booster seat—and looked at her dad, without smiling.

He chuckled, turned, and reached back to the island, then lifted a plate of peanut butter-and-jelly sandwiches on wheat bread he'd cut into heart shapes using a cookie cutter and set them in front of her. "Please share with Billy."

Her blinking lashes and sparkling green eyes charmed Jordan, as she knew they would. "Daddy, you know I'm a good sharer."

We laughed.

Love for my family rushed into every piece of me.

I'd pulled a chair for Billy. But exhibiting generosity, Bailey scooted to the side of her chair, patted the space next to her, reached for Billy's hand, and pulled him up the steps to sit beside her.

His internal sun shined through the clouds and spread across his face.

When we bowed our heads to give thanks, I peeped at him. He stared at each of us one by one. I'm not sure he'd become accustomed to our mealtime prayers, but he'd never said a word, just observed.

After dinner, while Jordan and Bailey cleaned the kitchen, I drove Billy home. It took all the will I possessed not to dunk him in the bathtub first. Baths were not a priority at his home, and I'd tried and failed to impact his household. But God had a plan and a purpose for this boy's life. I was certain.

#

On the drive toward Billy's house, he reached from the backseat and laid his hand on my shoulder.

"You okay back there, Bud?"

"Yep."

Still work to do on the "yes ma'am" thing, but my sphere of influence limited itself to one hour at the clinic and dinner on Fridays, and Cindy had him every day.

"I gots something to tell you."

"Good. I want to hear it."

"I think I want to wait till ya git me out of your car."

"Ya sure?"

"Yep."

"Okay, I can't wait to hear it."

I pointed my car into his driveway and scooted out before pulling him into my arms. "So, what you got, Billy?"

"Hug me fust."

I pulled him into a deeper embrace while he laid his face into my neck.

I hummed and swayed side to side.

He turned till his lips pressed against my ear.

"Miss Katie, I'm gunna love you ever and ever and slay all your dragons."

"Aww."

Cindy opened the door for him to come in.

Billy dropped to my side and gripped my hand.

"Could you go inside while I speak to Mommy?"

Looking uncertain, he slipped past his mother whose mouth curled around lower gums and sparsely appointed teeth, suggesting an unwillingness to talk with me.

"Cindy, this will take a second but I need to say something."

She grudged down the steps. "It's late and I'm tired."

"Same here but I've given Billy dollars as a reward for hard work at the clinic."

"What about it?"

"You've taken his money for cigarettes."

"Just borrowed it till payday."

"Payday? You're stealing from a five-year-old."

She flung words. "Katie, why do you make a big deal over everything I do?"

"It is a Big. Deal." I squelched a scream. "I've worked hard to show Billy what a healthy role model looks like."

She glared. "And she doesn't look like me. Is that what you're saying?"

"If you need money, get a job."

"I have a job. I raise kids."

"Then for Billy's sake do it right. Keep your hands off his money."

Cindy gathered her robe. "I'm going inside. And Katie, I'll do as I please." She stomped away and slammed the door.

"Why did you bring him to me?" I demanded of a dilapidated entrance.

Sickened by her attitude I crawled exhausted into my vehicle.

Billy's words rang in my head as I drove home, lightening my mood and leaving me humbled. He was a kid and failed to understand the full meaning of what he'd said. He knew he loved me and felt safe. But God love his heart. Wasn't that what every woman wanted from a relationship?

I decided during the short drive that starting with his next session he would leave the clinic some Fridays with squirt guns and sometimes with the latest animated DVD. Maybe new tennis shoes that lighted when he stomped his feet, or a yo-yo that Alicia and I would wind and teach him to throw. But he would never again leave with money.

How I wished stolen dollars were the only issue. While deplorable, conditions might be worse. I didn't trust Cindy to do the right thing concerning her kids. That same chill rushed through my body, leaving me shaken.

Chapter 7

Thoughts of Jordan and Bailey filled my heart and I savored the joy of having a family as I cruised toward home at day's end.

When I bounced through the door Jordan stepped toward me and kissed me. "I didn't expect you this soon, but sure am glad to see you."

He pulled me into the plushness of our over-stuffed sofa. We made out like teenagers.

"Yuck," Bailey said as she walked into the living room, eyes covered in mock horror.

"I thought you were napping," he said.

She jumped onto the sofa between us, wrapped one arm around each of us and said, "I love both of yous."

#

We ate an early dinner and agreed to a short night. After Bailey's bath we tucked her in together, helped her say her prayers, then trudged toward our room.

Jordan and I showered together then lay in bed talking about everything, but mostly about having a green-eyed daughter.

"She couldn't wait for you to get home."

"Good. And you?"

"Always." He rolled on his side to face me. "Always and forever."

"I love you."

"And I you, Katie Girl. Oh, I nearly forgot. I've invited a guest for dinner tomorrow night."

"Okay. Someone I know?"

"Doubtful. He's a graduate student and I'm chairing his thesis committee."

"Okay."

"He's also a cop."

I grinned. "Aha. I can see how a police officer would be interested in psych classes."

"Yeah. Real nice fellow." He reached over and brushed hair from my forehead. "His name is Steve Giovanni. You'll like him."

"Steve Giovanni?"

"Yeah. Do you know him?"

"Not until earlier today. I met him at work and your announcement just ended a professional relationship for me."

"How's that?"

"Think about it. The clinic is where I met him."

"Uh oh. I can't bring him here then."

"You can. I'll have to tell him why I can't see him again, as his therapist. I'll explain that we have a social worker and interns." I traced the outline of my husband's face. "He can see either of the other counselors."

"Are you sure?"

"I am. It's an important relationship you have with your graduate students."

He kissed me again.

"It'll solve a situation for me too."

"How's that?"

"Steve is the officer who showed up at the crime scene when Bailey's mother was murdered. He climbed over her body in the doorway." I took a deep breath. "He shared details about Bailey screaming in the yard, trying to run inside the apartment to check on her mother. It broke my heart." My eyes teared. "I already have more details about that day and the murder than my heart can stand, especially when someone draws terrifying pictures of our child standing there trembling and suffering." My breath quickened. "Jordan, remember the tiny bloody footprints we learned about?"

"Yes."

"She was so frightened she ripped herself from the officer's grip and barreled inside the apartment, even though he thought he had her secure. Thank God, the bodies had been removed by then but blood had soaked into the carpet and transferred to Bailey's feet."

He hugged me close, rocking me softly against his chest. Our noses touched. He rubbed soothing circles down my arms. "Sometimes I hate your job."

"Me too, when I don't love it."

"Did Steve know we are the couple who adopted Bailey?"

"Not a clue. But he kept looking at her pictures. Kept mentioning that she resembled the child he'd put in his squad car and drove to the station after he found her at the victim's apartment building."

"Did you tell him?"

"No. These sessions are about the clients. Not me. It would shift the whole focus if I revealed something like that." I lay there looking at my husband, loving every inch of him.

"You're right." His brows raised. "Baby, he'll find out if he comes here. Are you prepared for that?"

I nodded.

"You sure?"

"I'm sure."

"Okay," he said. "I'm feeling sleepy."

I leaned in and kissed him, and he reciprocated. Within a minute his kisses became urgent.

Mine too.

Love fills the holes in me.

Jordan, a happy but tired man, rolled onto his back, yawned, and slipped further beneath the covers.

I lay there watching him, memorizing every contour of his face. *Thank You, God, for bringing him home.* I listened to his soft whiffle. I reached over and tucked the sheet closer to his chin as though he were Bailey. *Lord, I can never thank you enough for a second chance and renewed love.* The scent of him filled my nostrils. I stroked his shoulder until my eyes grew heavy and I shimmied under the comforter myself. But sleep escaped me. My mind wandered to Alicia. On Monday, I intended to find out what had been wrong with my friend.

Chapter 8

Alicia waited at the hallway sink.

"Kat, no lunch again." She poured a fresh tea and placed it in my hand. "Cindy Thibbodeaux called." She grabbed yogurt and fruit from the fridge. "You can eat this."

"Is something wrong with Billy?"

"No. Cindy called about Sara Beth."

"Okay."

"She sounded upset, so I tucked Sara Beth into this hour." Her brows slammed together. "I know Cindy's different from your average client, but she sounded strange."

I scooped up a grape. "What did she say?"

"She babbled about Sara Beth. Reported her behaving even worse than Billy had before he started seeing you."

No surprise if she's living with the same family Billy lives with. "Are they here?"

"You don't hear her whining, do you?"

I laughed. "No." The day there's no bit of comic relief, I'll have to go.

She glanced down the hallway toward the front door. "They've arrived."

I drained my tea and poured another. "Send them back. I'll speak to Cindy then send her up front to fill out paperwork and, I hope, spend most of the session with Sara Beth." I paused. "How old is she? About three?"

"Yes, three."

The front door slammed behind my lunch client. I walked up front to greet Cindy Thibbodeaux—Billy and Sara Beth Martin's mother. "Hello, Cindy. How are you?" I held out my hand.

But true to her usual behavior, Cindy held too many things to reach for my palm. "Don't even ask."

"Come back and let's have a seat in my treatment room." I gazed down at Sara Beth who walked beside her mom. I patted her cheek, and she flashed a sweet grin. "Alicia, can you take Sara Beth into the playroom and set her up with toys or let her climb on the ladder and slide while I talk to Cindy?" We had designed a see-through window in the door. Alicia could spot her from her desk. And I knew she wouldn't leave this little one until she became comfortable.

The playroom took a rectanglular shape. Long enough that the furthest end neared my treatment room. Another clear plexiglass window nestled inside the door. I could check on Sara Beth at any time ... as I had with Billy. The room had been so childproofed, one would have to work hard to get hurt inside it.

Cindy clamored down the hallway behind me with empty stainless-steel mug, cigarettes and lighter, and a large purse that banged into both hallway walls. She stopped at the coffee bar to fill her stainless container. She'd been my client for over a year and had become familiar with my office.

I waited beside my door.

She stepped inside but turned around, "Can we sit on the back porch today? I'll die if I can't smoke."

"Okay, but I'd hoped to see Sara Beth for most of the hour—since you made the appointment for her."

"Well, she'll just have to wait her turn."

Same ole Cindy. She was my super-glue client. Once I touched her, I couldn't shake her loose.

"I need you to listen to *me*," she said.

"Okay." I gritted my teeth. Cindy had always tried to usurp Billy's time with me. Now, Sara Beth's.

We stepped through the back door. I walked across the long porch and sat on the swing. Cindy opted for the white wicker chair and turned it to face me. She tamped a cigarette from the pack and pushed down on the lighter wheel. She pulled deep, then blew smoke in curls like tiny tornadoes.

"Have you ever wondered if something might be wrong with Sara Beth?" she asked between puffs.

"Like what? I've spent little time with her."

"Slow maybe. Not exactly retarded ... but slow."

"I hadn't considered that in the limited time I've been around her, but it won't take long to find out." I pushed my high-heeled toes against the concrete. "You know how I work. I'll play games with her. Ask her questions. Watch her draw to observe how much detail she's able to put in. But she's a toddler. Are you expecting too much?"

"She can't talk well at all."

"How much time have you spent pronouncing words with her?"

"I switch on Sesame Street for her every morning."

"I see."

"That's what Sesame Street's for, isn't it?"

That's what mommies are for. "Has anything specific happened that caused you to bring her here today?"

"Not unless losing my mind is specific enough for you."

"Cindy, has there been a sudden change in her behavior or an accumulation of things?"

"Catherine, I don't think I was prepared to birth two more children. My first two are almost grown. This should be *my* time."

"But you have them, so can you give details of your concerns?"

"Sara Beth seems a little stupid."

"Stupid?" My gut felt stabbed clean through with her words. I stared her down trying to keep anger at bay. "I'd like to check on Sara Beth."

"No, Alicia can do that. I haven't said all I came to say."

There seemed to be a new sheriff in town. "I see." My teeth dug into my lip.

"You're responsible for Billy becoming a pretty good kid."

I tasted blood. "Billy's a great kid."

"Whatever. Oh yeah, Billy's birthday is next week, and I thought you would want to buy him a cake. And could you buy one large enough for me to take leftovers home for dinner?"

Why don't I have something catered for your whole family? "I'll have a cake for him Friday and we'll celebrate here."

"There should at least be a few slices I could take. And can it be that carrot cake like you brought for Christmas last year?"

An ugly knot formed in my throat. "Can you get back to why you brought Sara Beth?"

"She's not a likeable child. And if you can't help me, I'm not sure how I'll stay sane."

"What do you mean?"

"I don't know. I'm depressed and most days I hate everybody."

"Are you asking for an antidepressant?"

"No, I'm asking for a new life. A quiet household. Some peace. A whole new life with no kids driving me batty."

I clamped my jaws tight in an effort to regain my composure.

"You need to help me."

"I could recommend a good antidepressant, one with something for anxiety in it, but I can't erase two children."

"Medicine can't give me a new life."

"No, but it may help you adjust to the one you have."

"I doubt it." She spat on the porch.

How lovely. "That's my suggestion for now, since you've been in weekly counseling with me for more than a year. If talk therapy becomes inadequate, we look next to psychotropic drugs."

"What's that mean?"

"Mood altering meds."

"It's not *my* mood that needs altering."

"Your appointment is Wednesday. We'll discuss it further then."

She lit a third or fourth cigarette.

I stood. "I will see Sara Beth now."

"But—"

"We'll talk Wednesday." I marched across the porch and started up the steps but turned back to Cindy.

She whirled around as though she knew I hadn't gone inside.

My hand touched the familiar back door pull. "Cindy, you wouldn't hurt anyone, would you … including yourself?"

"I'm Catholic. I would never hurt myself."

"Promise?"

"Promise." But she dropped her head in a way that shrouded her eyes from mine.

"Wednesday then."

"Yeah."

#

Sara Beth looked up as I walked into the playroom. She didn't resemble Billy. Crystal blue eyes peered from a round face framed in blonde curls. A beautiful toddler with an impish smile. At three, she was more baby than girl. My heart warmed all over looking at the darling.

"I'm Miss Katie. I bet you remember me." Cindy had her in tow for her sessions most Wednesdays. The clinic would be familiar to her.

"Hewwo." She toddled toward me with outstretched arms.

I lifted her. "You okay in here?"

She nodded.

"So, what if we piece together a puzzle?"

She slipped from my arms and down my legs, then walked to the bottom shelf where I kept the beginner puzzles and pulled out a square box.

"Mickey," she said and pointed to the box cover then to her surroundings. She trekked to the festive wall and kissed Mickey Mouse on the hand. Two years before, Alicia and I had found an old transparency projector in a church yard sale, bought a Mickey Mouse coloring book, and one by one traced the pages onto the playroom wall, then painted the images in primary colors. It was magnificent.

Sarah Beth laughed when she kissed the mouse. That one moment rewarded all our diligent efforts.

She was cuter than Mr. Mouse. "Why don't we sit and put the Mickey puzzle together?"

She walked to the hard-plastic Fisher Price table and crawled onto the yellow bench.

I slipped myself onto the facing one. Those benches got smaller each year. My knees groaned. The puzzle, suited for toddlers, had larger, harder pieces with a built-in border.

Before I finished dumping puzzle pieces onto the table, Sara Beth began clicking them together. Usually, I started the puzzle for a three-year-old, but she didn't need me to. She fit the last piece together for herself, then clapped her pudgy hands.

I patted her blond head and started toward the shelves. I reached to the second shelf and pulled a puzzle with smaller pieces. Still for toddlers but designed for ages four to five. The puzzle had a built-in border but no lines that formed the shape of each puzzle piece.

Sara Beth surveyed the pieces, then without hesitation snapped each one in place.

"Can you tell Miss Katie your whole name?"

"Ser Bef."

"Sara Beth who?

"Ser Bef Markin."

"Can you excuse Miss Katie for a second?"

She grinned and nodded her head, blue eyes sparkling.

I strode from the room, opened the backdoor, and trucked down the three steps. Cindy remained in the chair. A cloud of smoke hovered over and around her. One glimpse of her face identified her as preoccupied and angry.

"Cindy?"

She startled. "What?"

"Has Sara Beth attended day care?"

"No. We can't afford it."

"Mothers' Day Out?"

"I told you we can't afford it. Why?"

"Just checking."

"Whatever." She reached for another cigarette.

I could tell you how to save enough money to send her. "Thank you." Cigarettes sold for over five dollars per pack.

I returned to Sara Beth and found her much in the same position. I took her sweet hands in mine. "Miss Sara Beth, who showed you how to put puzzles together?"

She threw another toothy grin.

"Sara Beth, who plays puzzle with you?"

"Biwwy."

Pride and sadness competed, my body their playing field. Jordan and I had taken similar puzzles to their home on Christmas Eve. I felt proud of Billy for teaching her but grieved that Sara Beth's only teacher was five.

Father, please bless both these babies.

I smiled at Alicia through the window and let her know I was leaving the room to chat with Cindy again. She shoved her desk chair back and advanced toward Sara Beth as I left the room through the other door. God love Alicia. Time had come to hire a file clerk because my assistant couldn't be everywhere at once. But she tried.

Retracing my steps, I neared Cindy.

She jumped again.

I'd never seen Cindy this antsy. I returned to the swing facing her. "Cindy, I'm not sure why you think Sara Beth is slow. In my opinion she appeared quick and smart."

"Who do you have in there, and what have you done with Sara Beth?"

"Sarcasm concerning your daughter won't help me and doesn't look good on you."

"So, what do you want me to say, Catherine?"

"Nothing. Nothing at all. I need to spend more time with her, but for now she appears to be a smart three-year-old who's had a bright five-year-old teacher."

"What?"

"Never mind. Book another session for her at Alicia's desk. And I'll see you Wednesday."

I left the porch and entered the playroom one last time to tell Sara Beth goodbye. "It's time for you to go home with Mommy, but I'll be excited to visit with you again soon. Okay?"

She toddled into my arms. I gathered her, then stood. She nestled her face into my neck.

Of course, like Billy, she wasn't bathed often. I didn't care. That baby could have snuggled me all day, and I'd have basked in the joy. But another client waited. I kissed her cheek and held my hand atop her head until she scrambled down.

"I'll see you soon." Where had this child come from? I taught Billy to behave, and he'd learned quickly. But Sara Beth presented so differently. At three, she exuded a loving spirit, unlike Cindy, or Billy in the beginning. This precious baby could only be what psychologists called the hardy child. Intrinsic goodness.

Chapter 9

I worked a long day. Nothing new. After my last client, I stood at the counter and stretched a mile. I sat all day during work and tension crept throughout my long body. Alicia packed my briefcase, and we prepared to leave. But the phone rang.

Alicia—already standing—answered. "Hello, Main Street Clinic." She squinted at me and frowned. "What, Cindy? Slow down." She listened for close to a minute. "Just a second, I'll check."

I already had my purse on my shoulder. A quick glance at the wall clock confirmed 6:15. "What?"

"This is Cindy. She wants to bring Sara Beth back."

"I saw her earlier today. And it's late."

"I wanted to say all that, but I never got a chance."

I reached for the phone. "Cindy, I'm almost out the door. What's wrong?"

"I'm at the pulling-my-hair stage. If you can't talk to Sara Beth again … I don't know what I might do."

I flinched. "Cindy, what are you saying?"

"I have to come back, that's all." She breathed hard. "Truth is, I'm sitting in front of your office with her right now."

I peeked through the window and there she sat. Exhaustion hovered. I placed my hand over the phone and gaped at Alicia. "God help me. This job makes me old."

"Come in." I laid the phone down. "Ali, call Jordan and go home."

"Anything you say, but you're tired. You worry me."

"Ditto." I opened the door for Cindy and Sara Beth as Alicia called my husband.

Cindy's face was colorless, ghostlike. Morbid. Her daughter ran toward me, wrapping both arms around my legs.

"Hey, sweetheart," I said as I lifted her. She snaked both arms and legs around my body as a frightened chimp might around his mother.

"It's okay, Sara Beth, I've got you." I held her. She didn't loosen her grip for three full minutes. I attempted to rub her back, but she cried out. The last time I remembered a child clutching me with that level of fear had been Bailey ... two days after her mother's murder. What on earth?

Cindy had already tromped to my treatment room.

With Sara Beth still coiled around me, I hurried to my office. "Cindy, what is wrong with this baby?" We sat in my chair.

She buried her face in her hands.

"You seem to need a medical doctor. Has something happened since earlier today?"

"Do I look like I'm fine and dandy?"

"I mentioned a medical doctor because I've never seen you like this. Are you ill?"

"I'm crazy."

"I see."

"No. I mean it. I'm losing my mind."

I cradled Sara Beth's head, caressing her hair. "What happened to Sara Beth?"

"To Sara Beth?"

"Yes. She seemed fine a few hours ago."

"Catherine, you've always been more concerned for my kids than for me."

"I'm sorry you feel that way. You have my undivided attention when you come to see me each Wednesday. I hoped that buying Christmas for the kids took a bit of financial pressure off you and Rob. I've tried to help in whatever way you needed me too, but Cindy, I'm your therapist, not the answer to every problem in your life. You are for the next many years the mother of two young children."

"Believe me, I know that."

"Fine. I'm still waiting to hear what's wrong with Sara Beth."

"Sara Beth. Sara Beth. Sara Beth."

I caressed the toddler's head while I hummed a soothing melody against her cheek.

"I guess I've been in a mood this afternoon."

"You were in a mood when I saw you earlier."

"It got worse."

"So I'd guessed. Your daughter is frightened."

"She wouldn't leave me be. Whenever I tried to have an alone moment, she followed me, even to the bathroom. She rattles non-stop, and she's such a clingy toddler. I can't get away from her. Ever." She pointed an ugly finger at Sara Beth's back. "I don't know if I'll live until she starts pre-K. She won't play by herself."

"Did you hit this baby?"

Silence.

"Cindy?"

"Who cares?"

"I do. And if you hit her hard enough, Family Services will care."

She glared. "Are you threatening me?"

"That depends. I would like to check under her clothes."

"No."

"My office had already closed, and you came here anyway. It's my responsibility to look." I gently soothed while stripping Sara Beth to her diaper.

Cindy wiggled through the fabric on the sofa.

Oh, dear Lord. Cindy's hand print emblazoned on Sara Beth's small back. Criss-crossed red and swollen flesh that resembled a scar. Switch burns covered both arms and legs.

"Cindy, how could you? If you lost control you could've called a hotline. You also knew I would have let you drop her here."

"You're making too much of this. People can spank their kids."

Unfortunately, I was well aware. "This is way too much spanking ... hitting. No one should be hit this hard, and she's three years old." Anger washed over me, tugging me under murky water. The kind of hurricane downpour that pulls trees from soil and houses from foundations.

"You heard me say I'm losing it. I couldn't stop myself."

Pulling Sara Beth's long-sleeved shirt down, I slipped her legs into pants. "You aren't allowed to leave with her until we have a plan. If you won't take an antidepressant, I don't think you have a choice about an antianxiety drug. Cindy, let me take her to my house for the night if you even think you might hit her again. You both could use a break."

"No. I can't deal with her dad too. He likes to play with the kids when he gets home."

"Should anything untoward happen to this baby, I will never forgive you. But I'm the least of your problems. I'll call Children's Services if you ever leave marks on her again."

She stood to her feet. "Okay. Okay. I'll call my doctor in the morning."

"No. I'll call. I need his name and number. It's my professional responsibility to fill him in on your state of mind and tell him you lost control with your child."

"No."

"Or, I can call Children's Services."

She pulled paper and pen from her purse and wrote both.

"I'm asking again. I feel the need to take Sara Beth home with me tonight. Just long enough for you to pull yourself together."

"I'd personally love that but Rob would be mad and I'd have to hear him nag me too."

The toddler turned in my lap and wrapped herself like a vine again.

"She's telling me something different. She's trembling." I kissed her hair. "Can I trust you not to hit this child again?"

"Yes. Rob will be home when we get back. He'll take care of her."

"Good. I don't want to be rude, but did you examine yourself in the mirror before you left home?"

"No. Why?"

"You've spilled a snack on your shirt. You're wearing two different shoes and you usually wear your hair in a ponytail, but it's kind of wild and in your face. I'm concerned, that's all."

She tried to finger comb her hair, but it tangled like wild grass she couldn't navigate. "Whatever."

"I'm trying to gauge the level of your distress. I'm still not sure about you taking Sara Beth."

"Rob is home, I told you."

"Okay, but if you need me tonight, you have my home number. And I will call your doctor in the morning."

I stood with Sara Beth and we all walked toward the front door. I couldn't pull her loose. "Cindy, open the van and maybe she will let me put her in her car seat. If she won't let go of me, I can't let you take her." I stepped out the front door to the white Dodge. Sara Beth allowed me to put her in, but when I buckled her, she stretched sweet pudgy hands toward me. "I'm still offering to take her with me."

"And I still said no."

I reached into the van and kissed the baby's soft cheek. The inside of the vehicle was dirtier than ever as if some homeless person lived there. The trash piled high enough to hide two bodies. Old soda cans, three months of McDonald's bags, food smeared on the floor and windows, curled fries. The smell made me gag.

Before I closed the door, I smiled at Sara Beth. "I'll see you soon. Be a good girl." She was a wonderful girl.

"K.T."

"What, sweetheart?"

She held both hands toward me. "K. T."

"Oh … Katie."

She shook her head yes. "Wuv you."

"Oh, baby, I love you too. And don't forget, I'll see you soon." Indigestion nailed me to the concrete. I watched as the rusted-out vehicle drove away. *Father, watch over that precious baby.*

Back inside, I stared at the phone and thought of calling Family Services. But I'd learned they would only step in when they saw clear and present danger. A fact that had caused the death of children. Those people were overworked and underpaid. I wasn't certain they cared enough anymore.

Shake it off, Katie, you have your own family who needs you at home. I locked the front door, walked out the back, then slid into my car. I drove toward home weary as a field hand.

But I would see Sara Beth soon. Right? Fear gripped my body.

And I hadn't found out what had been wrong with Alicia.

Chapter 10

Monday morning passed without my being able to approach Alicia. I had been so worried about Sara Beth. But it was Wednesday, and I determined to ask.

Happy as could be, she greeted me when I entered the backdoor, as if her strange attitude on Friday had never happened. I smiled, glad to see she had weathered whatever storm had plagued her. But in my heart I was certain a new wrinkle had developed between Kylie and Ali, and she didn't seem ready to share.

Concern for my friend caused me to push. "Ali, is there something about Kylie you're not telling me?"

"No. I tell you everything."

"Usually."

She squared her shoulders, almost looking like herself.

"Girlfriend, I'm concerned. You said you share everything, but I'm feeling shut out."

"If I had something to tell, I would."

"Why don't I believe that?"

"I don't know."

Her eyes didn't meet mine. "I'm here when you're ready."

She had duties at her desk. I ambled alongside her, chatting about work stuff. I wanted to check the schedule. One glance assured me of back-to-back clients until 6:00. Mostly adults. Fear gripped my belly. Something was wrong with Ali but I couldn't force her to share. I wanted to shake her.

#

I'd ended my 1:00 and stepped from my room for a breath of fresh air.

As my client walked out of hearing distance, Alicia turned. "Kat, I had planned to tell you there was a break for this hour. A client was sick and canceled." She leaned against the counter. "However, a new gal called this morning about an appointment. I told her you had no openings today, so she asked if I'd place her on a list in case you had a cancelation. When your 2:00 rescheduled I called her back."

"Is the appointment for her?"

"No. It's for her eleven-year-old son, Lewis, and they're here." She shrugged.

I raised my brows. "You're impossible. But yes, I'll see him." I strolled up front.

Lewis appeared darker than most African Americans in an exotic, beautiful way I was sure he couldn't appreciate. His huge brown eyes should have been filled with hope but weren't. He held his head, covered with close-cropped hair, slightly downcast. Now all his friends would know he was seeing a "shrink." Like most adolescents, he probably thought himself so transparent his forehead could break out in words and betray him. He stood in the foyer, shuffling foot to foot, pushing and pulling his hands in and out of his pockets. This eleven-year-old bathed in shame.

His mom sat in a waiting room chair.

"Hi, I'm Catherine Collier ... or Katie."

She stood. "And I'm Allison Davis. This is my son, Lewis, and my daughter, Whitney."

I winked at Whitney and smiled at the nervous boy. "Can you guys sit in the waiting room while I visit with your mom a minute?"

"Yes, ma'am."

Alicia pushed his file across her desk toward me.

Allison led the way after I pointed her down the hall. "The last door on your left."

Scurrying behind her, I scanned the form. I closed the door behind us, then offered the sofa or chair. She opted for the sofa facing me as I folded myself into my chair. "Can you tell me why you wanted Lewis to talk with me?"

Allison wrung her hands and tears played across her dark eyes. "Lewis wets his bed almost every night."

"I'm sorry. That's hard to deal with ... but for the child even harder."

Before me sat a lovely lady with impeccable taste in clothes and an air of sophistication. "He's humiliated by it. I've tried for the past two years to find help for him. My efforts have been fruitless. I'm not sure if you can help, but the bedwetting is escalating, and his self-esteem is plummeting." Sadness, even helplessness, cut frown lines into her forehead.

"Allison, we have hot tea, coffee, and water."

"A cold water, please."

I poured myself tea, handed her a bottle from the mini fridge, then returned to my chair.

"I have taken Lewis to his pediatrician who recommended a urologist. After running a series of tests, the urologist failed to find a physical cause for the bedwetting. I found two specialists in urology who work exclusively with children." She sighed. "The most recent one is on staff at The Children's Hospital in the Houston Medical Center, but she also found nothing."

"How long has he had this issue?"

"He potty trained at three, but at eight began wetting his bed."

"Was there a traumatic incident at home or school that affected him? I noticed on the intake form that you and his father are divorced."

"Michael and I divorced when Lewis was nine. Lewis's bed wetting became a source of tension between us." She shrugged, but sadness hovered over her. "Michael is an active, hands-on father, but gave Lewis grief about wetting his bed. Every. Morning. Lewis can't help it. Michael is embarrassed about it, but no one is more humiliated than my son. Ms. Collier, he would stop if he could." A tear slipped down her cheek. "And the harsh 'talking to' that Michael gives Lewis pretty much every time they're together breaks my heart. I still love Michael but his lack of empathy for Lewis's bed wetting is why I won't take him back." Her folded hands trembled. "I won't rear Lewis in a house where he's yelled at every morning."

"I wouldn't either." And I meant it.

"In the past school year, Lewis said troubling things that alarmed teachers. I teach at the same school he attends and have been called to the principal's office on several occasions."

"What has he said and to whom?"

"He's mentioned in front of his friends he might kill himself."

"Do you believe him capable of self-harm?"

"Not really. But then a lot of moms are shocked by what their kids do. And the new school year looms before us. I brought Lewis, hoping you might offer some relief we haven't found in physiological medicine. You're well-known in this community. Many of my friends trust you can help him."

"You're very kind, but I've always believed God called me to this work. All miracles come from Him. But let me grab this young man and have a chat." I stood and shook her hand.

We strode toward the front where Lewis waited, and I nodded for him to follow me.

I needed Lewis to trust me enough to tell me why he thought his mom had brought him to the clinic. I started with fun boy stuff, hoping he would lower his guard. We chatted about friends. Baseball. Football. Things I tried to maintain enough knowledge of in order to have these conversations. School. Girls? No, not much interest yet. They still "had cooties."

We walked two blocks to the Dairy Queen and ordered ice cream cones at the walk-up window. The warm day urged us to eat fast. As brown ice cream oozed from the side of my sugar cone, I ventured, "So, you talking trash to friends at school?"

His brown eyes saucered then narrowed into little slits. Vanilla ice cream trickled down the side of his cone, but he didn't notice, even when it dripped onto his fingers and crawled down his wrist. "I don't know what you're talking about."

I licked my chocolate again, noting that he blinked often. "Is that right?"

"Oops." He felt the sticky liquid snaking his wrist. He lapped the worst of it, then used both of our napkins to clean the rest. The huge eyes reappeared. "I guess my mom told you what I said to Germaine."

"No. Care to enlighten me?"

"I was mad, so I might have mentioned killing myself."

"Why on earth would you say that?"

"I guess I'm a troubled kid."

"Excuse me. Troubled kids don't tell me they're troubled kids. Who have you been listening to?"

"My mom talks to my dad about me."

"Of course she does. She's worried. Are you planning to kill yourself? You've said it to different people several times. Right?"

"Yes, ma'am," he whispered.

"Have you ever been serious? Had a plan?" My cone folded in on itself.

"No, ma'am."

"Got a gun? Gonna get one?"

"No, ma'am." Lewis twirled around to the can and tossed his napkins.

I did the same and gave him a few seconds. "Then knock it off and stop scaring your mom, teachers, and friends." I dropped my mess of a cone into the trash. "Lewis, I don't know you. So far, our relationship consists of fourteen football facts, a couple of sketchy descriptions of friends and two messy ice cream cones."

He glanced at me, mouth ringed milky white.

I smiled and pointed.

His tongue moved in a wide circle to clean his face, doing a fine job.

"What I believe is that you have something—some fact or secret about yourself—that you would like to kill off."

He stared through brooding eyes.

"It's okay."

Amid our chatter and stroll toward the office, and our rest on the swing that hung from long chains on the back porch, he radiated signs of an anxiety disorder. He blinked rapidly when I looked at him. He backed slowly against the swing, expecting to find it, but startled hard when it grazed the back of his knees.

I lowered myself onto the swing first and smiled.

He eased beside me but jumped when the chains creaked. "This thing gonna fall?" He looked toward the round hooks attached to the roof.

"I don't believe so. It's hung here for a few years and my husband is vigilant about overseeing the maintenance of this building."

"He got any WD 40?" Lewis asked. "These chains could use some."

"Probably." I grinned. "We do, after all, live in redneck country. You can't live in Texas without WD 40, duct tape, and 'an old aunt who refuses to take her cigarette out of her mouth before she tells the highway patrol to kiss her backside.'"

He grinned. "Jeff Foxworthy."

"The one and only."

"He doesn't say backside."

"You're correct."

"You were still funny though," Lewis assured me.

I pushed the swing gently with my feet. He stiffened and held out both hands as if to steady us.

"I won't spill you."

"Sorry." He settled his hands into his lap and bit his lip.

"Don't be. I didn't mean to push too hard."

"You didn't," he said, shaking his head back and forth. "Really, it's okay."

"Yes, it is."

"Sure is."

"Righto," I said.

"Righto."

Inability to let trivial topics settle without further need to say something more is a subtle sign of anxiety. Stiffening under the force of a slight push of a swing is not subtle.

"So, tell me what you say when you're mad."

"Whaddayamean?"

"You were mad when you said troubling things to friends at school. So, when you're angry at your mom or your dad or a friend, what do you say to let them know?"

Lewis shrugged. "I'm mad?"

"Umm," I scrunched my mouth like my granny used to, and she was as country as her outhouse. "Try again."

He looked over his shoulder then back at me. "The truth?"

"Always."

He ducked his head a tiny bit then peeked up. "Sometimes I say I'm going to kill myself."

"Get outta here. Because you're angry?"

"Bad, huh?" Lewis said.

I stopped the swing and faced him. "You're not bad, sweetheart. You have gotten into some ineffective habits. Saying, 'I'm going to kill myself' should be reserved for people with a loaded gun who have every intention of using it." I waited for the words to settle.

He stared at me.

"That's not you. Look me in the face and tell me that's not you."

"That's not me."

"Then we'll work on more effective phrasing." I reached to hug him.

He jumped too hard, even for someone not expecting a hug.

"Miss Katie, I need a restroom break. Like right now." He bolted for the door.

Chapter 11

L ewis rushed from the back door and folded himself into the white chair. "Feel better turkey?"

"Yes, ma'am."

"Good. Let's talk about what to say the next time you're mad at anyone."

He pulled back to glimpse my face. "What?"

"I'm mad."

"What else?"

"Nothing else." I shrugged. "That's enough. Right now, I'm mad."

He glanced with large questioning eyes. "What if I'm talking to my mom?"

"'Mom,' you would say, 'I'm mad.'"

He hunched. "Just like that?"

"Why not? It's not that complicated."

"Well, I'm not so sure. What if I'm mad at my dad?"

"Well, you pray ..."

He laughed.

"... then you say, 'Dad, right now I'm mad at you.'"

He shook his head. "You haven't met my dad."

"No," I held both palms in front, "but I've met mine."

We grinned.

Then his eyes clouded and his brow furrowed. "Your dad ever gripe you out for something you couldn't help?"

I nodded. "He did."

"Like what?"

"I felt ill often as a kid. My stomach hurt a lot."

"What about it?"

"My dad didn't feel bad and his stomach didn't hurt."

"Okay." Lewis jerked when a squirrel skittered down the trunk of a large oak tree near the swing.

"Want to put corn on the squirrel feeder?"

"Not really."

"No problem. Maybe you'll want to next time."

"I want to hear more about your dad."

"So, he thought I claimed my stomach hurt because I didn't feel well enough to do what he asked."

"Like what?" Lewis appeared interested in this conversation. "Like, clean your room and stuff?"

"No. I felt well enough to do that kind of thing. It was usually something that involved being outside in the sun."

"You didn't have to plow the back field hanging onto a wooden handle while singing, 'Nobody knows the trouble I've seen, nobody knows my sorrows,' did you?"

Too, too cute.

He air pumped his fists, aware he charmed me.

"No." I laughed. "Do I look that old?"

"No, but doesn't every parent have a story like that, whether or not it's true?"

"I like you."

"Thanks," he said, sounding genuine. "You still didn't tell me what your father was on your rear about, that you couldn't help."

"Let's see ..."

He narrowed his eyes. "Don't tell it if it's not the truth."

"Promise," I said. "We would go to a restaurant, which was rare for us. My family ate meals at home. I would be so excited about eating out, order something wonderful, like a hamburger with pickles, lettuce and mustard, and a pile of fries with lots of ketchup, then my stomach would get all sick and I couldn't eat it."

"Oh no," he said. "Why would *your* stomach get so sick?"

My stomach. Something made Lewis's stomach feel odd. Anxiety hits most kids in the stomach first.

"I didn't know then, but I learned it was because I'd been in the sun earlier that day or the day before."

"I don't like the sun either." His head oscillated from side to side like the table-top fans from my childhood.

"Really?"

"Nope."

"Why not?" I asked.

"No reason." He looked uncomfortable as though he wished he hadn't mentioned the sun.

No way. "I was in group therapy once, you know."

"Really?"

"Yeah. I went after a tragic family event." I didn't share with him the trauma

I'd experienced when I learned I might never bear a child.

Lewis squinted at me, like he still processed that notion.

"Sitting in a therapeutic circle off the cuff I said to the whole group, 'I don't like cold food.' The counselor stopped the discussion, looked at me ..." I made an oh-my-goodness face to amuse Lewis, "... and said, 'Everybody likes cold food, unless there is a compelling reason not to.'" I shook my head and held up my index finger at Lewis.

He smiled.

"'No,' I assured the group leader. 'There's no reason, I just don't like cold food.'"

Lewis eyed me.

"In group session that day, I wanted to move on with our original topic. 'No, no, there's a reason,' the therapist assured me.'"

His eyes fastened to mine, needing to hear this story.

"I protested. 'No, I told you already, there's no reason. I don't eat salads, cold sandwiches or anything that's cold except ice cream and pie—and, thank you very much, I prefer hot cobbler with my ice cream on the side.'"

"Why?" Lewis asked.

"I didn't have answers then. I thought she made a big deal out of nothing until I'd been in therapy a while. And to tell you the truth, I was put off that the counselor bugged me about it in front of the group." I deliberately stopped my story to find out if he would pursue it. I pushed my feet against the concrete porch to sway the swing.

"But you figured it out?" He studied me intently.

I swiveled to check if there were skittering squirrels. The shrub planted at the edge of the porch was within easy reach, and I plucked a gardenia blossom, inhaling its fragrance.

Lewis looked at me shrugging. "Are you gonna tell me?"

I laid the flower in my lap and glanced at him. "When I was a child, my father pastored a small country church in rural Alabama. We used to have all-day singings with dinner on the ground. Lots of Sundays we set up sawhorses and lined them end to end outside the church, laid sheets of plywood over them, added tablecloths to the wooden tables and loaded them with food."

"You are old," Lewis peered at me as though he was wrinkle checking.

I let the story rest again.

"Keep going."

"Mashed potatoes, corn bread, and fried chicken. At five o'clock on Sunday mornings, hardworking and willing hands prepared everything we would need later in the day. Before getting dressed in their Sunday-go-to-meeting clothes, folks loaded mountains of food, wrapped in their mothers' hand-embroidered kitchen towels into their cars and brought it to church, to share after service."

"Man, y'all had like a carnival at church. That doesn't sound bad if you like that kind of food."

"I love that kind of food ... hot. But we had no microwave oven, no way to keep the food warm. That should-have-been-delicious food floated in disgusting grease. Looking at it made my stomach lurch."

"So, you didn't eat it."

"My mother said I would eat it and smile, because I was the preacher's kid, and must set a good example."

"Oh," Lewis said nodding his head, "you ate it."

"Yes. I ate it, but once I left Alabama and those dinners, I ate no cold foods. Not even foods meant to be served cold."

"You're missing out on a lot of good food," Lewis said. "I love Subway sandwiches."

"Missed out."

"What?"

"Missed out. I went to therapy, remember? Knowledge is power. Once I understood why I didn't like cold food, all that old grease-soaked food lost its hold on me. I ate at Subway yesterday." I patted myself on the back, playfully.

"That's a good story ..."

His eyes turned a mental Rubik's cube. "... but I don't like the sun."

"Do you feel healthy in the sun? Does it make you get weak or nauseated?"

"No, I'm fine. Do you think my mom is wondering where I am?" Lewis scooted to the edge of the swing.

I glanced at my watch. "Another four or five minutes. She knows where you are, sweetheart."

"So, why didn't you like the sun?"

"I could tell ya ..." I said.

"But I'd have to kill ya," we finished together, laughing.

"I want to know. You're not black."

Oh my. There were multiple issues with this beautiful young man. "I'm not one hundred percent sure why the sun drains my energy, but it does. I like the sun, but my body doesn't."

"Did your dad understand about the sun making you sick? Ya know, when he was on your rear about stuff."

"No, he didn't. Not a clue then. It became more apparent when I was an adult." We sat for a moment. "With you—"

"I'm ready to go." Lewis looked away and prepared to stand.

"No. You're ready to stop talking about the sun."

"That's not it. I just want to go. But that's a nice car." He gazed across the driveway. "Is it yours?"

"It is. We'll take a spin sometime."

"No way."

"Yes, way, if you will—"

Lewis whirled around to stare me down, his face lit with anger. "Hey, lady," he said jumping up and looking away, "if I could stop wetting the bed I would've stopped a long time ago."

I jumped up behind him. "I'm not your father."

He stopped but didn't turn around. He spat words like a warning. "Don't rag on my dad."

"I won't rag on anyone. I tried to say we can take a ride in the car, if you'll practice one phrase this week. Just one and it only has two words."

He turned his head to stare.

I stared back.

"What is it?" He whirled around.

"I'm mad."

He twitched his head. "About what?"

"No. That's the phrase I want you to practice. All you have to say when you're angry is, 'I'm mad.'"

"What if I don't get mad?"

"Thus the word practice. Stand in the bathroom or bedroom and look in a mirror and say, 'I'm mad.'"

"And I can ride in the car?"

"Yes."

"With the top down?"

"Yes."

"I'm mad."

With my hand on his shoulder, we walked in the back door toward his mother.

I wanted to make a difference in this child's life.

With my arm slung across his shoulder we trekked to Alicia's appointment book. Watching her reschedule Lewis, I noted her lack of genuine friendliness. Totally unlike her. If she would tell me what was wrong, we could work it out together. I had confidence. Whatever it might be, she held it close to her vest.

Chapter 12

"Hey, Kat." Ali greeted. "Good morning. Glad you're here. Time to go to work. You got an angry teenager. A boy in your room who does not want to be here."

"Do I know him?"

"You haven't met him but his mom is Ellen Johnson and his sister is Karrie." I'd been seeing them for a couple years.

"And unlike him, they both want to be here."

"A typical Monday," I said. "So far as I can tell, teenage boys—at least the ones who come here—only come in one flavor. Angry."

Alicia, acting like my mother, pointed toward the treatment room. "I told you he's really mad," she reminded me, and shoved his chart in my hand. "His mom filled out the paperwork then ran to the store. She'll be right back."

"Okay." I grabbed my mug, filled it from the pot in the hallway, squeezed honey from the bear-shaped bottle on the counter, then scanned the new chart Alicia had thrust in my hand, gleaning relevant information. Aha. Drugs, anger, and truancy. I inhaled, transitioned from the happy banter up front to therapist ready to meet the angry boy waiting behind my office door.

A young man—so angry that anger became a smell, so needy that neediness took a shape—slumped down in the farthest corner of my sofa. He looked like a pile of laundry wearing a cap. The heavy interval between meeting a new male teenage client and earning his trust could be long.

I depended on God for that trust to develop.

This young man didn't stir or look up when I entered the room. Experience had prepared me he might not. He remained planted on the sofa. His sockless ankles rose from two-hundred-dollar Nikes.

"Hi, I'm Miss Katie." I walked toward the sofa, and extended my hand, but dropped it to my side when he didn't look up. I read the label on the chart and said, "Michael?"

"Mike," he muttered. Taut muscles roped his forearms. "It's just Mike. Mike Johnson."

Texas birth certificates are evidently issued for males after they are fitted for a baseball cap that grows along with their heads. Mike's face was shadowed, almost hidden by his sweat-ringed black hat, frayed around the bill's tip which sported a label advertising: Red's Grill and Pub. He had pulled the cap so far down it covered his face. I couldn't discern what the kid looked like.

"Okay, Mike, what can I do for you?" I stepped back and slid into my chair, feeling his anger, pulled by his neediness. I opened his chart.

"Nothin'," he groused, "except maybe show me the back door." His voice tinged with something meaner than anger.

"You barely missed it. When Alicia brought you down the hall you were headed toward it before you swung a left and came in here."

He glanced in my direction. "Well, I'll have to remember that." His words dripped sarcasm. His head dropped back down before I caught sight of his face.

"Other than the building layout, how can I help you?" The ceiling fan whirled above our heads. I stirred my steaming tea and scooped the honey that pooled at the bottom. I dragged the spoon across the rim, nursed the mug in both palms, and gave Mike time.

"You could leave me alone already."

"I could." I sipped and observed him over my cup rim.

"Duh. So, leave me alone already."

"Here's the thing, Mike, I don't arrest people. Your mother brought you here because ..." I read from his chart, "... you're in trouble. You can't go back to school until you talk to someone. I hope—"

"If my mom wants someone to see you, then let her come here." Mike's hands fisted then his knuckles crashed together, and he ducked further beneath his cap.

"Well, she should be in the foyer." I closed his folder and edged toward the end of my chair. "She planned to return after running to the store. I can ask her to join us—"

"No." His palm thrust stiff as a traffic cop and his mouth spit multiple obscenities. "Don't even think of doing that."

"Okay, I won't." Easing back in my chair, I opened his folder again and perused it. "So, it says here you're sixteen." I glanced at him, looking as though I had limitless time, knowing full well someone else needed Mike's seat in— my glance at the clock confirmed—forty-seven minutes. "Did you fill out this form?"

"Yes, I'm sixteen. No, I didn't. Like, can I go now?"

"No. You're old enough to fill out your own paper work here. Why didn't you?"

"I didn't want to. I don't want to." Mike's fists clenched to the sound of each word. "I. Don't. Want. To. Be. Here."

"Where had you rather be?"

"Anywhere. In my room. Smoking dope. Gettin' juiced up with my friends." His words majored in f-bombs.

There was a time when a kid sitting on my sofa cussing like Mike might have offended me. But I had occupied this chair for years—hearing angry parents, disillusioned spouses and broken-half-in-two children pour out pain in the only way they understood—so I smiled and gave Mike time, praying he would become more comfortable. "You love your barroom language."

"I don't like your questions and, well ... uh, ma'am, either I answer them like I want to or I'm outta here," he explained in a single breath.

Lord, forgive me, but I've got to meet this kid on his own turf. I tossed a couple cuss words of my own. "Let's just talk then." He peeked upward, showcasing a boyish grin allowing glimpses of a face barely old enough to shave.

I flipped through his intake form for additional information. "So, if you did want to be here, and you did want to talk, what would we talk about?" I directed the question to Mike's ball cap, considering he wouldn't maintain eye contact.

"How would I know since I don't?"

"Fair enough. Let's start then with why your mom thinks you need to be here." I read aloud: "Mike hangs with the wrong crowd. The faculty caught him at school with marijuana on three occasions. He's suspended from school for thirty days with mandatory counseling before he can return. I believe he is getting the marijuana from his friends." I looked up.

"That is so messed up." A choice blend of amusement and indignation colored his voice.

"Which part?"

"All of it."

"Then you tell your story."

I waited through his silence while fan blades whirled and floors creaked as other people walked through the building—my old renovated house on piers.

I picked up the water bottle from the table beside my chair, took a drink, and snuggled in.

"You drink two things at once?"

"Sometimes."

Circling eyes checked out my surroundings. "This is a girlie room."

I glimpsed his sapphire eyes. Eyes the color of surf off Saint Thomas, only locked tight. Blond fuzz framed his lips and ears. I wondered if his eyes were contact color enhanced but decided he didn't look the type. I shrugged, "I'm a girlie."

"No joke."

"So, the marijuana thing …" I made a circling motion with my hand and looked at him.

He giggled. "What marijuana thing?" His laughter started small then bubbled up.

I sensed when I'd walked in that he'd smoked marijuana, but his increased high signaled he'd taken a pill of some kind too.

I moved my foot to the rhythm of the fan and inspected him.

"What …" He guffawed. "Marijuana thing?"

"This marijuana thing." I regarded this small boy with perfect eyes whose laughter rolled over crooked teeth set too close together. Every time he stopped laughing and tried to say something, he giggled again.

"You're high right now."

"Not high enough."

"Is there something funny you can share with me? If there is, I'd love to hear it."

"No. Well … yeah. I do wanna tell you something after all."

"By all means.

"My mom is a … a … well, she's stupid and my stepfather is a drunken idiot who can't pour urine out of his own boot with both hands."

"Okay." Hoping he would say more, I waited, pushing my foot against the floor, taking another sip from my water. "Mike?"

"What?" he barked.

"Go on."

"Go on with what?"

"Your family. Keep telling me about your family. Your parents."

"I just told you."

He wasn't in great shape for a session, but he needed to be here and I sensed a great deal of hurt lurking inside a casual facade. "What about your father? Do you have a stepmother?"

"I told you. You not listenin'? That the deal? My mom pays you and you don't even listen?"

"You said your stepfather is an idiot. You didn't mention your father."

"Yes, I did. I said he's an idiot."

"I thought you said your stepfather."

"He's the father I have."

"Where's your real father? Your birth father?"

Fire fanned through sapphire orbs. "Real father?" Mike grew angrier causing his vocabulary to narrow to four-letter words. "Did you say real father?"

"I did."

"Why'd you ask that?"

"Because I wanted to learn about your family. About your life."

"You don't care about me. Don't know anything about me. If I thought you did ..." Mike shifted on the sofa.

"Say it. Let me in, even if it's a bit."

"What would you know about my real father? You strike me as a self-righteous bi—lady who sits back here and tells everybody else how to live their lives." He glared at me.

"What I really want is for us to get acquainted."

He kept talking over my words. "You haven't a clue who I am. You dress in smart clothes and judge people. Does that help you feel intelligent or superior?" He scowled, as his eyes raked over me. He spit each word as if it had a bad taste. "Look at you, I bet your dress cost five hundred dollars."

It wasn't a real question, not why he was here. I didn't answer.

"Did it? I want to know. Did it?" His nostrils flared. "I asked you a question."

"No."

"Four hundred?"

"Mike—"

"Three hundred?"

"Everything's not about money."

"Spoken like a person with money."

"Two-fifty for the dress, one-seventy-five for the shoes." I glanced at his own designer sneakers. "Less than yours?"

He ignored my remark. "What on earth would you know about real fathers and pain and suffering? And stepfathers, and moms jumping backwards to do everything they ask, and idiots?" Mike slammed his fist into the sofa with each word and hardly took a breath. "And sharing the same bathroom with siblings and stepfathers who come stumbling down the hallway in the middle of the night?" His anger boiled over, soaking his words. "And sisters who cry to go see real fathers, and moms who watch the clock when stepfathers are gone and who count the drinks when he stays in.

"Real? Father?" His cap slumped sideways on his head. "I get sick to death of my sister bellyaching about our real father not picking her up. About my mom not letting her go even if he would pick her up, but believe me he wouldn't." He righted his cap. "Oh believe me, he wouldn't."

"Okay," I breathed, more exhale than word.

"I doubt I'll ever talk about him, but if ... and that's a big if I do, it'll be when *I* say we talk about him. You get that? I need to know you get that, lady."

My eyes focused directly on his. "I got it."

"Remember, I don't want to be here." A near tangible rawness clung to his every word. "If I wanted to be here, I wouldn't talk about him."

Jordan had been right. One of these days I had to stop seeing kids. Not because I didn't care, but because I cared so much about whatever was eating this kid that every cell in my body ached.

Sometimes I hated my job.

Chapter 13

"Listen, and listen good, Miss High-and-Mighty. You think you know everything about everybody but don't know jack about nothing. You're a piece a' work who's spent your whole worthless life in a college classroom trying to figure out how to mess with people's heads. If you go down that little pig trail again, you have seen the last of me. Besides, I'm not coming back."

"You live with your mom and stepfather?" My gaze was direct. "The ones you call idiots."

His lashes blinked rapidly. "Wasn't that the part where you were supposed to close your little notebook? When you either dab at your pale face or turn bright red. Then slip out and stomp down the hallway to tell my mother I need a male therapist. Someone who can deal with me better?"

"Was it? Define idiot."

"Define non-idiot," he challenged.

"It's your session."

His eyes burned into mine. "This must be fun for you."

"No, I hate watching you suffer."

"You don't know me. I'm not suffering."

He suffered all right. Hurt reeked and raged from his every angle.

"What makes you think I'm suffering when you don't know me?"

The clock's ticking hung between us. Pulse points drummed in my temples and throat. "Non-idiot would be a person who makes the best decisions she can, helps whoever she can, and leaves others alone. Someone who has peace with her family, herself, and God."

"And that would be you, right?"

"No, not me always. But I work on it daily."

"You love your kids?"

"Unconditionally. I have a seven-year-old daughter."

"You listen to her?"

"Yes."

"Does she respect you?"

"I believe with all my heart she does. She shows every sign."

"Well, goody goody for you."

I prayed, needing him to say something that mattered.

Three minutes passed before Mike said, "My friends hang with the wrong crowd. Me. I'm the wrong crowd." He shifted on the sofa. "I supply the weed. You should see my truck. It's a large black one with leather seats and custom wheels." He attempted a smile. "I can get any drug and enough alcohol to keep this whole town flying. Mom and Jeff think I cut lawns for money, and listen to this," he said leaning toward me, "my lawn mower has been busted for two years. How stupid would you have to be to buy that?"

I said, "Sounds like they may not be paying close attention."

"Okay, you getting the picture? Hey, you gotta admit though, I have this innocent-looking face. I could pass for the right crowd as long as my parents keep their heads up their ... anal sphincters."

This child laughed a lot, but I recognized it as an attempt to hide suffering. It wasn't humor. "Not to mention the blond hair and blue-eyed thing," I said. "It all adds to the innocent look."

"It's a pretty good gig."

"But you aren't happy. What are you going to do about school and life?"

He appraised my girlie office with skepticism. His eyes loafed around the walls, scanning everything but showing interest in nothing. His brows knit at the little red-haired girl clutching her bundle of pink posies in the painting above my head. "I have a life. I bet I make as much money as you do, and I'm quitting school, thank you very much. Don't you go to school to learn how to make money? Well, I've mastered that already. You follow me?"

"I understand what you said. I'm not sure that's the same as following your logic."

"Whatever. I'll sit here with you for an hour, my mom will get off my back for today, and we'll all be happy."

My eyes roamed over this kid. Something about his birth father ate at his guts. Without someone reaching him soon he would die on the street behind the wheel of his fancy vehicle or his body would show up inside some dumpster. That's what drugs were best at.

On the spot I decided to try something desperate. "What about your kid?"

"What?"

"Your kid?" A decided long shot, but I needed his attention.

"Well now, you've gone nuts or you've read the wrong chart. I ain't got no stinkin' kid. I ain't even got a serious girlfriend. Just ... hey"—he leaned forward and pushed his ball cap further back on his head—"do you know something I don't?"

"No."

"You are off your rocker. Are you high right now?"

"No," I leveled my eyes at his, like I knew where I was going with this. *Help me, Father.* "I don't mean now. I mean in ten years, when you'll have a child and you're home—well, if you're not in jail for the drug thing—sitting in your mighty fine house, listening to your stereo—"

"Home entertainment system."

"That too," I nodded, "and you and your wife have dinner—"

"Steak. Filet mignon."

"Oh yeah, I hear ya. And as you're settling in, getting comfortable in front of your home entertainment system, your blond-haired and blue-eyed son asks you on a homework night to help him solve for x and graph the solution on a number line."

"What?" He scratched the blond bangs that peeked from the front of his cap. "That's a bunch of crap. This little story hour started out fun, but I ain't playin' no more. And, like I said, it's a big bunch of crap."

"Yeah, the crap you learn in school then help your son to learn."

Mike left the building. Not his person. His body stayed on my sofa, but his air up and left. His face blanched to a sickly white and his soul searched for a place to grab hold.

Looking into his eyes, I observed as his Ghosts of Christmases Past buckled before the knees of his Ghosts of Christmases Future. A panoramic view of more emotions than he could ever have named rolled from his eyes.

"You're okay, Mike."

The clock ticked and a boy fragmented.

Lord, in your mercy, help me help this child.

He rose gingerly and walked across the room. He leaned against the dark wood molding that framed the old windows and stared through handmade screens that overlooked the long back porch. Mike didn't flinch when a bird banged its beak into the window, an inch from his nose.

Please. Don't run away.

He shoved hands deep inside his pockets. He took them back out, turned them over and examined them like searching for clues, then turned from the window. His hands found his pockets again and he started to say something, but appeared to find no words. Fifteen minutes of our fifty-minute session found Mike staring mutely into my backyard.

Don't run away, Mike, don't run away. I held my breath, pulse timing itself to the clock.

"You're a tough broad," he said when he turned. "I didn't expect that."

"You're pretty tough yourself."

"I need to say something."

"I need to hear it."

He struggled to speak. "I. Will. Never. Have. A. Son." His heartbeat thrummed against the smooth skin at the hollow of his throat. His mouth clicked, sounding dry. "I will never have a child. Because I will never ever abandon and humiliate a little kid."

"It's okay, Mike."

He dropped into the armchair to my left.

I looked at the top of his bowed head.

He gripped the chair arms and shoved his cap between his knees while teardrops dotted his jeans. "I intended to hate you, Ms. Katie."

"I didn't intend to hate you, Mike." This poor boy. "Is being a father and a failure one and the same to you?"

His eyes burned into mine. "I already warned you about my father."

"This was a more general question."

"Yeah, right." He cleared his throat. "I think I'll come back Thursday. Okay?"

Thursday. I was hoping to have free time with Bailey since school had closed for summer break and I left the university early. Mike didn't look up, so I laid two tissues on his knee. "I'm not here on Thursdays."

"Fine. I'll see you around … sometime … maybe." He stood up, wiped his face on his shirtsleeve. "I have a cold," he mumbled. Clean folded tissues dropped to the floor.

"I can be here Thursday," I said.

"Don't be doing me no special favors. I don't need to be here."

"Ditto."

"I'll be here at noon," he said.

"Me too."

Chapter 14

I thought about Mike as I cruised toward the clinic. If he showed, I'd be stunned. Prayer for him had been a constant since he'd left my office the day before. There were moments he'd verged the brink of saying something. He'd said a lot, really, for a kid swearing he didn't want to be in my office. Looking so tired, so small, he'd dropped into my wing chair yesterday.

I was likely driving to the clinic for nothing but I would check on Alicia and get back home early.

I lifted my cell and speed-dialed the number to Jordan's desk.

He answered on the first ring. "Psychology."

"Hey,"

"Well, hey yourself."

"I'm glad you could answer." I slowed for a red light. Took a breath. "I love you."

"I love you too. You don't usually get to call during the day. A treat."

"Yes. A short treat but I'll see you tonight."

#

A few minutes later I pulled into the parking lot. Well, thank you, Lord. Mike showed. But the little turkey had parked dead center of the driveway, making it impossible to nose my Beamer around him.

His truck—a Cadillac Escalade EXT with a deep black shine—dominated my parking lot. I thought back to the car I drove at Mike's age—my mother's hand-me-down 1960 Ford Fairlane 500 that looked more like a boat than an automobile. I growled.

My BMW parked behind his truck then I walked around the monster. Couldn't verify the leather seats through heavily tinted windows, but I estimated the custom wheels alone rivaled the sticker price of Jordan's redneck truck. I reckoned crime didn't pay long term, but it did pretty well in the short term.

Mike spotted me from the front office window. He strode down the hallway from the reception area to meet me.

"No joke," he said. "A back door."

I looked straight into his sapphire eyes. "I won't lie to you about anything. Ever."

"Uh huh," he said.

It was okay that he trusted no one over eighteen. He'd come back. Maybe he didn't have faith yet, but he must have some level of hope. Many moons ago—many more that I could count—King Solomon said, "Hope unfulfilled makes the heart sick." The verse rang out in my mind because that Scripture painted a perfect picture of the boy in front of me.

"Let me say hi to Alicia." I grabbed a drink from the hallway fridge, then offered Mike one. He declined. I closed the door with my foot then he walked into the room. "Have a seat. I'll only be a couple minutes."

"Hey you," I said to Ali after scurrying toward her desk.

"Hey." She didn't smile.

"Something's troubling you."

"I've already told you it's not."

"I love you."

"And I love you." She offered a half grin. "Go to work, Kat."

"Okay, but …"

"Go to work. I'm fine."

God, please convince Ali to tell me what's wrong and in the meantime, please lift her heavy heart.

With Evian in hand I slipped onto my chair and addressed Mike. "I'm glad to see you."

He'd dropped onto the sofa. "You had to come here today because of me."

"Coming here was my idea. Remember? Glad you came back." I placed my drink onto the chairside table.

"Feeling silly right now."

"Don't. How are you?" I hadn't grabbed his chart because I wanted this visit to be informal. "Relax."

"Relax," he mused. His hands shook.

I smiled, hoping it would be infectious. "Where were we Monday?" I remembered, but needed him to start the conversation.

"Is being a father and being a failure one and the same?" Mike looked up, his eyes burning into mine.

I maintained my smile, inviting him to make himself comfortable. The clock clicked away one second at a time. Hundreds of seconds passed. Click. Click.

I held my position.

Click.

Something powerful brought this child back, and I was in no hurry.

Click. Click.

My mouth went dry, but I refused to drink.

#

Mike jumped when the wind peppered the tin carport roof outside my office window with acorns.

I smiled. "Just acorns."

Click. Click. Click.

He clenched and unclenched his fists. "This was a bad idea."

Click.

"Cool truck," I ventured.

"I don't hate you."

"I'm glad."

We gazed at each other.

Click.

"You have something to tell me or ask me. I don't know which yet," I said.

The toe of his sneakers tapped the floor once. "No."

Click. Click.

Until he decided to talk, I sat without ammunition. Hundreds more seconds clicked by. In a fifty-minute session I felt pressure to pull a little, but today we had the gift of time. I tuned in to any move, any gesture, any anything.

"My sister comes here and talks to you. She trusts you."

"She does."

"Should she?"

"Yes. She can."

"My mom too. She thinks you're a saint."

"That's unfortunate. I hate failing people. I think she just counts on me a lot."

"Are you some kind of saint?"

"Absolutely not."

"Even close?"

"No."

"I hate saints."

"Thank goodness I said no."

We laughed again.

Click.

"What I came for is an appraisal."

"If you're talking about the truck, we're in trouble. I don't know 'nuffin bout birffing no trucks," I teased.

A furrow dug into his brow. He was unfamiliar with the line. "I didn't come here to talk trucks."

"I'm relieved."

The bushes outside the windows, stirred by a blast of Texas heat, scratched the screens. "Azaleas," I said.

"This building makes too many noises."

I shrugged. "Does it?"

"I bet this room makes less sound than it hears."

"How's that?"

"All the things people say in here," he said. "Their secrets, all their skeletons, all their filth, all their ..." His palms turned up then rolled into fists again.

"All their pain," I whispered, "all their hurt, all their anger, all your disappointment, your reservoir of broken promises."

His eyes rebelled against the shift in pronouns. "I thought we were talking about other people."

"We can be ... or not."

Come on, Mike. Come on, Mike. *Come on, God.* Come on, Mike.

Click. Click.

Warm breath traveled through my chest. My soul, in that moment, marched closer to the tune of a cardiac surgeon than a psychologist. Surgeons, having cut through the chest wall, can touch—and hold—a throbbing heart. But even when their incision is precise and perfect, the exposed body parts are slippery and only the exact amounts of skill and pressure will save the patient. In this case, too much emotional pressure and Mike would leave again. Too little, and his tiny heart would slip through my caring hands.

Come on, Mike.

Click.

Come on, God.

Click. Click.

"What about the appraisal?" I asked.

He looked at me. We had already reached a critical point. He appeared ready to bolt or tell me why he'd come back.

"It's me." He stared at me without flinching.

"What's you?" I asked.

"The appraisal. It's me. In your professional opinion, what do you think I'm worth?" An awful thing smoldered in those blue eyes.

"Exact or approximate?" I stalled, praying to divine what he meant.

"You can go for a ball park figure because I already have a first opinion in exact dollars and cents." His eyes stared right through me. "How. Much. Money.

Do. You. Think. I. Am. Worth?"

"Six billion, nine million, eight hundred ninety-six thousand, nine hundred and twelve dollars."

He tipped a pretend hat. "You are an optimist, ma'am."

I kept silent, allowing his feelings to hang in the air between us, like sheets on a summer clothesline in rural Alabama that haven't seen sunshine through the winter. "Mike," I said, "what are we doing? You have my undivided attention, but I'm flying blind here. Help me help you."

Mike slowly pulled himself to his feet.

He was leaving, and there was nothing I could do about it. My heart broke, but I couldn't help him if he didn't want it.

Chapter 15

He faced me, layered pain pushing his chin in my direction. Mike started to turn, first weaving then almost posing. He pumped his muscles and flexed his arms. His motions became dance-like.

My gaze followed his movements.

His mouth smiled, but his eyes hinted heartache. This boy danced out the steps of some heartbreaking waltz playing within his head.

I couldn't hear the music but I had crawled inside his pain.

Something ate at Mike's guts. He stared directly into my eyes. The clock took on a more melodic click, echoing the only sound in the room. Mike swayed slowly, soft tears dropping one by one. He kept smiling, focused on me all the while. His eyes were pleading, but devoid of any trace of sexuality or impropriety. Silently, he begged me to help him. The tears washed into a steady stream from which neither of us could or would look away.

I had a front-row seat to something Mike had probably never shown another living soul—his naked, breaking human heart. He rocked back and forth until we were both spent. Exhausted, he thumped back into his chair, dropped his chin to his chest, and let the crying overtake him.

And I waited for God to do something.

His head down, he searched blindly for tissue.

I stuffed both his hands full.

"Sorry," he said reaching for a second and third handful of tissues to sop the remains of what I gathered to be the biggest cry of his life.

Handing over the Kleenex he needed, I teased. "We don't charge by the tissue."

A post-rain freshness bathed his face, yet I sensed we had only experienced the painful prelude to whatever Mike had come to say.

"I'm worth twenty-two thousand, three hundred, sixteen dollars and twelve cents. Ask me how I know," Mike instructed.

"Mike, how do you know?"

"I've read the papers."

"What papers?"

"The legal papers."

"I see."

"Ask me what legal papers."

"What legal papers?" But I already knew the demon's name who ate at Mike.

"The legal papers my real father signed." He eyes hardened. "Ask me why he signed them."

"I know why he signed them."

"Ask me anyway."

"Mike, why did your father sign away his paternal rights?"

"You mean why did he sell me?"

"All right."

"When a sorry, good-for-nothing father gets twenty-thousand dollars behind with his child support payments, a mother has the option to petition the court to have a father pay up or sign away all rights to the child."

"Yes."

"So, she did. And he did. Not pay up ... he signed up."

"Okay." I chewed the inside of my lip till I tasted blood.

"He could've told the judge he would try to make any kind of payments and the judge wouldn't have terminated my father's paternal rights."

I hoped I didn't look like I felt—as if his big shiny truck had plowed me over.

"He didn't even show up for court. The sorry, lousy jerk was served with the papers two days later and he signed them."

"I'm so sorry, Mike."

"Heck, it ain't your fault," he assured me.

"I'm sorry, anyway."

"I don't want pity ... I want ... oh God, I don't have a clue what I want." He paused for the briefest of seconds. "Yeah, I do. I want not to hurt so much."

"May I hug you?"

"No," he said. But he dropped from his chair onto his knees and crawled toward me, looking all of four years old. He crossed the short distance between us and laid his wet face in my lap.

I touched his hair with feather-light strokes while I silently asked the god of all wisdom to make this child whole again.

For forty minutes Mike cursed his father with one breath then begged him for love with the next. On one hand, Mike blamed his father for his own decision to use and traffic drugs then implored his father to be proud of him for becoming entrepreneurial and making more money than his dad would see in a lifetime. He agonizingly apologized for doing anything that would cause his father shame or validate his decision to walk. Then he railed against a man who would bring a child into the world only to dump him like garbage. In the end, he begged his father to love and accept him.

And he sobbed.

I felt his frame stiffen. He looked me in the face but his eyes glazed over.

"Daddy, please love me. Daddy," he said, tugging at my hands, "love me. I can love me if you can love me."

"Son," I whispered, "I love you."

His head collapsed back into my lap while his body sagged at my feet.

A song pushed inside me. "Hush little baby, don't you cry, Daddy's gonna sing you a lullaby. Hush, little baby, don't say a word, Daddy's gonna buy you a mockingbird ..."

Feeling raw with emotion and sick to my stomach at the thought that anyone on earth could so fail a child, I reached for the wastebasket, sensing Mike would need it.

He grabbed the can and violently emptied two days' food and sixteen years of pain into it.

I reached backward toward the stacked towels, turned on the faucet, and dampened one. I applied it to the back of his neck until the siege passed. New clients, like Steve Giovanni, who have been curious why I have a sink in my treatment room, haven't met kids like Mike.

"I need to rinse my mouth," he said.

"Check under the sink and you'll find a stack of plastic cups and a bottle of Scope. Help yourself."

While he busied himself at the sink, I tied the bag lining the trash can. It couldn't control all the stench, but it helped. Later, I would spray the room with a can of air freshener—also stowed under the sink. He wasn't my first puker.

When he felt better, he walked back in front of my chair and knelt at my knees. "Is that what you shrinks call a breakthrough?"

"Pretty much."

"Now can I hug you?" he asked, a sheepish grin on display.

"No," I said, pulling him into my arms.

#

Mike went straight from my office to rehab. I sent Alicia along to guide him through the intake process. He would return to my office to continue counseling, but only after he was detoxed and stable.

#

"Stay," I said to Bailey as I walked through the door at home.

"Did we get a puppy, and I didn't notice?"

I dropped to the floor where she sat playing Barbie. "No," I laughed, pulling her into my arms. "I want you to stay forever at the age you are now."

Jordan's face peeked around from the kitchen. "We're getting a puppy?"

Bailey and I laughed.

"She just wants me to stay seven, but I thought growing up might be fun."

He walked into the living room and dropped beside us. "Just hold your horses. I've thought of putting bricks on top of your head to stop you from growing myself."

Later, when we were in bed, I turned to my husband. "She's growing so fast. How do we keep her safe?"

"What's bothering you?"

"I had a teenager today who spoke about his parents with such anger ... even ridicule."

He pulled me into his arms. "She's growing, but not a teenager."

"It's what we do between now and then that will make the difference."

"We're doing everything and she loves us very much."

I snuggled deeper into his arms and fell sound asleep.

Chapter 16

"Good morning."

Alicia sounded friendly. I was glad. She was keeping up all her responsibilities. Still her gracious self. But something was eating her lunch. Not one client seemed to notice, but she had been my close friend and confidant for too many years for me to not see it ... or sense it ... or whatever. *God, help my friend.*

She poured herself a strong Folgers. "Kat, you have a new client named Elizabeth. She's eight and an absolute beauty. Her mom is sitting with her up front. Judy Gibson."

"I'm still waiting for our plan to see more adults."

She grinned. "Didn't I schedule the police officer recently?"

"You did. You did try to suggest Angie?"

"Yes, but that only works when they didn't meet you at the university, or haven't heard you speaking somewhere. Like, when they've read the sign or found our ad in the paper."

"Judy was my student. It's been a while but I recognize her name."

"Three years ago."

"Good. That would put her safely past the two-year requirement before students can be seen as clients."

"She didn't come as a client, she brought her daughter."

"Yeah, yeah. Bring her file, I need to glance through it."

"Sure." Ali's grin looked forced. Fake.

Lightning shot through me. Her constant chatter had ceased. In the past, Alicia hadn't told me the time. She'd explained how her watch was made. But my hands were tied by the ropes of her unwillingness to talk. The urge to pry her mouth open rose within me.

Instead, I walked up front to greet Elizabeth and her mom, Judy. Wow, the little girl was a beauty. I shook her hand and introduced myself. "Hello. So, I hear you're eight."

"Yes, ma'am, going on nine."

I winked at Judy. Elizabeth's face had been kissed with round rosy cheeks and her beautiful brown hair spilled full and heavy down her back. She stood large for her years. Judy had called ahead to tell Ali why she'd be bringing Elizabeth. Alicia had also received a call from Joey Gibson, Elizabeth's father, promising to help in any way to assure Elizabeth made the easiest transition possible.

I'd returned his call and listened to his concern for his daughter. He'd moved out, and divorce was imminent.

Sure enough, Judy looked familiar. "You attended Lamar."

"Yes. I took your intro to psychology class years ago. I graduated as a sociology major with a psych minor." She brushed her hair back. "I've learned enough about human behavior to know divorce, even in the friendliest of circumstances, is a kind of civil war that takes children as hostages." She hunched. "Elizabeth is the youngest of my three children. I never saw this divorce coming and am taking it hard myself. I want my baby to have the benefit of talking to someone."

She wanted an assessment of her daughter to determine if I thought she could weather the divorce without suffering long-term trauma.

Was that even possible? I wasn't sure. I knew her chances for growing up to be well adjusted were better with counseling than without. And I wanted to help.

I asked her to step from the foyer so we could speak privately.

#

Inside the treatment room, she continued. "This divorce signals major changes in her life and routine. Her dad moved from our home and her daily life." Judy looked tired and anxious.

"Oh, and if this wasn't hard enough on Elizabeth, the timing of the divorce has coincided with her older sister, Jessica, turning sixteen, taking up bad habits, and pushing Elizabeth to the corner of her life. Another deep hurt for my baby girl." She clutched at the small black bag hanging on her shoulder from a silver chain. "Elizabeth feels as though she's lost them both. Joey has a girlfriend whom I suspect will become Elizabeth's stepmother. The gal has a daughter one year older than Elizabeth. Maybe they will bond and that could be helpful." Judy gazed at me. "I hope. I hope. I hope."

After a few minutes and additional facts, I asked Judy to return to the waiting room and allow me to begin my session with her daughter. Elizabeth looked furtive.

Walking back down the hallway with her I asked, "So, would you like to spend our session outdoors on the swing?"

"Yes, ma'am, that sounds great." She relaxed when I suggested we go outside.

She and I spent our time together on the swing. Kids—and I saw lots of them—hated treatment rooms. Swinging or sitting in one of the white wicker chairs out back helped facilitate the feeling of visiting with a friend. Elizabeth proved to be intelligent, open, and friendly.

"I miss my dad and don't think he's coming back. He has a girlfriend." She bit her lip. "We didn't know about her until he moved out."

"I'm sorry." I hurt for her. "That has to be painful. But my guess is he's missing you too."

She shrugged.

We chatted about trivia until she became comfortable enough to talk about her parents.

"Miss Katie, why do moms and dads get divorced, anyway?"

"Yours or parents in general?"

After stripping off her socks and shoes, Elizabeth pushed her feet against the concrete, propelling us into smooth motion causing the old chains to squeak. She hoisted her feet in the air and wiggled her toes, letting the wind filter through.

"Both." She scrunched her mouth into a tight knot. "But mine for sure."

"Did you ask them? You have the right to do that, you know."

"I did. They both talked a lot." She shrugged. "But after all the talking they didn't say much. I still don't know."

"Would it surprise you if I told you they probably don't know either?"

She studied, thoughtful. "No, ma'am. Well, really, that's what they kinda said."

"That's what your mom kinda said to me too."

"How can they split up when they don't even know?"

"Life is tougher than people imagine it will be. Sometimes money is a problem when it's time to pay the bills. Couples fight about how the money is spent. The fight … any fight … can lead to defensiveness and accusations. One person gets really unhappy." I paused.

"Please go on, Miss Katie."

"In many cases an unhappy spouse meets another person. Life seems simpler with that person. A mom is tired. A dad feels like he does too much. One may feel as if the other does too little."

"Like Carla," Elizabeth said.

"Your mom said your dad has a girlfriend. Is her name Carla?"

"Yes, ma'am."

"Okay, then maybe like Carla, or if not Carla then—"

"I guess my dad thinks life will be easier with Carla."

"It may be."

"It may not be."

"Do you think it will?"

Elizabeth made a fish mouth. "I hope."

I raised my brows. "Since this appears to be what's happening, I hope so too."

"You have talked to both my parents, right?"

"I talked to your dad on the phone before you came."

"Did they say whether any of the divorce is my fault?"

"They mentioned it."

She snapped her head up and looked anxious.

I touched her arm. "They both said it was not your fault at all." I squeezed her hand. "I talked to your mom and read her paperwork. You have a sister and a brother."

"Yes. Jessica and Joe."

"Nothing you, nor Jessica, nor your brother, Joe could ever do would cause your parents' divorce."

"Honest to God?"

I dragged my finger in an x across my chest. "Cross my heart."

"My mom says you never lie to kids."

"No, I never do."

"That's why we pay so much money to come here."

I laughed. "Is that right?" I kicked off my shoes too.

"I wonder why they never thought of not lying … to their kids."

"I don't believe your parents meant to lie to you." I crossed my heart again.

"But what if I'd made all A's on my report card when my dad still lived at home?"

"You'd have better grades and your parents would be getting a divorce."

"What if I'd kept my room cleaner?"

"You would be able to find your carpet and your parents would be getting a divorce."

"What if I had been perfect?"

"You seem pretty perfect and your parents are getting a divorce."

She reached for my hand. We sat swinging, holding hands and I felt good about Elizabeth.

"Will I still be my dad's baby girl?"

"You will."

"Can Kathy take my place?"

"Kathy?"

"Carla's daughter. My dad lives with them now, so maybe she'll take my place."

"No. He can love her, but she cannot take your place. He assured me on the phone that he has room in his heart for his daughters *and* for Carla's daughter."

"What if they have another baby?"

"They won't."

"You don't know that."

"Normally I wouldn't, but your mom said your dad had a little operation after you were born so he wouldn't have more babies." I patted her knee. "She mentioned it because she felt relieved there wouldn't be half siblings."

"An operation?" She frowned. "What if it grows back?"

I laughed out loud.

"How come you know everything?"

"Cuz you pay me s-o-o-o much money." I nudged her naked toes with mine. She scrunched her nose and wrinkled her brows. "Will I always get to see him?"

"I believe you will."

We swung, quiet for a few minutes.

"There is at least one more question stuck inside that head of yours."

"How do you know?"

"I just know."

"There is something I think about when I wish I was asleep, instead of lying awake." Elizabeth placed her hand across her middle. "It's the thing that makes my stomach hurt the most."

"Can you tell me what that thing is?"

"My grandparents." She took several breaths. "Not my mom's parents, but my dad's parents ... my Grandma Jenny and my Grandpa Joe."

I wondered how many names there could be that started with a J and why one of them hadn't been assigned to Elizabeth.

"If th ... umm they ..." she stuttered.

"They will always be your grandparents no matter what."

She glanced at me, surprised that I'd guessed what she'd been about to ask.

"Grandparents don't divorce their grandchildren."

"Well, since he's the one that moved out, well ..." She made a rolling motion with her right hand.

"It doesn't matter who moved out. You are stuck with the same grandparents for life. Guaranteed." I held my right hand out.

Elizabeth shook it.

"And the same parents," I said. "Almost always the relationship that parents and grandparents have with the child turns out in the end, to be the 'til death do us part' one."

"Till they die?"

"Till they die."

"Does that mean they'll always love me?"

"They'll always love you."

"When will Jessica love me again?"

"I haven't met her but I'm certain she does now. She's growing up and wants to hang out with friends. I predict when you're both older, you'll be best friends again."

"My brother, Joe, says she's lost her mind."

"Amazingly enough, she'll get it back."

We sat for a few minutes watching the sun crawl higher in the bright sky. Warm wind tickled our skin and ruffled our clothes.

"I'm glad my mom brought me here. I like you, Miss Katie."

"Ditto, kiddo."

"I love your neat clothes and your fancy car."

"And I'm jealous of your hair."

She touched her head and grinned.

"And thanks, but clothes and cars are just things that I've been entrusted with for now."

Elizabeth sang a little tune, making up a song on the spot. "I need to know how to make a lot of money."

I joined in the impromptu sing-a-long, strumming an air guitar. "Well, little girl I can help you with that," I sang soulfully.

Elizabeth giggled, while her hands strummed her own air guitar.

"Stay." I held the notes out dramatically. "In. School."

She abandoned her guitar. "How long?"

"However long it takes, sweetheart." I hugged her. "Let's ask your mom when you can come back."

"Oh, good."

Chapter 17

Home. Walking through the doors and into the arms of my family was a dive into a pool of lemon meringue pie … ooey gooey sweetness I melted into. A delicacy so perfect it tantalized me anew each time I stepped inside. I could fret and exhaust myself with worry about a client, but then there was home. Unconditional love laid bare. It wasn't true for all my clients' homes. I drank in what Jordan and Bailey offered me—the sustaining force in my life. Each came from opposite ends of the house when they heard the garage door. Both faces smiling and loving. *Thank You, Father.*

Jordan kissed me. "There's a plate of pasta and a salad waiting for you. Bailey and I were starved and Alicia called to say you would be late, but she had no idea how late."

"Thanks."

"Mama, do you want to color with me after you eat and shower?"

"I would love to."

"I'll get out the crayons. I'm so glad you're home."

"As am I." Jordan kissed me again.

I colored in her *Frozen* book and laughed with my girl while Jordan watched the news. Sara Beth Martin's face and legs and back pushed their way into our circle. Had I done the right thing? No. I should have demanded Cindy surrender her for the night. *God, be with her. You brought her to mind for a reason.* I could keep Bailey safe. But for a moment I imagined living in a home with fifty bedrooms so I could take care of the suffering children.

#

I dreamt about the house of endless rooms when my cell phone on the bedside table pulled me from deep sleep with incessant ringing. Someone had to be kidding me. I rolled over and grabbed it, squinting like the phone was my enemy. "Hello."

"Kat?"

The clock on the dresser read 2:10. "Alicia? You okay?"

"I'm in jail."

"What?" I sat up in bed. "Say that again."

"I'm in jail and I need you."

"This might be funny at eight o'clock." I laughed.

She didn't.

"This is a joke … or you've taken up heavy drinking."

"Shh … don't let Jordan hear you."

"What? This isn't for real."

"Either that, or I've stumbled inside a bad movie."

I pulled for a bad movie. "I'll come wherever you are and try to help, but I'll have to wake Jordan and tell him I'm leaving, and that he's on kid duty by himself."

"No. Promise not to tell Jordan."

"Why on earth would I not tell him?"

"You are married to the best man I know. I'm ashamed for him to know I've been arrested."

Dread crawled into my stomach creating little tremors. "Alicia, there is nothing I wouldn't do for you, except lie to Jordan. I let him believe a lie one time in our entire life together and it broke his heart. He moved out for months, caused the darkest time of my life. Things are perfect between us again." I swallowed. "What are you asking?"

"You've told me he's a sound sleeper."

No. No. No. "Why can't I tell him?" I touched Jordan's shoulder. "Alicia, don't ask this."

"I'm asking."

"I can't." I won't.

"I'm begging you, Kat."

Her breath caught.

"When have I ever begged you for anything?"

Then I heard her cry. Unlike me, she never cried. "Dear Lord, girlfriend."

"Kat, God as my witness, I am locked in the Jefferson county jail and I need you to bail me out."

Little knives stabbed me all over. "You're serious." I rolled out of bed, stumbled to my closet, clutched the phone between my shoulder and ear with one leg already shoved in my jeans.

Reality slapped me. No matter how much I wanted to help my friend—and I desperately wanted to—nothing could be done concerning a judge or an arraignment in the middle of the night.

"If you're in jail, I can't help before tomorrow morning."

"What?"

"We little church girls have no experience with jail."

"I'm getting some."

"You aren't familiar with how the system works. But Ali, I'm sure I've mentioned that during my internship I spent long hours sitting in a courtroom listening to a judge arraign person after person. No matter what the charge—and I have no idea why you are there or what you're charged with—the persons appearing before the judge, even on misdemeanors, had spent the night in jail waiting for arraignment the next morning."

"God help me. Kat, I cannot stay the night here."

"Sweetheart, in a town our size, no judge will make herself available for night court."

"Oh, dear Lord. They want me off the phone. This isn't exactly a hotel."

I heard more gentle sobs.

"I don't have an attorney, so they let me call you."

"Quickly. Where were you when you were arrested?"

"Driving my car near the clinic on Murray Avenue."

"Was anyone with you? Hurry."

"Lexie."

Oh no. The cop had arrested her in front of her oldest daughter.

"Where is she now?"

"I have to go."

"Quick. Quick. "Where?"

"I told her to go home. She—"

Silence screamed in my ear.

"I'll do what I can," I said to no one. Think. This was Alicia. My nerves were plucked like guitar strings. Sitting in my closet I started to "church laugh." My mother surely had dropped me on my head.

I pulled my leg from my jeans, still in the closet, and called Alicia's house.

Lexie answered, crying. "Hello."

"Lexie, what is going on?"

"Did Mom get to call you?"

"Yes." I took a deep breath. "She called from jail, but I don't have a clue why or what happened. I hope she had a blown tail light and an overzealous cop arrested her."

"Not exactly."

"I can't help without information and she didn't have time to give me any ... except she's in the county jail."

"Miss Katie ..."

"Lexie, what?"

She sounded terrified. "She doesn't want anyone to know why she's there."

"Your mother needs my help." I was baffled that Lexie played hush-mouth too. "I cannot help with what you won't tell me. She only had a couple minutes on the phone." I searched for patience. "That just leaves you."

"Miss Katie, she'll kill me if I tell you."

"Well … I'll kill you if you don't." I verged on meaning it. "This has something to do with Kylie. Let's start there."

"How'd you know?"

"It doesn't even matter. Just spill."

"Kylie's a good kid."

"Sweetheart, I know that. But her mother … your mother … is in jail." I closed my eyes and leaned against the closet door, the church laugh long gone. "And I know she didn't deliberately break the law. Now help me help her."

"Kylie has a new boyfriend. Rikki."

"All right."

"He's bad news."

I'd tried to drag this out of Ali for weeks. "Okay."

"I told Mom I'd heard at school he's always been bad news." She exhaled. "A reputation for using drugs."

"Please tell me marijuana." Not that I thought marijuana was okay. If drugs had been found—planted maybe—on anyone, a small amount might be a misdemeanor.

"Mom and I feared it might be harder drugs. Kylie's changed a lot and Rikki looks higher than a Georgia pine most of the time. But we weren't sure." Lexie hesitated. "Until tonight."

"Tonight?"

"Promise me—"

"Lexie, don't make me crawl through this phone."

"Yes, ma'am, I know how much you care about my mom. And I know you'll help her."

"Of course I'll help but talk to me." Talk, so I won't have to jerk you bald-headed.

"Kylie didn't come home tonight."

I dropped my head into my hand. I could imagine Lexie doing the same. She loved her sister.

"Okay. Then?"

"She didn't answer her phone. Kylie always answers."

I fingered my hanging clothes, waiting and agonizing.

"We even called Rikki. One day while Kylie showered, I peeked in her cell, found his number, then made note of it. When she didn't come home and didn't answer, Mom and I called."

"I'm sure I would have done the same thing," I said with honesty. "Then what?"

"Nothing. No answer." Lexie mumbled something to someone else. "Miss Katie, I have to put my brother back to bed. Can you hang on?"

"Yes." I heard soothing words whispered and doors closing.

Then, "Are you still there, Miss Katie?"

"Yes, of course." I slid down the door resting on my heels. "Keep going. But Lexie, bless you for caring for your brother till your mom can get home."

She sniffled. "Yes, ma'am."

"So, Kylie didn't answer and …"

"We didn't know what to do. But I thought we should check Kylie's room."

"All right."

"We checked everywhere but couldn't find anything at first. Then we noticed her baseboard dangled. It was kinda just shoved against the wall."

"What did you do then?" My nerves jerked with every word.

"Mom pulled it loose with her hand."

"And?"

"It was not marijuana."

I wanted to throw up. "Okay."

"I'm sure Mom has told you my dad smoked marijuana, so we knew what it looked like." She exhaled. "We found white powder and some rock-like pieces." Lexie swallowed hard. "There was a small pocket mirror, a razor blade, and a short straw."

I felt a strong urge to grab a trash can and fill it. "Oh, mercy. I don't know what you did next, but you did something."

"It was my fault and I can't take it back." Moaning and groaning crawled through the phone. "But Kylie is my sister."

"I know, honey. Just try to tell me."

"I told you earlier that I'd found Rikki's number in her cell."

"Yes."

"I was worried for her, so later at school, I asked around until someone told me where he lived."

Dread walked into my closet and squeezed. "And?"

"And we packed the drugs and other stuff, Mom shoved the whole mess into her handbag, then climbed in the car, and tried to take it to Rikki." She fought for breath.

Fear slid down the closet door, perched beside me, and grabbed my hand.

I could intuit much of the story from there. "How did she get pulled over?"

"Mom was crying so hard she missed a stop sign and drove right through it."

"Oh, no."

"When lights flashed behind us, she became hysterical. Out of control. The cop didn't know why, so he asked her to blow into a breathalyzer."

Every cell in my body cringed.

"It's a blur after that. Mom tried to explain that she was hunting her daughter and a bad boyfriend who used drugs."

A refrigerator door opened and closed, and I heard Lexie swallow with deep thirst.

Listening parched my own throat.

"Mom babbled and babbled."

Oh yeah. My friend could do that.

"The cop lost patience. He told her he didn't have all night, so just blow."

"And she did, right? When a cop says blow, you blow."

"No. She became more upset. And before I could stop her, she grabbed her purse, opened it, and held it up so the cop could see inside and explained that she just needed to get Kylie's boyfriend's drugs out of our house and back to him."

"Oh no. No." My sweet, naïve Alicia.

"She tried to tell him about the baseboard when he opened the door, pulled her out—she didn't even hear him ask her to get out—and cuffed her on the spot."

"I'm so sorry. I'll find a way to help her." Lexie couldn't see me shake my head. "But she thought I could bail her out tonight and I can't. I will call the jail tonight and attempt to find out for sure what the charges are, but I believe our hands are tied right now."

"My mom can't spend the night in jail. She'll just die." Frustration colored Lexie's voice. "Can't you do something?"

"I will. Like I said, I'll call the county jail tonight and ask what to do in the morning."

Her crying bled through the phone.

"If there was another option, I'd take it." I stood, my body creaking all over. "Try to sleep and when I find out something, I'll call you." I ended the conversation. I had to find out what I could do.

But not before I told Jordan. Alicia was my best friend, but my husband centered my world. Her shame wasn't lost on me, but I'd kept my last secret from Jordan. I woke him and explained Alicia's dilemma.

Chapter 18

My call reached a friendly and comforting police officer. I told him what I needed … that my friend had been arrested earlier in the evening and I needed to know the exact charges, what would happen next, and when I could bail her out.

"Well, little lady—"

"Ms. Collier."

"Officer Jacobs. You officer Collier?"

"No. A licensed counselor."

"Don't be shrinking me now."

I laughed. Whether nerves or mirth, the relief of it soothed me like warm milk. "What are the charges that have been brought against her?"

"Can you spell her name for me?" he asked.

"Yes."

The sound of tapping computer keys filled the empty space. "Let me get her profile pulled up in front of me."

"Yes, sir." I waited without breathing.

"She will be arraigned on a felony charge for possession."

Alicia. A felony? What were we going to do? "When can I get her out?"

"Your friend will be with us tonight."

A pit dug deep into my belly. I knew it … but still …

"She'll go before the judge first thing in the morning, for her arraignment, and the judge will set her bail."

"How much?" I asked.

"Well, little miss counselor lady, the judge will decide that."

"Yes, sir. What time?"

"Oh, can't say for sure." Sounded like he took a drink of something. "Court will start by eight, but I'm not sure what time she'll stand before the judge. They van the felons over to the courthouse."

Felons. "Yes, sir." I soldiered on. "Then what?"

"There are bail bondsmen littering the highway across the street from this place. I suggest you contact one." I heard him piddling with something. "Tell him how much the judge sets the bail for and he'll tell you how much money … cash only … to bring."

"Are you putting up the cash?"

"Yessir."

"You believe she'll show for her court date?"

"Yessir."

"Well then, my dear, you should be all set."

I thanked him, hung up, and called Lexie.

#

Jordan and I discussed Alicia over breakfast.

"Katie Girl, I understand that you will bail her out. You should." He patted my arm. "Are you prepared for the cash you will need? I have about a thousand on me."

"That's about what I have."

"It won't be enough for a felony. You'll need to run by the bank before you show for her arraignment."

"Thanks for understanding. I love you." I kissed the top of his curls and left the house at seven-thirty. I hated early morning, yet I went after kissing Jordan and Bailey and assuring them I would try to be home early.

I'd rescheduled all my clients and waited in the courtroom.

I'd been wrong—way wrong—about cattle-call court where people walked in on their own and waited their turn. When I'd sat in the courtroom as an intern it had been family court. This was criminal court.

Alicia and several others were vanned to the courthouse and escorted by policemen into the courtroom at eleven exactly. They filed into the courtroom, the whole line of them. I spotted her immediately, and she looked like she'd spent the night in jail.

I squirmed, aghast. Her detainers must have provided a comb, yet her hair was pulled back in a ponytail—something I'd never seen before—and her face was clean-scrubbed. And mercy, a hideous orange jump suit and ink-stained fingers.

The judge called out with authority, "Alicia S. Green, case number 094671."

She peeked over her shoulder, searched for me, and looked as though she'd rather die than face the judge. I nodded her forward and made a zipping motion across my lips, not knowing what she might say.

She trudged toward the judge's bench.

He scowled like a bulldog looking for a fight. "Ms. Green, you have been charged with a felony drug possession."

She started to babble. "Oh, Judge—"

I coughed like a flu victim.

She silenced herself.

"Have you ever had a felony charge before?"

"No, sir."

"Have you ever been charged with possession of drugs?"

"No, sir."

"Do I understand then, that you are a first-time offender?"

"Uh—"

I coughed like I might be dying.

"Yes, sir," she choked out.

"You are a first-time offender, but you're charged with a felony. I'm setting your bail at one hundred thousand dollars."

"Yessir."

The only acceptable way to answer a judge. He is the god of his courtroom.

"You'll need an attorney." He banged his gavel. "Bailiff, return Ms. Green to her cell, pending bail." He called the next felon by name and case number.

I watched helplessly as a cop led her away.

She glanced toward me. "Kat—"

I shushed her.

#

I drove across the street. Sure enough. Bail bondsmen everywhere. Choosing the cleanest looking one, I ducked inside. The heat wrapped me like a damp blanket. A bail-bonds woman, one not particular about her surroundings, hunched in the corner. Four years of newspapers piled everywhere. Stacks of magazines were strewn haphazardly across tables next to gray metal chairs. General disarray was the order of the day. A scratched industrial desk and a chair that squeaked when she moved to turn her jowled face.

"How can I hep ya?"

"I want to post bail for Alicia Green. Her bail has been set at one hundred thousand dollars. I'm paying her bonding fee."

"Ya got a case number?"

I pulled a scrap of paper from my purse. I'd scribbled it when the judge called it, thinking I'd need it. "094671."

She faced her computer. "Le' me look."

"Okay."

Her cheeks warbled when she said, "On a bail of one hundred grand, she can bond out at ten thousand dollars, but you'll have to fill out papers as the one bailing her out."

"Okay." I zoomed through the paperwork. Prepared with cash, I laid it out. I would sell my car and take a second mortgage on the clinic before leaving her in jail.

"Ya think she's a runner?"

"No."

"'At's good. Cause I'll come after your butt for the other ninety thousand if she don't show."

I glared at her. "I know. She'll be there."

#

My car pointed its way back across the street where I arranged for Alicia's release. She squinted into the sun where the heat and humidity slapped both our faces like a warning.

She wept a river. "How much did I cost you?"

"We'll talk about it later." My arm gentled around her, soothing her. "It's okay. We're getting out of here. I've paid your bond, and I'm taking you home."

She couldn't look up, just nodded.

"God knows your heart. This will somehow be okay."

She shook her head.

I understood. "I love you."

"I love you too."

#

In the car, I turned to Alicia. "I'll call my attorney. I talked to Lexie last night. She told me everything. So—"

"Everything?"

"Yes."

"I told her not to tell the drugs were Kylie's."

"And I threatened her life if she didn't tell."

"Kylie is my baby."

"Yes. And the drugs were hers and Rikki's." I turned her chin toward me with cupped hand. "Did you need my help or not?"

"Yes, but Kylie is still my baby and I'm not telling any attorney or the judge that the drugs weren't mine."

My brain screamed for oxygen and for a moment I could not speak through a collapsed throat.

"Kat?"

"Ali?" I said when I could. "Are you saying you are willing to protect Kylie and her strung-out boyfriend and throw yourself on your sword?"

"Yes, I am."

"Oh, no, you will not. I won't let you."

"I love you, but it's not your decision."

Though I'd switched the air conditioner to high, I felt sweat gather in every body crevice. "Well, let me say with unconditional love, since I feel like your sister," I reached into the console for a tissue and swiped it across my forehead, "if you think you will proceed with this insane plan—though you and I are joined at the hip and have been for years—you have lost a screw or two." I tried without success to calm myself. "Maybe even a few nuts and bolts. And now's as good a time as any to inform you I've told Jordan everything."

"You said you wouldn't."

"I did not. You told me not to, but I couldn't do that."

"We'll both do what we have to."

I sat stunned. "Loving your child is one thing, going to jail for her another. Who are you?"

"Kylie's mother."

I barked my tires as we shot from the parking lot. We didn't speak another word until I nosed into her driveway.

My eyes glued to the steering wheel. "Are you coming to work tomorrow?"

"Of course." She opened the car door, retrieved her brown leather purse from the floorboard, then left my car without saying thanks or goodbye.

We'd never had a cross word between us.

An anchor dropped to the pit of my stomach.

Chapter 19

I arrived home and walked through the garage door, grateful I'd told Jordan everything. I strode toward him and he pulled me into his arms but stared at the television.

Bailey barreled from her room, thrilled to see me earlier than she'd dared hope.

We both wrapped our arms around her.

She released her dad's neck first, then slid to the floor.

"Do you have homework before dinner?" I asked.

"Yes, ma'am. I was jus' about through when I heard you come in."

"Can you finish it while I talk to Daddy?"

"Yes, ma'am. 'A course. But talk to Daddy quick cuz I'll be right back." She grinned and blew kisses.

The yes-ma'am and yes-sir thing she had down pat. We seldom corrected her these days.

She scampered down the hall to her room, and I turned to Jordan.

He held the television remote in his hand. "I know from your demeanor you need to tell me about Alicia's arraignment and hopeful release, and I want to hear it, but you need to see this first."

He rewound the TV to the beginning of whatever ...

"When we bought Christmas for Billy and Sara Beth and drove to their house in our Santa hats, you introduced me to their parents."

"Yes. Why?"

"Just watch this," Jordan said, "I believe this news story is about her." He hit play and pulled me back into his arms.

A news reporter, wearing a navy jacket, white shirt, and dark tie broadcast from a large parking lot.

I didn't know why but a swarm of bees flew into my stomach, their sting more than a little uncomfortable. I turned to my husband. "What is it?"

He laid the remote aside, then gathered me closer. "Just listen, baby. And watch closely." He turned me toward the television.

The reporter spoke into his microphone, saying, "Last year in Port Arthur we aired two stories of children in our small town who died from being left inside the car during the hottest part of summer." He dropped his blond head for less than a second, then continued, "These tragic deaths rarely occur this early in summer, but the weatherman warned us last night we would—and we did—have extreme temperatures today." He gripped his microphone. "I'm here at Walmart, where reportedly someone left a three-year-old in a car. A lady who was willing to speak has said," … he glanced down at his notes, "when she walked by the car where the baby's head showed through the back window, she knew the little girl didn't look right, so she called 911, then remained by the car until police officers arrived. As we speak, a woman—perhaps the child's mother—is running from the store. The police informed me they'd paged her." He paused.

The camera swung around to focus on Cindy screaming. The reporter turned toward the shrill sounds. "We're experiencing ninety-six-degree weather, dipped in humidity meshed with the concrete temperature rising beneath the car. Our meter registered one-hundred-thirteen degrees when placed on the parking lot. The police arrived before I did. As you can see the mother of the child is hysterical. The baby …"

The reporter stopped speaking, but Jordan and I stared at the television while a small body was laid on a gurney and covered—face and all.

Water dripped from me.

Jordan ran the TV backward, paused the television on the mom's face. "Katie Girl, isn't that Cindy Thibbodeaux? Billy and Sara Beth's mom?"

I slipped from the circle of Jordan's arms onto the floor.

"Baby … baby, perhaps I should have warned you before I played the story."

I'd become a volcano and brains spewed from the top of my head.

"It's Cindy, isn't it?" He dropped to the floor beside me to comfort me.

But volcanos can't speak. They erupt. I crawled through our bedroom and on to the bathroom. I reached the commode, and the lava poured in phases into the bowl. Finally, I whispered the words, "Sara Beth." I fell into Jordan's arms.

#

He washed my face as I tried to pull the room into focus. He didn't try to move me, but wiped the cool cloth over my face, arms, and neck.

When I could, I sat up. "Where's Bailey?"

"Still in her room, but not for long."

"Get her out of here. Take her someplace she loves."

"She loves nothing more than grocery shopping."

"Then take her … and be slow about it." I lay back on the floor, knowing I couldn't walk right then. "Jordan … it's Sara Beth."

"I know."

"How did the reporter get there so soon? And show pictures of Cindy?"

"The reporter explained that later in the newscast." He wiped both hands across his face. "He was on assignment for a different story, but driving back to the station, he saw police cars and lights flashing. On a whim, he pulled into Walmart and got a two-for-one."

"What time did the initial report air?"

"2:15."

"What time is it now?"

"4:30. Why?"

"Last year when Bubba killed himself, the police notified Tabbi. Thirty seconds later she called me, shrieking and screaming for more than half an hour before she hung up."

He wrinkled his brows. "What are you saying?"

"I don't know, but this is a small town and my clients depend heavily on me. Even when my kid clients are acting out, their moms call me asking what they should do. Cindy's kid is dead, and she doesn't call me?"

"Sara Beth isn't your client."

"Yes, she is. And even if she wasn't that wouldn't stop Cindy for a minute. She considers her whole family my clients. She's my client."

"Baby, we'll talk as long as you need to tonight, but I need to take Bailey to the grocery store until you're okay."

"Yes, go now before she comes in here. I'll be okay."

He leaned down and kissed me. "I love you so much. Somehow, it'll be okay."

I didn't answer. I wasn't so sure.

Had this been a tragic accident or had Cindy left that baby in the car on purpose?

#

I lay on the bed, losing my mind. My body was racked with chills, and the heavy cover didn't help, so I left the bed, stripped my clothes, then pulled on a pair of sweats. The ninety-six-degree weather had smothered me this morning but failed to warm me now.

Cindy hadn't called.

I walked to the kitchen and brewed myself a cup of coffee. I hated the stuff but hoped it would warm me. Random thoughts haunted me. The beating Sara Beth suffered at the hand of her mother. Cindy had said disparaging things about Sara Beth from the first day she'd brought Billy to see me. What all had she said?

I needed to go to the office and pull her file. It was Billy's file but Cindy had taken most of his session. Alicia had resorted to transporting Billy to keep Cindy from usurping all his time with me. I had to reread that file.

I stumbled to my car as Jordan and Bailey pulled into the garage, their back seat filled with groceries we didn't need. Bailey liked to have the fridge and pantry overflowing. Whatever made her feel safe, Jordan and I were willing to do. Our little one had been hungry before she lived with us. I didn't care if she lined food around the kitchen.

Jordan inspected me, concern brimming his eyes. "Where are you going?"

"To the clinic. There's a file I need to read."

Bailey assessed me. "You don't look so good, and you never go to the clinic in sweats. You go all frou de frou'd."

Leave it to Bailey to make me laugh on this awful day.

"Do you need us to drive you?" he asked.

"I'm better. I can drive myself." I shrugged. "And I'm not sure how long I'll be."

"We have enough groceries for two years, so if you'll tell me what you want for dinner, I guarantee I can make it." He rubbed Bailey's head.

I hugged them both and held on tight. "Make it something mild on the tummy. I feel like I'll never be able to eat again."

"Got it." Jordan's schedule was more flexible than mine. He served as dean of the college, therefore teaching fewer classes, resulting in a malleable schedule. He did most of the cooking because he wanted to. "We'll come up with something perfect."

I kissed them before leaving.

Cindy still hadn't called.

I walked into the clinic, praying I had an overactive imagination and that what had happened to Sara Beth had been a terrible accident.

Alicia walked into the clinic right behind me.

"What are you doing here on a day when we've canceled all our clients?" I asked.

"I could ask you the same." She grinned.

It felt wonderful to see her smile again. "Did you hear about Sara Beth Martin?"

"Not till a minute ago." Her face pinched. "I left the house to buy groceries, but the story aired on the radio. They're calling it a terrible accident." She hunched her shoulders near her head.

"And?"

She stared, piercing my eyes with hers. "I don't know why I thought you might be here, but I need to tell you about a call she made to the clinic a month or so ago. On a Friday."

"What did she say?" My tummy butterflied.

"She cried. She said you had to see Sara Beth, and you had to see her that day."

"Go on."

"I explained to her you had no opening at all. She asked if you could stay late." Ali twisted her hands. "I told her you were already staying late because a judge had court-ordered someone to come here."

"Okay."

"She asked if you could come in on Saturday."

"I see."

"I told her I knew you and Jordan were taking Bailey to the beach."

"What did she say?"

"That she hoped she didn't have to do anything desperate."

"What?"

"Yeah, like kill the kid maybe."

"Dear Lord, she didn't say that, did she?"

"No. I just said that to you."

"Thank goodness," I breathed.

"Kat, can you honestly say you didn't think of it?"

"I can't say my brain hasn't turned over every possibility, but I didn't know she'd made that call." We were standing in my treatment room. "Let's try to calm ourselves, but when you're ready, pull the file on Billy's first session. Cindy said some un-mother-like things that day. I want to take another peek."

"Want tea while we're sitting?"

"Yes, but I'll make it myself. You're not officially working today."

She stood. "Doesn't matter. I'll make us both a cup."

I felt too drained to resist. "Thanks."

She walked toward the door but turned back. "I usually drink coffee, but my tummy is a little off today."

When she returned with hot Red Zinger tea, she clutched the file beneath her arm. After she handed over my tea and settled hers on the coaster resting on the end table, she pushed the folder toward me and collapsed in the chair. "I'm normally not here when you read a file, but I sense you may need me."

I reached from my chair to squeeze her hand. Her presence eased some of the angst from the morning. I sipped my tea for several minutes before opening the dreaded file.

I laid the open folder on my lap and flipped to the front. Transported backward in time, Cindy stood once again in my foyer surrounded by the contents of a small house—clutching a basket load of odds and ends in her hands. She had a huge baby stuffed in an infant carrier—Sara Beth, who I learned later was two years old and walking—but strapped in tight. She'd tried to break free of the carrier but Cindy hadn't even noticed her. Sara Beth had the appearance of a fat finger wearing a flesh-biting wedding ring.

I'd said to Billy, since the appointment had been made for him, "You must be Billy Thibbodeaux."

But Cindy had jumped in. "No. He's Billy Martin. My name is Thibbodeaux, but their name is Martin." She had gestured toward both Billy and the stuffed carrier. "Their father's name is Martin. My name was Martin because I married their daddy, but then we divorced, so I took my maiden name back, but then we still met up so I got pregnant again with him." She'd pointed at Billy. "I moved back in with Rob and got pregnant with her." She fingered toward Sara Beth. "We didn't remarry, so I will not take his name again."

I'd wondered how many times she had introduced the kids as, "This is Billy and Sara Beth, the reason I'm living with their father, whom I will not marry and whose name I don't want."

Cindy had brought Billy, hoping I would medicate him. I hadn't. As to Sara Beth—I flipped though the file pages—the only thing she'd said about her was, "She's cute, but I needed another baby like I needed a hole in my head, if you know what I mean." She'd laughed through jack-o'-lantern teeth, and talked non-stop.

I wondered then if she ever stopped talking to breathe, but she soon discovered her cup was empty. I'd been thankful for the bottom of a cup.

When she'd left the room for more coffee, Sara Beth had strained to peer over her carrier to see where her mother disappeared. But she hadn't cried. I had the specific feeling she'd learned crying wouldn't change anything.

I glanced up at Alicia. I had read some of the file text aloud to her. An unusual thing, but this was a crazy situation.

"During subsequent sessions, Cindy had said she hadn't wanted her last two kids—Billy or Sara Beth. She and her husband Rob had two older children who were fifteen and sixteen. She hadn't wanted to start over." I sipped tea. "She repeated those words recently."

Alicia, hesitant to speak, said, "She's made remarks in the foyer—basically to anyone willing to listen—saying pretty much the same thing. Her theme became: it's my last two kids who are making me crazy. I wish most days I'd never had them."

"And when she brought Sara Beth in, she asked if I thought the toddler might be slow." My hands trembled. "Sara Beth is … was bright and absolutely delightful."

"I thought so too when I checked on her. Cute as a bug."

"The last time she came with her daughter, Cindy looked awful. Near a total breakdown. I never should have let her leave with that baby." I rose, hugged Alicia, and stepped toward the door. I wanted my family.

"It's not your fault."

"You sure?"

Sometimes I hated my job.

Chapter 20

Summer soared—all three hundred days of it. While I grieved but didn't know what to do about Sara Beth's death except attend the funeral, when everyone in our part of Texas endured hot, steamy weather and sought relief with air conditioning, while Alicia waited for a court date, and she and I could talk about anything but Kylie, Elizabeth Gibson's dad married Carla. Elizabeth, her brother, and her sister participated in the wedding. Joey and Carla wanted all the kids, including Carla's daughter, Kathy, to help decide on the theme and help pick the color scheme. Elizabeth's dress—a concoction in lavender—had a matching flowered headpiece that perched atop her crown of glorious brown hair. At Elizabeth's behest her mother fetched the outfit to the clinic so Ali and I could ooh and ah over it. It was a beautiful dress, and she would look stunning. The wedding meant Elizabeth suddenly had a new sister, and she seemed delighted.

Elizabeth turned nine in early summer, and her stepsister, Kathy, turned ten. Elizabeth came to visit me weekly, appeared happy to be there, and she was always delightful. Her eyes brimmed with mischief and fun. She embodied a healthy, well-behaved child.

#

Everything about Elizabeth's demeanor changed by midsummer. Subtle things … I couldn't put my finger on it.

Elizabeth, Joe, and Jessica spent two weekends each month with their dad, Kathy, and Carla delighting in summers filled with surf, sun, and laughter. The camp had always been a comfortable place for the Gibson kids. Their family had owned the property and house before any of the kids were born. They'd always summered there and frittered away every available weekend that wasn't locked into one of the kids' athletic events. The new parties to the beach weekends were Kathy and Carla.

When Elizabeth first told me about these weekend trips after the wedding, she glowed with excitement about going to Dad's. But as summer moved toward scalding temperatures, and the tender blossoming plants died on the vine, so did Elizabeth's joy. The changes didn't jump in my face but certainly signaled my nerves. I couldn't decide if a huge problem brewed or if a simpler issue of family-dynamic changes had become problematic, but would work out with time, patience, and counseling. Elizabeth reported being happy about the trips. But as she talked, I realized she might be pleased, but something was wrong all the same.

A Wednesday appointment found the two of us in my treatment room. Not my favorite place to visit with a child, but rain blew in on a strong wind, leaving the back porch swing uninhabitable.

As we chatted, wind swirled through the oaks. Branches banged against the window screens and acorns dropped by the dozen onto the carport outside my window, causing a persistent peppering.

"So, this is the weekend you spend with Dad?"

"Yes." She half-smiled.

Maybe she didn't feel well, or she was tired.

Lightning shot through the darkening sky and thunder shook the building, threatening to rattle our teeth.

"Looking forward to it?"

She nodded on cue. "Yes, ma'am."

Didn't I remember that Elizabeth was afraid of lightning? Perhaps not. "What do you think you will do?" I asked.

"Camp."

"What, sweetheart?"

"Go to the camp."

"Will y'all still go if this weather persists?"

"Yes, ma'am. We go no matter what."

I scrutinized her face and didn't like what I saw. "And this is a good thing?"

"Yes, ma'am."

"Bethy, are you all right?" I walked over and sat on the sofa beside her, then cupped her chin with my palm and peered into her face.

"Sure." She smiled, but not like she had when I'd first met her.

Same beautiful face. Same deep brown eyes. But something was different. "Okay." I touched her chin with my thumb. "Have a nice weekend."

When I accompanied my charge to the front to meet her mom, I asked Judy if she had a moment to chat. Stepping back into my treatment room, I asked whether she'd noticed any recent changes in Elizabeth's affect. Did she appear sad or bothered about anything? Judy thought she seemed fine, but possibly tired from adjusting to the new routine of two houses and additional family members.

I asked Judy to keep a close eye on Elizabeth and to call me if she needed anything.

#

Elizabeth crept into my thinking during my weekend. This once effusive, expressive child had become monosyllabic. I couldn't shake the notion this newly adopted saying-almost-nothing style spoke volumes. Had she tried to tell me something without telling me? I related to Anne Sullivan trying to decipher what Helen Keller needed to say. Elizabeth was speaking but not telling. I'd been well trained to counsel people with emotional problems. Some things can't be taught, however. They must be felt. Bingo. I did not feel like this child was okay. I had absolutely nothing to substantiate this but my gut. But my gut was fine-tuned.

Multiple client problems kept me awake for much of the weekend. A follow-up report aired about a child—whom I knew to be Sara Beth—dying in the Walmart parking lot from being locked in a hot car. The television station warned parents against leaving kids or animals in the heat—especially cars—during the summer. The incident signaled the year's first death from heat exposure.

Sara Beth had become a statistic. I smothered as though someone had left me in a hot car. My breath came in shallow spurts. I had the horrible sensation she had been the first child murdered by her mother that year.

Many nights Jordan woke me, telling me I had been crying in my sleep.

I had to do something about this persistent suspicion lodged in my heart, but couldn't figure out what.

#

Steve Giovanni. Thank God I had kissed him off as a client. He was now being counseled by our social worker, Angie. Even better, we had become friends when he visited our home as a graduate student. Steve had nearly swallowed his tongue when he saw Bailey in our home. We'd explained why I didn't tell him at the clinic. He not only understood but thrilled in the knowledge that Bailey was safe and happy as our daughter.

I wanted to run my fears about Cindy and Sara Beth by him and see what he thought. I called on Monday morning to ask if I could meet with him about a sensitive and private matter—a police matter. He agreed to be at the clinic on Tuesday morning at 8:00 a.m.

Meanwhile, Cindy had not called.

I knocked on her door. Waiting on the steps, I wilted in the heat and humidity. Through the door I heard her scream at Billy and tell him to respect her time on the computer. Nausea threatened me. Ali had continued to pick up Billy for his sessions and I picked him up for Friday night dinner, but I rarely saw Cindy's face. She shoved Billy out the door when I arrived and shut the door behind him. She had either canceled or no-showed for all her appointments after her daughter's death. She'd never missed an appointment before the incident.

She screamed at Billy a final time. She opened the door with a big smile stretched across her face … not a pretty sight with top teeth sparse and her lower dentures missing. But the second she realized it was me, the smile dissolved, and she fell into my arms crying.

I held her a few minutes, patted her back, then pulled away. "How are you holding up?"

"Oh, Catherine, it's been horrible. First my kid died, then the police called me in for questioning … routine you know, but still …"

"I'm so sorry about the whole thing and I've been surprised you didn't contact me."

"Oh, I've meant to call, of course, but it's been one thing after the other. Not to mention Rob has seemed mad at me since the accident."

I had long been aware Rob was a kind and loving man. Always working two or three jobs to support his family while she, a college-educated woman, chose not to work. Rob was the crown jewel of the family. Both he and Billy. If Rob was angry at Cindy, he had a reason.

"You've missed appointments, and I worried about you."

"I'll try to come in soon. And Catherine …"

"Yes?"

"The things I said about the kids …"

I stared at her.

"It's nothing … except, you know I didn't mean them."

My gaze never wavered.

"Catherine, I didn't mean them. If you can't say anything to your therapist … even running off at the mouth … well, what's the point of having one?"

"That's true."

"Well, I'd hate for you to go running off at the mouth about something I might have said."

"Cindy, you are hurting but I won't stand here as you insult me. Our visits are private. And when have you heard me 'go running off at the mouth' about anything?"

She sobbed again. "Oh, never. I just wanted to be sure."

"I have to go to work. I've wanted to check on you."

"Okay. Thanks." She smiled.

Way too much smile for a woman having so recently lost a child. I've counseled moms whose children have died for assorted reasons—including murder. It took a long time and lots of work in my office, to smile again. Some were never the same. Losing a child is every mother's worst nightmare.

When she ducked inside and closed the door, I stayed for a couple minutes. Her words leaked through the flimsy door. She screamed at Billy for eating a Twinkie without permission. I heard her hit him. Then, "Go to your room right now, and I'll be on the computer, so don't bother me." I ached to bolt through the door and rescue him. I couldn't, but oh how I wanted to.

Could she have murdered Sara Beth?

Chapter 21

I left for work as late as possible to give Jordan and Bailey special attention they needed from me.

I loved my family with abandon, but another client, Lewis, awaited me at the clinic.

He sat in a waiting room chair when I walked up front to greet Alicia and Lauren, the new file clerk.

"Hey, Kat." Alicia seemed all right—not great but at least all right. She smiled.

"Hey, yourself."

Lauren turned from the filing cabinet. "Good morning, Ms. Collier."

"Good morning, Lauren. Alicia is pleased with your work." I picked up Lewis's chart. "We're glad you're here."

"Me too."

I nodded for Lewis to follow me. We passed my treatment room and descended the steps to have our session out back.

"I'm glad to see you again, Lewis." I slipped onto the swing and he plopped in the wicker chair. I waited for him to settle in. "What is the worst thing you've ever done?"

He joined me on the swing. "I wet the bed every night."

I could never have gotten away with asking that question to this eleven-year-old boy inside my office. But outside on the back porch, swinging together with sticks in our hands, poking at bugs crawling slowly by, I not only asked, but he answered. And he answered with honesty. Lewis became candid with a baseball-knowledgeable, ice-cream-licking, bug-poking, stick-wielding therapist.

"Why do you think you wet the bed?"

"Duh, I don't know." His mouth sneered. "If I knew, I would stop. Like, I hate it more than almost anything."

"Almost anything?"

"No, I said I hate it more than anything."

"I thought you said almost anything."

"No. That's not what I said."

A passenger plane, an American Eagle, flew low over our heads. Lewis startled so hard the swing chains would have squeaked, had Jordan not come down the afternoon before and squirted half a can of WD 40 on them. No one could live in our small area without planes sweeping pretty much right over their rooftop. Jefferson County airport sprawled beside Highways 69 and 287. If you lived in Port Arthur, or even Beaumont, you lived close to Highway 69. Sitting on my deck at home, almost daily I paused phone conversations as planes flew over.

I took a second to glance in Lewis's chart. Sure enough, he lived on Michigan Street, a street that intersected with 287.

"So, how did you do with the 'I'm mad' assignment?"

He grinned.

"What?"

"My mom seemed surprised when I told her I was mad at her, and my dad didn't care for it at all." He continued smiling. "Actually, I liked it pretty good."

"Did we discuss attitude when you're speaking with your parents?"

He shook his head.

"You can use the same three words with your parents as you use with friends or your sister, Whitney, but your tone has to change significantly."

"You should have mentioned that last week." He forged his mouth into an uh-oh.

"I purposely didn't, because now that you are wearing an I-did-it-wrong face, you will listen more carefully to that part of the lesson today."

"If you say so."

"Give it a chance. I'll show you how to deal with friends and peers. Remind me of your best friend's name."

"Germaine."

"What do you like to do with Germaine?"

"Shoot hoops."

"Okay, let's say he fouls you or is too rough with you or whatever ..." I rolled my open hand in a circle. "What would you say to him?"

He crinkled his brow and moved his hand in a circle. "I'm mad?"

"Get into this, Lewis." I glanced across the driveway and pointed. I had deliberately left the top down when I parked the BMW that morning. "The car is waiting."

He narrowed his eyes. "You weren't serious about that."

"Try me." I kicked off my shoes and reached for a basketball that lived on the back porch. "Pretend I'm Germaine."

His face said, what?

"Let's role play," I said. "What would you say to me? I've fouled you." I bounced the ball a couple of times.

He shuffled his feet and hunched his shoulders but glanced back and forth from the car to my face, then back to the car, then to the ball in my hands.

"I'm Germaine," I encouraged. I swayed and passed the ball from hand to hand.

He relaxed and bobbed and weaved with me. He reached for the ball.

I wouldn't let him touch it but bounced it again.

He darted toward the ball.

I ignored him. I bounced it again and again, refusing to let him take a turn. He reached for it three times.

I hogged the ball, half offering it then sweeping it out of his reach, dribbled it across the back porch then sailed it straight into the net mounted on the front of the carport.

His eyes registered surprise.

"I played in high school."

He grabbed the ball when it dropped from the net.

I stood taller than Lewis. I surprised him by lifting the ball smooth out of his hands, sinking another basket. I pushed, needing to see an honest, angry reaction.

"I want a turn," he said.

"Too bad. It's my ball." I tossed it again. This time it rolled around the rim, but away from the net.

He reached the ball first, but I grabbed it from him again, sinking my third basket.

Angry eyes narrowed, his muscles taut across his forehead. "Miss Catherine..."

"She's busy. I'm Germaine." I blocked his way while bouncing my ball.

"Then I hate you," he said, sprinkling enough four-letter words to warrant grounding for life.

"That's not what you mean. You don't hate me. I'm Germaine. I'm your best friend." I stopped dribbling. "You're just mad at me."

"I'm blazing mad." With slumped shoulders he turned to stomp back to the swing.

I walked behind him. "I hated doing that to you."

"Why'd ya do it then?"

I touched his shoulder.

He sluffed my hand away.

"Let's have a seat. I need to explain the benefits and disadvantages of words."

"Whatever."

"Your words must accurately mirror your feelings with few expletives that will, after all, require an apology later. The words, 'I'm mad' will work with almost everyone in your life when you're angry, but it will be necessary to remember with whom you are speaking. Your parents and other authority figures will require a different demeanor and different tone of voice."

After a few trials, with me playing everyone from Germaine, to his sister, Whitney, to his dad, Lewis started using appropriate words. "You really know how to make a guy mad."

"So, ready to go for a ride?" I'd checked his folder before he'd arrived to be certain his mother had signed the forms giving me legal permission to transport her child in a moving vehicle.

He jumped to his feet. "I gotta pee. Sorry"—his eyes opened wide—"I meant I have to use the restroom first."

I laughed. "I'll be in the car."

Running from the building and toward the car, Lewis opened the passenger door and slid onto the seat beside me, grinning.

"Seatbelt," I said, watching him with my hand resting on the gearshift.

"Oh yeah," he said, searching for the strap.

"It's farther back in a convertible," I leaned across to show him.

His body tremored. "Sorry."

I patted his arm.

Normally, after checking for oncoming cars and finding none, I'd squeal my tires coming out of my driveway, especially when my passenger was an eleven-year-old boy. I didn't do that with Lewis. Anxiety causes a gut-check reaction that can be rather intense, even painful. I had already made him angry. I chose not to add an anxiety attack.

#

I sent Lewis and his mom back to see his pediatrician with a note requesting Lewis be put on a mild anti-anxiety medication. Miraculously, the bedwetting ceased. In Lewis's case, the solution to the bedwetting problem was so simple it was heart-wrenching to realize how long its secrecy clouded his life. The "planning around the bedwetting" and "covering up the bedwetting" had colored the life and routine of his whole family. His primary diagnosis was an anxiety disorder. He became more anxious at bedtime. Anxiety about wetting the bed potentiated the behavior. The vicious cycle perpetuated itself.

Lewis received a two-fold benefit from the anti-anxiety drug. The hated bedwetting went away, but he became much calmer during the day. He reported relief from butterflies-in-the-stomach symptoms, and his mother and I both noticed visible signs he felt better about himself. The startle response all but disappeared, and he became more confident.

In the beginning Lewis hadn't wanted to take his medicine. Lewis may only have been eleven, but he was male. Men don't need help and they sure don't need medicine.

We sat outside again. "If you'll take your medicine, I'll pay you one dollar every day you wake dry for the first two months."

Doubt clouded his eyes. "No, you won't."

"Try me."

"Hey, that could get into some serious money."

"Hey, we could get you some serious relief." We struck an instant shake-of-the-hands deal. One dollar for every dry day.

Chapter 22

I rushed in the door to my family after a long workday.

Bailey tore from the kitchen when she heard the door. "Mommy, Daddy and I pa'pared somethin' that will make your tummy feel good." She jumped into my arms and I nuzzled her face and neck. "How 'bout chicken and rice cas'role?" She stayed put.

"I can't think of anything more perfect."

"Honest?"

"Honest." I leaned away from her and crossed my heart.

She grinned, slid from my hip, and ran to the kitchen. "Daddy, Mommy said chicken and rice is perfit."

I walked into the kitchen and straight into his arms.

"Perfit, huh?"

We gathered around the table. I hadn't realized how hungry I'd become.

We assembled in the living room after the kitchen cleaning. Jordan reached for his Bible, lying on the table beside his La-Z-Boy. The three of us curled on the sofa. He read from Jeremiah 29:11 in the Living Bible, hoping it would be easier for Bailey to understand. "For I know the plans I have for the Collier family, says the Lord. They are plans for good and not for evil, to give you a future and a hope." He looked up.

"Wait a second," Bailey said. "The Colliers are wrote in the Bible?"

"Every family can find themselves in the Bible."

"Huh?"

"Sweetheart, the Scripture I read tonight says, 'I know the plans I have for you'. But many times, I've found that inserting my own name, or my family's name in a passage, helps me realize every promise in the Bible is a promise to me."

"And me?" Bailey asked.

I tousled my daughter's hair. "Yes, sweetheart, it all applies to you."

"Is that why we sing in children's church, 'ever' promise in the book is mine, ever' chapter, ever' verse, ever' line?'"

Jordan and I answered together, "That's why."

"Well, I be." She studied him. "Daddy, is Collier anywhere else in the Bible?"

"It is anywhere we want to put it, to help us remember how much God loves us and that Jesus died on the cross for us … for you, Bailey."

At first, she looked confused. After a minute, she brightened. "Well, I like that. I must be pretty special."

Jordan answered, "The most special kid I know."

"I'm ready for my bath. I'm sleepy."

I led her to her bathroom. She had more questions as she stripped off her clothes. "Mommy, did Jesus really die on the cross for me?"

"Yes, for you and for me, and for Daddy. And every person."

"Oh."

"But Bailey, I believe if you were the only person on earth, He would have gone to the cross for just you. That's how much He loves you."

"Wow," she said as she crawled into the tub.

I helped her soap all over and wash her hair. Once out of the tub, I assisted as she dressed in her favorite bunny jammies and I blew her hair dry. "Now before you leave this room, check the wall chart to make sure you don't forget anything."

She glanced at the chart—complete with pictures I'd drawn. Checking the chart often, she brushed her teeth, put her clothes in the hamper, hung her towel on the bar, filled her glass from the faucet, and used the toilet.

I tucked her in bed, placed her water on the table, and called Jordan to join us.

He walked into her room wearing his own pajamas and navy-blue robe. "Ready?"

"Yes, sir."

Before he prayed, he pushed her bangs from her forehead and kissed her all over her face and sweet-smelling hair.

She giggled then folded her hands and bowed her head.

I relaxed on the side of her bed and followed suit.

"God, thank you first for my wife, Katie, and for our precious daughter you so generously brought to us. We love her. And Lord, we ask that you be by her side when we can't. Help her always be respectful of other people, and most of all, never let her forget that she belongs to you. We will love her every day of her life and rear her to love you. Amen. Your turn, pumpkin."

"Okay, Daddy. Now I lay me down to sleep … in a really good bed."

I chuckled.

"I pray the Lord my soul to keep." She paused. "I don't want to do the 'if I should die' part."

"We told you long ago, you never have to say that part. It scared me as a child." I shuddered and winked.

"Just saying …" She prayed again. "I know I'll live through other days, so I pray the Lord will guide my ways." She cocked her head. "Oh, amen."

He gathered the covers around her chin and I tucked her ballerina bear close beside her.

We both said, "Good night, angel girl."

We switched off the lights in her room and left the door, leaving the bathroom light.

Jordan asked as we walked toward our room, "How on earth did we get along without that child? And what did we do with our time?"

I laughed. "I don't have a clue." We nuzzled all the way to bed and afterward.

When he felt chatty again, he said, "You came home to tell me something a few weeks ago, but I stopped you because that was the night Cindy Thibbodeaux was on the news. I forgot to ask you about it afterward."

"I waited for you to ask. So much happened after that."

"Katie Girl, you think Cindy left Sara Beth in the car on purpose, don't you?"

"There's no way I can be certain without more information, but I think she's capable." I gazed deep in his eyes. Mine probably said a thousand things. "But before we get distracted again, let me say what I came home to tell you that day."

"Okay."

"It's about Alicia and Kylie. You know Alicia had Kylie's boyfriend's drugs in her purse. I went to court and bonded her from jail, but I've had no chance to tell you she's refusing to release facts about the owners of the cocaine. She won't tell anyone—judge or lawyer—the paraphernalia found in Kylie's room is not hers. Not Alicia's. She's willing to enter prison for the crime."

He kissed me. "I'm sorry."

"I'm unable to reason with her. It's like she's sleep-walking concerning Kylie."

"What are you going to do?"

"Right now I'm praying, but somehow I will stop her."

"My baby is convinced she can save the world."

"Well, sometimes God needs arms and legs."

"Go to sleep. I would try to dissuade you, but I gave up on that notion ten years ago."

We both snuggled under the covers.

It would've been the perfect time to tell my husband I was meeting with Steve Giovanni first thing the following morning to discuss Cindy and Sara Beth. "Baby?" Awe, he slept.

#

I waited for Steve while I made fresh tea and filled the coffeemaker. Ali would be there soon, but I'd arrived early because I had a full day starting at 10:00.

The clinic was small—1,300 square feet—and from the wet bar I heard Steve's car pull into a parking space. I walked toward the front door and glimpsed a white SUV.

He surveyed the room. "I thought you couldn't see me as a client again."

"I can't. But your relationship with my family has been worth it."

"For me too. Boy, was I relieved to learn you guys adopted Bailey. I don't have nightmares about her anymore."

"That makes me happy, but today I want to talk to you about a child I'm having nightmares about."

"Oh?"

"Steve, remember the baby dying in the Walmart parking lot a few weeks before? The one whose mother left her in the car?"

"How does one forget that?"

My voice shook. "Steve, I believe Cindy Thibbodeaux left Sara Beth in the car with the intent for her to die."

He sipped the coffee I'd placed in his hand and didn't speak for several minutes.

The clock seemed louder than usual.

"It's rare to talk police matters with anyone outside the department."

"Right, but you have the same confidentiality now as when you were my client."

"I trust you totally, but this is unusual to say the least." He retrieved a tissue from the ever-present box and swiped his forehead.

"I'm sorry to be making you nervous, but what if a baby died and the mother who may have killed her is walking around free to mistreat her son—a child I love, by the way."

"Katie, do you vow you won't say anything to anyone?"

"I vow."

His edginess was apparent. "There is buzz at the department. Some agree with your theory, but we haven't been able to prove it. No district attorney will take a case she can't win. It's the DA's decision." He took another sip. "Police officers have a lot of responsibility but no real power. We can beat the street till we wear holes in our shoes, but all we can do is turn over what we've found and wait until the DA decides."

"So, have you?"

"Excuse me?"

"Beat the streets until you have holes in your shoes?"

"Yes."

"And?" I asked him, while slipping to the edge of my chair and leaning toward him. "Did you have Walmart check their security video?"

"That's police 101. Of course, we checked, then subpoenaed their tape."

"And? What?"

"Surely you don't want me to lose my job?"

"No. But I'm losing my mind. Cindy killed her baby."

"Katie, it doesn't matter what you believe. It's what we can prove."

"What was on the video?"

"Is anyone else in this building?"

"Alicia won't be here till 9:30."

He checked his watch. "That gives us over an hour."

"Steve?"

"First, tell me what makes you think this wasn't a tragic accident."

"Well, it's my turn in the hot seat. I have never once told anyone, except Jordan, anything that took place in this clinic."

"We'll have to hold each other's information close to our vests," Steve said, the stress easing from his face.

"Yep." Little prickles started in my feet and climbed to my throat. "From more than a year of being around Cindy, I can tell you she never wanted her last two children." I grabbed a tissue from the box on the chairside table and dabbed at my lipstick. "I have never heard a mother whine about her children the way Cindy did."

"Not enough."

"There's much more."

Chapter 23

"Cindy would have called me from her car two minutes after the police asked her questions, had this been an accident."

He shook his head, but I kept talking. "She seemed more distracted than upset at the funeral. And to this day she has not called me and has not shown up for her appointments."

"Your opinion. I was there too, in the back row, very low key. We took her attitude into account but she could have still been in shock."

"What about the appointment thing?"

"People can stop seeing a therapist any time they want to."

"I know that. But she had a standing appointment every Wednesday morning at 11:00. Never missed. Didn't call in sick. Never no-showed. I haven't seen her since the funeral until I appeared on her doorstep yesterday morning."

"Katie, are you trying to do my job?"

"No. Well, not exactly. Just checking on her."

"And?"

"Different. She usually talks till she loses breath. But she said almost nothing, then ducked inside. I often have to go to my car with her following, talking all the while."

"Still …"

"Alicia has more details. She said Cindy spoke openly in the waiting room about not wanting to start over with little children. She told anyone who would listen that she was sorry she had her last two."

Steve winced. "Not everyone who whines about their kids kills them."

"You never said what you found on the video."

"I was hoping you'd forgotten."

"I have a memory so long it exhausts me." I half frowned. "Well?"

"She's definitely on the video. It shows her driving into the parking lot, getting out, and never glancing back."

"What did her face show? Was she nervous?"

"The video never showed her face until she came out of Walmart screaming. There was a light pole that blocked the front view when she arrived at the store and left the baby."

"That could have been deliberate."

"Or not," Steve said.

"You're killing me, man." I scrubbed my right hand through my blonde, pixie-cut hair. "But I have something else."

"Okay."

"Alicia told me Cindy called here about a month before Sara Beth died. She asked if I could see her daughter that day. I couldn't. I had a court-ordered client Alicia had booked late." I held quiet for a minute. "She asked if I could come in on Saturday to see Sara Beth since she acted like Billy had before Cindy brought him here." I grabbed Steve's eyes with mine. "Cindy ended with 'Well, I hope I don't do anything desperate.'"

"It's good information, but are you willing to testify to this?"

"I cannot. I'm bound by confidentiality."

"What about Alicia?"

"Not in the same way, but I had her sign an agreement that stated she would never disclose anything she heard here. It's probably not legally binding, but it reassured me about hiring her." I wiggled in my chair. "I haven't told you that Alicia is in legal trouble. She's innocent, but she's facing a felony charge. The defense would run down every detail on every witness. They would decide she's not credible. I won't put her through that."

"Wow, I had no idea." He massaged his lower jaw. "I've lingered at her desk to chat. She's a great person, easy on the eye too." He chuckled. "Apprise me if I can help."

"I will."

"May we speak of another matter?"

"Of course."

"There's an issue I'm working through in my sessions with Angie, but I haven't told you or Jordan."

"You can tell me anything. I'm your friend."

"Have you wondered that I'm in your home often and never mention my wife?"

"Yes. I questioned you the second time you came over but your face flashed a stop sign."

"I couldn't discuss it then, but she moved out." He glanced away. "That house we built wasn't good enough for her. I suppose, neither was I."

"I'm sorry. For real. But she never took time to know you if she believes you aren't enough."

"She has higher goals than marrying a cop."

"I wish she'd figured that out before the wedding."

"Me too. Let's talk about your suspicions again. I'm depressing myself."

"In a jiffy. When did she leave?"

"In May. Not long after my session with you."

"Do you miss her terribly?"

"I miss having a person in the house, but if I'm honest, no, I'm not grieving her."

"That's a very important distinction."

"Angie enabled me to sort the difference between lonely and missing my wife."

"Good for her."

"Yeah. She's a good therapist. But we need to talk cop."

"You sure?"

"Very."

"Was there any additional information on the video?"

"Dang it, Katie."

"There's more."

"At first we thought not. But I went back to Walmart and asked to see video from the whole day."

"Bless you, my friend."

"We had skipped from watching Cindy park the car to her running back out the door."

A drummer invaded my chest and head. "What did you find on second pass?"

"About two hours after she'd arrived, she came out and opened the passenger door to drop off packages. Then went back inside the store."

I sensed his desire to say more.

"What?"

"The two hours bothered me."

My body stretched toward him. "That's a long time to remain inside a store."

He hesitated. "Not if you're waiting for your kid to die."

I thought I would smother in my chair. "Did she look toward the back seat?"

"We couldn't tell. Remember the light pole. Those posts are huge at Walmart."

"Excuse me for a second," I said, leaving my chair and starting out the door.

I stumbled toward the bathroom. With sweat on my lip, I clung to the vanity and stared in the mirror. I looked like a caricature of myself. After two hours in stifling heat, Cindy could have smelled Sara Beth—not her flesh, but at high temperatures she would have released the contents of her stomach and bladder. I remembered the Hasidic prayer my dad loved. "Lord, I know you're gonna help me, but please help until you help me." Usually I smiled when I read or thought about that prayer. But I'd become mighty Casey and had just struck out. Out of patience, out of caring too much, out of hope. Another kid, Bubba, had died on my watch the year before. I'd struck out of everything. *God, please help me.*

I washed my face, ran a brush through my hair—supplies I always left at the clinic for days like that one—reapplied lipstick, and pondered running away. But Steve waited.

I filled a new cup with tea and walked back into the treatment room, nudging the door with my elbow.

"You okay?" Steve asked.

"Yes." No. "What do you need that would be real evidence?"

"Do you know if Sara Beth had been potty-trained?"

"Let me think. Billy wasn't at four. Alicia and I finished potty-training him here. It takes a lot of work and Cindy is rather lazy." My brows pinched. "Wait, remember she is a constant talker. When Alicia picked up Billy on the Friday before Sara Beth died, she said she'd run out of diapers for the baby, and wanted to get to the store while Billy spent the hour with me." I paused. "Alicia, who is a talker herself, told me about it after she returned with him. So, that's a no on potty-training." I blew upward, my bangs dancing across my forehead. "Is that important?" An invisible string pulled me toward Steve.

"Well, I told you about the buzz at the department."

I couldn't answer and held my breath.

"The department never released this information to the public. But the police went through her shopping bags." He coughed. "There was nothing for a three-year-old and nothing for a baby girl."

I sat numb, stared at him.

"We found a couple boy outfits in a size 5-6. There were cartons of cigarettes, a blouse sized medium, assorted food items, but nothing for a three-year-old. No diapers even. Of course, she could have bought them another place."

"I've known her a while. She buys everything at Walmart." Nausea bubbled in my belly. Sheets of sweat ran down my face. I grabbed one of the hand towels he had asked about on his first visit to the clinic and swabbed my face.

"You don't look good."

"I'm okay. Surely a shopper noticed an untoward occurrence. Maybe a passerby you haven't thought of. Steve, have you questioned everyone who was in the parking lot that day?"

"Everyone. I think I questioned a couple of dogs that hung out there."

"I'll think of … I don't know but I'll chew on it."

"Katie, you're a therapist and I'm a cop. It's my job to 'chew on it.'"

"Okay, I heard Alicia walk past my door. You can slip out the back if you'd rather."

"Yes. Thank you, I will."

I walked with him. But as we slipped down the three steps and toward his car, I said to myself, "I'll absolutely determine the right thing." The no-diaper issue had pushed me over the edge. "Steve, what time did all this happen?"

"According to the video, she first parked at 10:14 a.m. and came screaming out the door at 2:06 p.m."

"And the piece you found where she returned to her car?"

"12:04 p.m." He searched my face. "Katie?"

"Just wanted to know. No reason."

"Uh huh."

I waved as he backed from his parking spot. Scarlett O'Hara swallowed me. "God as my witness, I'll never let this go."

Chapter 24

Elizabeth visited with me on Wednesdays. She loved pizza, Taco Bell, and her new stepsister, Kathy, who at ten, had not lost her mind yet, which for Elizabeth seemed mighty convenient.

We were at Taco Bell for our session; her mom had signed all forms. Elizabeth ordered her favorite, which she usually ate in three bites. This time, she stabbed her fingers into a misguided version of pizza. Taco Bell cut tortillas into wedges, slapped on beans and cheese and proclaimed it taco pizza. I prided myself on being able to watch her eat it without shuddering.

"So, how did the weekend go with Dad?"

"Huh?"

"Did you enjoy the camp?"

"Nyes." Her eyes showcased two disparate emotions.

"Are you okay?"

"Yes. Could I also get a taco? I'm still hungry." Flat. She presented low affect.

"Yes, ma'am," I said. I still couldn't touch it. The thing that had changed. Could I pinpoint when it had happened? If I pushed, I would become a parent. If I became a parent, sweet Elizabeth would grow sullen and suspicious of my motive. No one wants an extra mom, and this child already possessed a crowded roster. "I think I'll get us both one."

"Okay," she said.

Headed back to the office, I ventured, "So, Elizabeth, you like Kathy?"

"Very much."

"Lots of things in common?"

"Yes, ma'am, lots."

"Carla treating you well?"

"Really well."

"You think your dad is happy?"

"Yes, ma'am, real happy."

"Bethy?"

"Yes, ma'am?"

"The card I gave you with my home phone number on it, the first day you came to see me ..."

"Yes, ma'am?"

"You still have it?"

She gave her purse a little pat. "Yes, ma'am, right here."

"And remember you can use it anytime. You wouldn't even have to ask anyone's permission."

She gave her purse another pat and nodded. She turned and pointed out the window toward a towering oak tree. "Miss Katie, look at that little family of squirrels."

"Precious." She avoided the question successfully.

Back inside my treatment room, I hugged her close before she left. She hugged me back, hard. Maybe too hard. I stood with my arms around her, needing her to be whole. When I first met Elizabeth and our visits ended with a hug, I did not sense this desperate fragment.

"Next Wednesday, Elizabeth?"

Releasing my arms, I meant to let her go, but I put my hand under her chin and lifted it. I searched her face again.

"When you hold my face like this," she said, "I feel like I'm supposed to say something. Like you're waiting for me to tell you ... whatever."

"Is there something you need to say?" I looked at her another moment before letting her chin go.

"No, ma'am."

"Scout's honor?" I asked, cocking my head to one side.

"I'll see you next week." She'd slipped under the question again.

"So, next Wednesday, then?"

"Yes, ma'am."

The clock told me I had three other clients before I could go play detective.

#

I ambled toward Alicia's desk. "Did you look in Cindy's file and find the family photo she brought me a few months ago?"

"I snapped a picture with my phone and cropped out everyone but her." She passed it over the counter.

I studied it for a minute. "The clarity is still there. Good."

"Kat, what are you going to do with this picture?"

"Show it to a few people and ask if they witnessed her in the parking lot the day Sara Beth ..."

"When did you add detective to your credentials?"

I stuck my tongue in her direction.

"Are you going to Walmart now?"

"Yes."

"Well, we're finished here for the day. I'm coming with you. Please don't get us in trouble. I'm in enough hot water already."

"You don't have to come. I'd planned to go alone."

"I'm not letting you go without me. I'll lock the front door and we can leave through the back."

#

"Kat … do you have a plan?"

"Sort of," I said.

"Do you want to enlighten me?"

"I want to find the manager and ask what cart guys were on duty on July twelfth. Specifically, the shift that would be on duty at 12:04 p.m."

"Will they give you that information?"

"We're about to find out. Make sure you have the picture handy on your phone."

"Yes, ma'am."

We slid from the car and the smothering heat accosted our senses. Inside the store we asked several employees before someone directed us to the right guy. At the courtesy booth, a pudgy gray-haired gal paged him. In less than two minutes he appeared, smiling all the while. He wore an inexpensive dark-gray suit, white shirt and dark tie. He looked vaguely familiar, but nothing came to mind. He wore a name tag: Randy Tearman. That sounded familiar too, but I was on a mission.

"Mr. Tearman, is there someplace we could talk privately for a second?"

"I hope our store has not offended you in any way?"

"Oh, no, sir." I don't shop at Walmart. "It's about another matter altogether. A private one."

"You can come to my office," he offered.

"That would be great."

He led us through aisles that covered a city block, then into a small room. Two straight-back chairs faced a desk piled with ad layouts.

Alicia and I sat down. And for the second time in her life, she kept silent.

"Mr. Tearman …" I had it. I knew why his name sounded familiar. "I wanted to ask a few questions. Really one, about July twelfth. The day the baby died in the parking lot."

"That was a wretched tragedy, but the store has no liability."

"Of course not. Let me get to why I'm here. Somebody saw something. I was wondering if you would give me a list of the guys assigned to gather carts that day, specifically at 12:04 p.m., which would be a shift covering a few hours."

"I am sensitive to what happened that day. However, that information is not public knowledge and would only be available to the detective assigned to that case."

"Begging wouldn't help, would it?"

"I'm afraid not. We've cooperated with the police, though."

"I have no doubt."

I tried to hold it together but couldn't keep the disappointment from my eyes. I felt myself look pitiful. I felt pitiful. I stood and Alicia followed. "Thanks for your time, Mr. Tearman." I shook his hand.

We walked toward the door. But Mr. Tearman said, "Ms. Collier?"

I turned, "Yes, sir?"

"You saw my wife and daughter a few years ago, didn't you?"

"Yes, sir."

"You made such a difference in our lives. I only met you once, but the impact you made in their relationship trickled down to me. Our house is a nice place to be now."

"I'm glad. But they put in the work themselves. I was just their shepherd."

"What is your interest in the guys who were working the parking lot that day?"

"I was thinking maybe one of them noticed something and hasn't told anyone."

He asked Alicia to excuse us.

He pulled a large, tattered schedule book from his top drawer. "I probably shouldn't do this, but I feel like I owe you and I know I can trust you."

"You don't owe me, but you can trust me."

He smiled, then flipped his massive book to July twelfth. "Well, the 10:00 morning shift comes in—their main job is bagging but they gather carts during slow times—and they stay till 4:00."

My body tingled all over.

"Let's see. That morning Gary Morris, Travon Smith, Terry Richardson, and Lee Simon were on duty." He looked up. "Does that help?"

"Yes, and if this leads to anything, no one will ever find out where the information came from."

"Had I not believed that in my heart, you wouldn't have the information."

"May I copy their names?"

"Yes. But I can tell you that Terry Richardson doesn't work here anymore. He moved to Dallas."

"When?"

He looked at his book again. "July twelve was his last day."

"Do you know why?"

"No, they don't have to give a reason."

"Thanks again, Mr. Tearman. I appreciate your help more than I can say."

"That day stands out as the worst in the minds of most people who work here. I hope in some small way I helped."

"Yes, you helped me."

#

On Monday morning, when I walked to the front office, Alicia stood over Lauren, training her to schedule and file.

"Good morning Alicia, good morning Lauren, I'm glad to see you again. Alicia needed your help."

Her green eyes twinkled at me. Glorious auburn hair fell around her face. "I love the job. Alicia said y'all would let me work around my college classes."

"We will." I looked at Ali. "Are you teaching her to answer the phone?"

She nodded. "Trucking as fast as we can."

"I'm glad to have you, Lauren. You'll spend a lot more time with Alicia than me."

She flashed white teeth when she tossed a wink. "She told me, and I'd already noticed."

I put the list of names I'd received from Mr. Tearman, on Alicia's desk, hoping she could work her magic on the computer and find addresses for the boys employed at Walmart.

"I have to get busy now," I told Lauren. "I really am grateful for you." I turned to Alicia. "Let me know about the list I put on your desk."

"Of course."

But Ali stood outside my treatment room when I opened the door for my ten o'clock to exit. She nodded toward the vacant office next to mine, meaning she needed a private moment with me and we both knew my eleven o'clock would come down the hallway when my ten o'clock came out. We ran a casual office.

"So, Linda," I said to the client who walked from my treatment room into the hall with me, "make your way to the front, and Alicia will be right with you."

"Okay," she said, disappointed I wasn't walking to the front with her.

"Linda."

She looked back at me.

"Do your homework next time." I made a writing motion in the air.

"I did it this time," she insisted.

"Write it down." I shook my head. "Journaling only counts if you can read it to me."

She sulked away.

Stepping inside the room, I closed the door, and looked at Alicia. My brows pinched into a question mark.

"Judy Gibson called."

"Elizabeth's mother," I said, watching her. "I don't see Elizabeth until Wednesday."

"I know, but Judy was crying. More than crying. I could hardly understand her. She had to identify herself three times on the phone before I could be sure. Man," Alicia said. She flung both hands out. "You have crisis cases and you never take a lunch. You trouble me."

"Judy Gibson …" I prompted.

"Yeah, poor thing. She called several times. There were four messages on the machine when I got here, but before I could listen to them all, she called again. She said she and Elizabeth had to come today."

I nodded. "Okay."

"She's not one of your panicky mothers who thinks her kid needs to see you because she had a bad dream. When she said they had to come, I figured it was an emergency, especially with all the tears and stuff. I tacked them onto the end of your day."

"That's fine but call Jordan and tell him I'll be late. He'll explain to Bailey. And you're right, Judy doesn't do hysterics." My brows pulled closer together. "Did you get a sense for the problem?"

"I already called Jordan, and no. I could tell something awful was wrong and there are marks on Elizabeth."

"Marks?" I hated the taste of the word on my tongue.

Ali frowned and nodded. "I don't know what kind or where, but there are marks." She looked tired and concerned. It took a big heart and wide shoulders to be a part of my clinic. Alicia had both. It had become our clinic.

Chapter 25

Six clients later I walked into the foyer to greet Judy and Elizabeth. Judy sat in the chair closest to the door, crying. Elizabeth hunched in the chair furthest from her mom, with her head down, gripping her purse as if a known thief hovered.

"Elizabeth." I could tell she heard me from the set of her shoulders, but she didn't glance up.

"Well, come on back." I motioned for them both to come with me.

"She doesn't want me to come back with her." Judy looked a miserable and frightened mess. I hardly recognized her with no makeup and swollen eyes. Hollow eyes sunk deep in her pale face. Everything about her screamed, "Something horrible has happened."

"Okay, E." I knelt in front of Elizabeth and laid my hands on her knees, but she kept her gaze fastened on hands, still grasping her purse. "What if I chat with Mom a minute first, then we can visit?"

She nodded.

I reached to squeeze her hand, but found it fisted.

As Elizabeth's mom wept and twisted an endless multitude of tissues into a pitiful pile at her feet, I absorbed the story. Jessica, the red-haired beautiful sister who liked boys and had taken up smoking marijuana, had stumbled into Elizabeth's bathroom last evening. Elizabeth had been lying on her back in the tub, not expecting company. The rather stoned redhead instantly sobered by the sight of what should have been her sister's unflawed prepubescent body lounging in a bubble bath. But Elizabeth lay in the water with teeth marks ringing her nine-year-old nipples. There were angry places where someone's teeth had pierced and broken the white skin around the pinkish-brown flesh. Disbelief and horror had sent Jessica to the floor as her knees buckled.

Panic and hysteria left their household in splinters. After hours of threatening and pleading, a tearful and frightened Elizabeth revealed to her mother that her stepsister, Kathy, had taught her two new games: "Mama and Baby," where one child sucks the other's breasts, and "Boyfriend and Girlfriend," where one child inserts her fingers into the other's vagina.

"Elizabeth," I said to her when she joined her mother and me in my treatment room, "I need you to lift your shirt so I can see what your mother is upset about." Judy remained disheveled and wept on the sofa.

Elizabeth didn't hesitate. She peeled her shirt over her head, revealing her chest. Obviously, Kathy had been vigorous with the "Mama and Baby" game. Elizabeth's small breasts bore teeth marks new and old. Her tiny nipples were swollen and bruised. Some welts were brownish yellow and some blue and purple.

I pulled my Nikon from the top shelf of an antique sideboard, stored there for this exact heinous purpose. After I snapped several pictures from the front and side view, I nodded at her. "You can get dressed, sweetheart."

Slipping her shirt in place, she sat and closed her eyes.

"Bethy ..." I said.

She shook her head.

"Judy."

"Yes, ma'am?" Judy was as fragile and weak as if she were the child victim.

"Can you give me a few minutes alone with her?"

"If she wants me to."

We both peered at Elizabeth.

She nodded.

Judy's shaky legs almost failed her. Mopping her ashen face, she left the room.

I perched beside her child for several minutes before speaking. "Elizabeth, please look at me." A dark sadness settled in my bones. I could work twenty hours a day, seven days a week, but there would never be enough of me to pick up all the pain. *Only you have the right words, Father.* "What are you thinking, little Miss Gibson?"

She glanced up. "I'm thinking I'm glad you know. I'm glad everybody knows."

"I'm glad too. Why didn't you tell me about the games?"

"Because I like Kathy. Because I love her. I was afraid if anyone knew, I couldn't see her ever again. I hate the games, but I love Kathy. Can you understand that, Miss Katie?" She peered with begging eyes into mine.

"I think I can."

She appeared relieved at my answer. At nine, she didn't hear the sadness.

"I'm glad you're not mad at Kathy. You're not, are you? Please. Miss Katie, don't be mad at Kathy. She's great. My mom hates her now. My sister wants to kill her. Hey, are you mad at her?"

"No, I'm not mad."

"Well, you are the only one in the world who isn't."

"I'm not mad, but I am concerned."

She studied me to see what concerned might mean.

"Concern is very different from anger. My guess is Kathy is a good kid."

"She is, Miss Katie." Elizabeth smiled exactly the way she had when I first met her, eager and warm. "You would like her tons."

I stopped her with my eyes. "These games are bad."

"I hate the games. I never wanted to play the games. I just wanted Kathy to like me. I never had a sister close to my age. She lets me wear her clothes. She paints my nails for me. Look, purple." She held up both hands, her fingers splayed into a deck of cards. "Can you believe she has purple nail polish?"

"I like it," I whispered. "But the games cannot happen between you and Kathy or between you and anybody or between Kathy and anyone. No one, not even another child, can engage in sexual exploration against the will of another—touch you in places you do not want to be touched—and call it games. No one can."

"Thank you, God," Elizabeth almost screamed.

I took an audible breath.

"I wanted so much to tell you." She squeezed my hands in hers. "I laid awake at night practicing telling you, but I was afraid Kathy would get in trouble."

"How did Kathy learn about these games?" I asked.

"Oh, her uncle showed her."

"I see." I held her eyes with mine. What? What? What?

"I think he's probably a bad man," she announced.

"I think you are a great thinker. But Elizabeth, what do you want me to do?" I held up my hand to delay her response. "Lots of things have to happen and I will see to all of them, and many of the things you won't find pleasant."

She sucked at her lip.

"But," I continued, "for tonight, what do you want me to do for you?"

"I want you to make my mother stop crying and my sister shut up. Don't let my mother call her attorney." She wrung her hands. "Tell my mom not to blame my dad. I want you to tell my dad instead of my mom telling him." Her eyes pled. "I want you to help me see Kathy without playing the games." She shook her head. "Help me figure out how to tell her I'm not mad at her. I don't want to talk to Kathy's mom about this. I want you to tell my mom to stop looking at me funny." Her eyes opened wider. "Tell her to stop breaking dishes and stop vacuuming the carpet when it's not dirty. I want you to tell her I'm okay. Please help me."

Elizabeth bolted through her monosyllabic barrier.

"You can. You can. I know you can." She nodded. "Oh, yeah, and tell my mom I don't want us to move far away and never see my dad again. And did I tell you, Miss Katie, I don't want anyone arrested?" She arched her brows. "Why does someone have to be arrested?"

"Well, I like a girl who knows what she wants." I smiled. "Elizabeth, I will address every single one of these issues with both of your parents."

"That means you'll help me, right?"

"That means I'll help you."

A light tap sounded at my door.

"Who's that?" Elizabeth jerked up with open suspicion.

"It will either be your father or Alicia telling me he is here."

"I don't want my dad to be mad at me."

"No one is mad at you, sweetheart." I rose to pull the door open. "No one."

Alicia stood in the doorway. "He's here,"

"Give us five minutes," I said. "Then send him back."

#

When I opened the door for Elizabeth's Michael-Brady-really-meant-to-be father, he looked confused and defensive ... and ready for a fight. He entered the room smelling of Texaco Refinery.

"Please, come in."

"What is so important it had to be handled in the middle of a work shift? We have the boiler room shut down and my crew is waiting for me to tell them how to locate the gas leak, then put that muthah back together." He stopped talking, taken aback when he noticed his daughter perched on my sofa. Joey peeled off his cap. "Elizabeth, honey, what are you doing here on a Monday? Didn't you tell Daddy you come to see Miss Katie on Wednesdays?"

She shrugged.

"Does this pertain to Judy hunched over her steering wheel and refusing to glance my direction? I tapped her window but her eyes glued straight ahead."

"Probably," I said.

Joey glanced at me, then back at Elizabeth. "It's Wednesday. When I dropped you off at your mom's yesterday, we went over your schedule for the week." He scratched his forehead. "Today was the dentist, not your appointment here." He shook his head. "She asked me to pick you up because she had to stay late at work. I scribbled in my planner to avoid confusion." Joey glowered back and forth from her to me. "Wednesday."

"Daddy." Elizabeth's voice sounded small.

"Baby, what's wrong?"

I motioned to a chair. "Joey, can you sit down?"

"That boiler room ..."

My face turned to stone.

"Sure, I can sit." He shoved his cap in his back pocket and joined his daughter. He gripped his hands together, tossing a nervous smile in her direction.

"Elizabeth, would you like me to talk to your dad alone or would you prefer to be here?"

Her father cocked his head to one side. "Alone? What do you have to say to me that you can't say in front of my kid?"

"Elizabeth?" I prompted.

"Daddy," she said, scooting to the edge of the sofa, "I am going to the next room while Miss Katie tells you something. But," she said with the relief of truth ringing in her voice, "I will be right here if you need me." She opened the door for herself and walked out.

When I closed the door, I heard her walk into the next office to wait.

"What?" Joey said, exhibiting confusion. "Did my nine-year-old just tell me she would be available if I need her?"

"Joey, there is a situation at your house, I—"

"A situation? What situation?"

"Judy called this morning to tell me that after you dropped Elizabeth off—"

"No. Whoa." Joey put his hands up to stop me. "What could have happened that Judy would call you instead of me? No, no, we agreed we would never do that. We would never use the kids against each other." He squinted. "If there was an issue that came up at either of our houses, we would call each other. We agreed to always act in the best interest of our kids."

"You are both to be commended for that. Judy could not have foreseen—"

"Commended for that?" Joey shook his head with a quick jerking motion. "Did you say commended for that? Judy and I are to be rewarded for loving our children, for putting their welfare above our pettiness? You mean they give commendations for doing the right thing?" Cuss words are evidently comforting to hurting Texas men. Joey Gibson spewed them.

I waited.

He didn't know the details yet, but Joey, like cornered prey, smelled bad news. "What?" he said.

"I am waiting for you to calm down."

"I'm calm," he said through clenched teeth.

I kept waiting.

He took a deep breath. "Okay, I'm okay. It's nerve-wracking being called from the job. Ya know?"

I searched his face. "There are marks on Elizabeth's body."

Chapter 26

"The heck there is. Is that what this is? You think I beat my kid?" He glowered at me. "Did she say that? Did Judy say I hit my own kid?"

"Oh, no," I said, but he didn't hear me.

"Nobody would lay a hand on my kid … not and live. Nobody would hurt Elizabeth. I would kill anybody who touched her."

"No one hit Elizabeth, Mr. Gibson."

"So, it's Mr. Gibson, is it? Wasn't it Joey when I came in here?" He glared at me. "It was Joey every time I dropped Elizabeth off here since the first day I met you. Now, I get promoted to Mr. Gibson?"

"Joey, there are marks on her that—"

"No, there isn't," he shouted. "There honest-to-goodness isn't. " Joey jumped to his feet.

Elizabeth startled us both when she walked back into the treatment room as her father leapt from the sofa.

"Bethy," I said.

"Don't scream at her, Daddy." Elizabeth peeled her blouse over her head with a single motion. She faced her father, naked from the waist up.

Total silence screamed inside the room.

Elizabeth bared her body and her soul before her father.

I watched Joey Gibson's face, chiseled with pain, as he slipped from the sofa onto his knees at her feet.

Don't turn away. Don't turn away from her, I prayed. If you can't look, she will feel damaged.

But Joey laid his calloused hands on her shoulders. "Thank you for showing Daddy." His hands left her shoulders to cradle her face for a long loving moment. "Let's get your shirt back on, now. Do you want to put your shirt on? Catherine, Carla and I picked this shirt out for Elizabeth for her birthday. She loved it, didn't you, sweetheart?" He made a valiant effort to smile for his baby girl. "Not purple, we scouted everywhere for purple. But pink is her second favorite color. She was such a sport about it not being purple."

His large hands fumbled, but he helped her raise her hands and guided her head through the neck opening, over all that lovely hair.

"Look at my girl in pink. I don't think you could look better even in purple. Although at the wedding that was a shade of purple you were wearing." His hands trembled. "Yes, lavender, I believe. Her picture is stuck right here in my wallet. Keep it by my twenties. Showed it to everyone at work." He dragged his wallet from his back pocket and there was Elizabeth smiling at his wedding.

Beside her in the photo stood a child I'd never met.

"See? Oh, have you met Kathy, Catherine? Has Elizabeth told you about Kathy? She has a sister close to her own age now, eh, sweetie?"

Elizabeth nodded at what should have been her father, but kneeling in his spot, a life-size wind-up talking toy, whose string had been jerked. Confusion wrinkled her brow. She couldn't decide what she was supposed to do.

"Elizabeth." I touched her shoulder. "Maybe you could go beside your mom. If she's not in the waiting room, check with Alicia."

She studied her father's strange behavior. "I'm okay, Dad."

Joey cradled her lovely face in his hands. "You will be fine, sweetheart. You are daddy's brave girl. We'll go to Dairy Queen after I talk to Catherine. I will make everything okay." He still knelt.

"Taco Bell," she said.

"Taco Bell. What was I thinking? Taco Bell for my girl coming right up." His head nodded mechanically up and down.

"Okay, Bethy," I said.

"Daddy, can you get off your knees so I won't worry about you?"

Joey blinked hard.

I'm not sure he realized he'd continued to kneel.

"Oh, yes," he said struggling to stand, "I'm fine, honey. Oh, and Elizabeth, don't sit in the room next door, please."

"No, sir, up front with Mom like Miss Katie said." She started to leave then spun around, pulled him to her level and kissed him hard on the cheek.

I felt the same impulse. His pain clawed at my throat like a wounded animal had crawled in there.

"Who?" The single word crashed from his throat the second I closed the door, behind his daughter.

"Joey ... I—"

"I. Asked. You. Who?"

"Please, sit down. I was hoping to—"

"A name." Joey stared at me. "No sitting, no waiting, just a name." But he dropped into the nearest chair.

"Kathy."

"Kathy?" Squinting fiercely, he perched himself on the outer two inches of the sofa cushion. "Kathy who?"

Oh God, help both of us.

"Kathy, may-god-in-heaven help me, whoooo?" he screamed.

"Kathy Fontenot."

His brows pinched, almost touching.

"Carla's daughter."

Joey's mouth fell open, suspended in time.

For a minute, he froze. I waited to see if he would move. "Joey," I said. "Joey?"

His body shook. "Not Kathy. It can't be Kathy. Give me another name, any name, but not Kathy." Loud wordless sounds escaped him.

"Joey, I need to tell you something about Kathy."

He stared at nothing.

"Kathy has been molested by her uncle." I swallowed. "Kathy is a victim as surely as Elizabeth is."

"My God, my baby girl. Oh, holy God, my baby girl."

"Joey."

"What have I done?" He looked drugged. He fisted his right hand.

I watched as he bit at his knuckles.

"Joey, we can help Elizabeth. We can get help for both girls. That's the good news." I crouched on the end of my chair too. "Now that we're aware, we can help."

Joey wept. Blood drops appeared on his knuckles.

"Her pain is hard for you to swallow."

"Where was I? What was I doing that I didn't know?"

"You were right there with her. Elizabeth told no one because she lived in fear of getting Kathy in trouble."

He gnawed deeper into his knuckle.

I grabbed a towel, wet it at the sink faucet, and offered it to Joey.

He didn't see it though I waved it in front of his face.

I reached across and dabbed at his knuckle.

He jumped but didn't resist. "Tell me what you said about what happened to Kathy."

Still dabbing at his hand, I said, "Kathy told Elizabeth that her uncle—I'm not sure who the uncle is yet—showed her two games."

"Games," Joey said.

"Yes. One was 'Mama and Baby.' The uncle evidently sucked at Kathy's breasts and called it the mama and baby game."

Joey turned to stone. He stopped crying.

I waited.

"What other game?" he asked, his throat hoarse.

I kept dabbing at the blood seeping through his knuckles. "Boyfriend and Girlfriend."

He grimaced.

"Kathy inserted her fingers into Elizabeth's vagina—"

"No, oh no."

"I can only assume until I have talked to Kathy that her uncle inserted his fingers into her."

"What else? Spit it out. What else?"

"There isn't anything else yet."

He stared at me, braced to hear whatever else I had to tell him.

"If I had more information, I would give it to you. You have the right to know. I would never withhold facts from you about your child."

"Somebody's been holding a lot of stuff … a mother-hauling truckload."

"Joey?"

He didn't answer.

"Joey. How many uncles does Kathy have?"

"One. Carla's brother." He jumped to his feet but misgauged the physical drain of his suffering. Unsteady on his feet, he sank down.

"Joey, I will make all the calls that must—"

"Calls? When I can stand up, which will be in just a minute, I won't need any telephone. I got me a date with my brother-in-law. I'm sure you'll understand if I eat and run," Joey said.

"Joey, I want you to stay put another minute and listen."

"That's too bad, Catherine. I'm not sure I can hear anymore."

"Joey, don't make me call the police to have them pick you up."

"Me? Pick me up? That's the way my luck is running today."

"I will have you arrested if I need to, to keep you out of harm's way."

Joey grunted and snorted.

My heart weighed a ton. "You cannot care for your family if you are in jail for killing your brother-in-law."

"I'll shuffle the deck and let the cards fall where they may." His resolve was clear.

"Joey, I will make sure both girls get help. I will talk to Kathy, to Carla, to the police department, Child Protective Services, and anyone else who will listen. I live next door to a criminal judge."

Joey made that clear-out-the-cobwebs shake of his head again. "Carla's brother is a registered sex offender. Lawrence Hubbard."

"What?"

"Yes, Kathy's uncle is a sex offender."

"Well, well," I said, "that will surely speed things right along."

"Not a pedophile. I would have paid more attention if he were a registered pedophile, but a sex offender all the same. Raped an old girlfriend, two years ago."

I gaped at him.

"It never occurred to me he would touch a child. My God, my child, Carla's child. Oh, heavens, Carla." He jumped up again, and this time stayed on his feet.

"I have to tell Carla. Has anyone told Carla?"

"Not that I know of."

"I gotta go. I gotta tell her. Oh no, Elizabeth. Did I tell her we would go to Taco Bell?"

"Joey, sit still for a second and I will help you."

He flinched.

I took his hands in mine. "I can't let you leave until you listen."

We both waited for Joey to calm himself.

With his hands in mine, I prayed. "Father—"

His hands jerked from mine. "His help comes a mite late."

I waited. If I thought it would change anything for either of those girls, anything at all, I would bite through my knuckles. "Their father being in jail wouldn't help them."

Great broken sobs jerked his body. He placed his hand in mine again while his body jolted and heaved, but he bowed his head.

I allowed him time before I prayed. "Father, Joey Gibson is a father. His heart and spirit are broken. For today all I ask is that you enter that brokenness. Joey can't carry the sorrow alone. Father, those beautiful girls—"

"Oh, my girls," Joey cried.

"Father," I continued, "those girls can be healed and their lives still be bright and happy. Be with Joey as he talks to Carla. Don't let bitterness grow between Joey's home and Judy's home. They have been generous of heart and spirit with their children."

"Go on," Joey said. "Finish your prayer."

"Amen," I said.

"No. Not Amen. If we gonna stand here lollygagging around talking to God, then you need to ask Him to kill Lawrence Ray Hubbard. Don't just pray pretty prayers. Put some meat behind 'em. He can plant a bolt of lightning in the right blasted places, can't He? If He's unable to handle that little job, why we wasting time talking to Him?"

"God has a much bigger job to do helping you with your anger, and your family with their pain. When I get through making calls, the state of Texas can handle Lawrence Hubbard."

"You promise?" Joey asked, sounding pitiful.

"God as my witness." I raised my right hand. "There's something else I can do."

"What?"

"I can take Elizabeth home with me for tonight. You need to go talk to Carla and Judy needs a long bath and a longer nap. She didn't lie down at all last night."

"Are you sure about taking Elizabeth?"

"I'm sure. My daughter will love a sleepover."

"I would appreciate it." He studied me a long time. "Catherine," he said, "if I trust you to make the calls and handle this, and nothing happens ..."

"Plenty will happen. That registered sex offender thing changed everything."

His voice cracked. "Thank you."

"My pleasure."

"You really gonna take Elizabeth for tonight?"

"Yes. Of course, I'll talk to Judy first."

"She'll appreciate it. I do too."

I ushered him out the door. "You're welcome."

Chapter 27

"Am I going with you because my parents are mad at me?" Elizabeth wanted to know.

"Absolutely not. You are going with me because I asked your parents, and they said yes." I turned and smiled over my shoulder. I had belted Elizabeth into the back seat. "I thought if you came home with me tonight, your parents would have time to talk about a new plan, and your mom needs uninterrupted sleep. Both your parents trusted me to take care of you." I glanced back again. "Are you comfortable going with me?"

"Oh, yes. One, because I like you, and two, at my house tonight it might be terrible like last night. I hated last night."

"It had to be hard for you ... and for everybody."

"Yeah."

"Well, I wanted you to be away from any drama tonight, and I thought you might have a nice time with my daughter."

"You have a daughter?"

"I do. She's about your age. Seven."

#

When I walked into the house, Bailey ran into my arms. I kissed both her cheeks and held her close, cherishing her. As I put her on the floor, I introduced her to Elizabeth and told her Elizabeth had come for a sleepover. Then I scanned the house for Jordan. I couldn't wait to lose myself in the comfort of his arms.

I found him in the kitchen. "Hard, hard day," I whispered in his ear, as I laid my tired head on his shoulder.

"Your days all seem hard." Jordan pushed away.

"What?"

"What did I hear Bailey say a moment ago?"

"Oh, I brought a sad little girl, Elizabeth, home to spend the night. They're getting acquainted."

"Maybe," but he walked around me to enter the living room.

His cheerful disposition had crawled from his face.

I trailed behind him.

Jordan studied our daughter.

She looked sheepish.

"Do you want to introduce your new friend?" he asked her.

"This is Elizabeth. We're not friends."

Elizabeth appeared as though Bailey had struck her.

Dumbstruck, I stood beside Jordan.

"Sweetheart," he addressed Bailey. "What's wrong with my friend-loving baby girl?" Wearing a troubled face, Jordan asked, "What did I hear you ask Elizabeth?"

"When?" She wouldn't face her dad.

"While your mom and I were still in the kitchen. Bailey?"

"Nothing."

"Bailey?"

"Oh, I asked her who killed her mother."

I cupped her face. "Sweetheart, no one killed her mom. Her mother just needed a good rest tonight, so I brought her here for a sleepover."

"Well, I needed to know."

"Why?"

Her insecurities stamped lines across her forehead. "I knew if her mom were dead, you'd keep her."

I suggested Elizabeth make herself comfortable. I said she could go upstairs to visit the Victorian room—where there were lots of beautiful dolls—if she wanted.

"Yes, ma'am." She couldn't get up the stairs fast enough.

Jordan took Bailey in his arms and we both snuggled on the sofa with her.

"Sweetheart, what causes you to worry that we'll adopt another daughter?"

Her bottom lip drooped. "Just cuz."

I lifted her onto my lap. "We have no plans now to adopt again." I squeezed her. "We love having you." I brushed my hand across her sweet forehead, pushed her bangs aside, then kissed her. "You fill our hearts."

"Well, if you're both sure, I'll go upstairs and be her friend."

Jordan stopped her by tugging on her hand. "Bailey, I understand you're still adjusting. However, you cannot be unkind to others." He touched her face. "We love you to the moon and back, but we can't allow it."

"Sorry."

We waited until she'd climbed the stairs. "Jordan." I turned to him. "What else can we do to calm her fears? We adore her."

"Katie Girl, it may be time to get her additional counseling. You counseled her before she came here to live, but I think it's time to call in someone else."

"I'll talk to Angie, my social worker, tomorrow."

He kissed me. "Good idea."

When the girls came downstairs, they were holding hands, laughing.

#

After dinner, I helped both girls with their baths and dried their hair. Bailey wanted to bathe together but Elizabeth whispered in my ear she didn't want Bailey to see the marks on her body.

"It'll be okay," I promised.

We were in the bathroom with water running. I turned to Bailey. "Sweetheart, Elizabeth is a little shy about bathing with anyone else."

"But we're friends now," Bailey insisted.

"You sure are, but what if I have Daddy read you a story while Elizabeth bathes? Then it'll be your turn."

"Okay. What about *Goodnight Moon*? I know it's for lit'ler kids but I still like it."

"I'll tell him right now."

Jordan and I tucked in both girls after they bathed. Sadness had settled itself on Elizabeth's face again.

I walked around to her side of the bed and eased down. "What's wrong, Bethy?"

She clamped her bottom lip with her teeth.

"It's okay."

"I'm afraid about going home tomorrow."

"You don't have to be. No one, *no one* is mad at you." I took her cold hands in mine. "Your mom didn't sleep last night because she was upset—"

"At me?"

"No, about what had happened to you." I squeezed her hands. "And your dad needed time to talk to Carla."

"Carla might hate me."

"She won't."

"Miss Katie, sometimes you pray for me at the clinic. Can you do that now?"

"For sure."

Bailey peeked at Elizabeth. "Her and daddy always pray, anyway."

Jordan took Bailey's hand, and I held Elizabeth's. "Father, look down on Bethy, especially tonight. Last night proved difficult for everyone in her home. But one touch of your hand can calm her and everyone in her family. I ask that you touch Elizabeth right now. Amen"

Jordan, Bailey, and Elizabeth said, "Amen."

I remained at her side. "I promise to be part of the healing process. I'll be available to your family for as long as y'all need me."

"What if we need you for a long time?"

Bailey jumped in. "Oh, she'll be there for as long as it takes. God keeps calling her."

"Does He call her on the phone?" Elizabeth asked.

"I'm not real sure."

Jordan and I rolled our eyes at each other as we closed their door and walked away. We would need to have a discussion with Bailey about the giftings and callings of God.

#

The next morning Jordan delighted Elizabeth by serving breakfast in bed to both girls. I dropped her at the clinic before I scooted to the university to teach my classes. Judy—whom Alicia reported to be feeling much better—came to the clinic and retrieved her baby girl. They would have to find a way—with God's help and lots of counseling—to begin to heal.

Chapter 28

I handed Lewis his first six crisp one-dollar bills on a sunny Texas day. I was thrilled and excited for him. He was taken aback that I kept my word.

He woke dry. I shelled out money.

Together we celebrated.

He held up the six dollars one at a time, watching the sunlight peek through each one. My bank always put brand new one-dollar bills aside for me. Somehow, new bills seemed more special to kids.

He turned every bill over and faced them in the same direction.

I winked at him.

His brown eyes, though still troubled at times, held more hope. "Now this makes two hundred and sixteen dollars."

"Wow," I said. "I'm not sure I have two hundred and sixteen dollars on me. Where in the world did you get the other two hundred ten?" I expected stashed birthday money, Christmas money, chore money, etc.

"Well, I don't actually have it, but my dad owes me two hundred ten."

"For what?" I leaned toward Lewis, needing to hear a good explanation.

"Well, my allowance is five dollars a week," he made a circling motion with his hand, "and he hasn't paid me for forty-two weeks."

Liquid fire spilled down my spine. "Oh, you're keeping book on him?"

"Of course. Maybe my dad will love me more now."

"What do you mean, love you more?"

"My dad doesn't love me as much as Whitney because I wet the bed."

"I'm certain that's not true, Lewis."

"And I'm pretty certain it is."

Without breaking eye contact, I scribbled unobtrusively on the yellow sticky-note sheet that stuck to the front of his chart: Book session with Dad ASAP.

"Enjoy your money, bud," I said. "See you next week."

He drew a brown leather wallet from his back pocket and tucked the crisp bills inside. "I'll be waking up dry, ya know," he said.

"I'll be counting on it." I hugged him.

He didn't jump.

#

At 6:15 on the day Lewis told me his dad owed him money, I burned tire rubber coming out of my office driveway for my own amusement. Here I had this kid I'd worked hard with. Something ate his guts out, and he wouldn't talk about it. That something was connected to the sun and being black. Those two components would signal a psych major after one year of education that Lewis feared the sun would make him blacker.

He had come to me with an overwound coil instead of a stomach, a self-loathing because he wet the bed, an emotional clothesline that could string from Texas to Alabama with pee-soaked sheets. He had a reputation at school for threatening to kill himself and a father who had nagged him for years about something he couldn't help. Now I'd found out his dad owed him two hundred and ten fire-trucking dollars.

No parent does everything right. But one must have credibility with their kid. Without integrity, one cannot parent.

Two hundred and ten dollars?

Could the going rate for integrity be so low? Why not a million dollars? If a parent is going to steal from their kid, for the love of broccoli, can't it be a million dollars? Be a real thief. Don't nickel and dime a kid's respect.

Two hundred and ten dollars?

Thank God for a convertible. I needed that blast of air blowing over me on the drive home. Jordan did not deserve for me to walk in whining about parents stealing from their kids.

God, please help me help Lewis.

I loved it when there was a breakthrough with a kid. I loved it when we found the right medication for a child. I loved it more when we found that a child didn't need medication—but rather a chance to talk in a safe environment and be heard and understood. I loved it when parents learned to express themselves meaningfully to each other and to their children. I thrilled when a child determined to hold his head high and like himself. I loved being involved when a child discovered she had a learning disability in reading—that there was help for—but she was gifted in math. I loved every hour I had spent helping children learn to love themselves.

I hated cleaning up behind bad parenting.

Two hundred and ten dollars?

For the love of Pete ... whoever Pete was ... Lewis was my Let's-Make-A-Deal client. That poor baby had an issue behind door number one, door number two, and door number three.

Sometimes I hated my job.

Chapter 29

My first client was Lewis's father. Michael Davis, though he gave Lewis grief about bedwetting and owed him money, was not a bad parent. He presented as pleasant and affable. During our first moments together, however, he tried to be an I-don't-need-no-therapist, my daddy-didn't-need-no-therapist, and my-son-sure-doesn't-need-no-therapist kind of dad. "Mr. Davis, your son came to me suffering over wetting the bed. He's been ashamed and humiliated and has tolerated near debilitating anxiety."

With his eyes locked on mine, Mr. Davis dropped all pretense of protest about being in my office.

"He doesn't have to suffer like that anymore."

He remained silent for a long moment.

Because of Lewis's deep color, I assumed his father would be a darker shade of black. I was wrong. He, like Allison and Whitney, was a creamy latte color—the color we white folks hope to achieve when we stand in line and pay lots of money at tanning salons. To our chagrin, we usually walk away looking rusted around the ankles and elbows.

Upon arrival, Michael had leaned comfortably into the cushions, but now slid closer to the edge and clasped his palms together, lacing his fingers. "I don't want my boy to suffer."

"Me neither."

"I'll do anything you tell me to do."

"Thank you. I'll only ask you to do things that are in your son's best interest."

"I didn't know he couldn't help wetting the bed."

He clamped his palms together and searched for words. "It embarrassed me."

"Believe me, Lewis knew, and it devastated him."

"I thought …" His voice broke, and he swallowed hard. "… I could shame him into stopping."

"It doesn't work that way." I felt drawn in by the sincerity of his tears.

Misery peeked from his eyes. "Obviously."

I handed him a tissue. "Obviously." I waited while he wiped his nose. "It works in the opposite direction. Disparaging remarks drives the unwanted behaviors underground instead of away and usually creates tension between family members."

"No joke." He shook his head back and forth.

"He's so proud of himself now."

Fresh tears winked in Michael Davis's huge, luminous eyes. "He's a good son."

I nodded.

"He reminds me of my grandfather."

"How's that?"

"My grandpa on my father's side. A large man. Real quiet, but kind and polite." He chuckled. "He was as black as my grandma's wash pot. She used to tease him. She'd say 'Lewis—I named my son for him—'you better keep your eyes open at night or you'll disappear in the dark.'"

"Sounds like you loved him a lot."

"Yeah." He shoved his tissue into a front shirt pocket. "He's gone now. We lost him nine years ago to congestive heart failure. But a finer man never lived." Looking embarrassed, he dragged the tissue back from his pocket. "The second I saw my son, Lewis, I knew that was his name."

"What about your grandmother? Still have her?"

"No. She died not long after him. I think she grieved herself to death. She stayed on the move, healthy as a horse, until my grandpa died."

"What was her name?"

"Abigail Louise Davis." Michael smiled while reminiscing about his grandmother. "She was the daughter of a wealthy Louisiana family. A wealthy white Louisiana family who disowned her for marrying a black man. I never knew her to be unhappy for a single day until my grandpa died."

"The happiest happy you can be is happily married."

Michael dropped his head, then looked at me again. "I failed at that kind of happy."

"I'm sorry."

"I have failed my boy." Tears trekked down his handsome face. "I didn't mean to, but I let him down." He pressed his palms together sandwiching the soiled tissue. "I could use a little help."

"Okay."

"I will never ever fail him again. I didn't understand him. But with your help I won't taunt him again."

"Good." I gave him a reassuring nod.

He nodded.

"There's something I need to ask you." I said.

"Anything."

"Lewis said his allowance is five dollars per week."

"Is that not enough?"

"The amount is not my concern. That's between you and your son."

"All right."

"So, when is payday?"

He wiggled in his chair. "Uh oh."

"If your boss tells you payday is the first and the fifteenth, when do you expect to be paid?"

He wiped his brow. "Uh, the first and fifteenth."

"When did you tell Lewis you would pay his allowance?"

"Weekly, on Fridays."

"Okay."

"No, it's not okay." He opened his palms and wiped the tissue across his damp forehead.

"Why not?"

"I can't recall when I last paid him."

"I do. It has been forty-two weeks. You owe him $210.00."

"You're kidding me. I had no idea."

"Do you think kids won't hold us to our promises, and when we fail to deliver, they won't keep book on us?" I stared at him. "Don't lose his respect. And don't sell it."

"I'm embarrassed."

"Talk to him, apologize, and pay him. All of it."

"I'll take care of it this afternoon."

"Good. And next Friday?"

"He'll be paid five dollars every Friday. As a matter of fact, he'll soon be twelve—a good time to raise it to ten dollars."

"What a great idea."

I accompanied Michael to the front door. As I pondered the whereabouts of Alicia my phone buzzed from her desk. She texted me: *Sorry to leave but am chasing leads. You'll be happy with my news. On my way back.*

Chapter 30

After class—I taught summer sessions also—I called Jordan, who didn't teach summer classes, and told him I had to go to the office. He wasn't surprised. Disappointed, but not surprised. "I love you and will be home as soon as possible."

"Love you too. I'll pick up Bailey from aftercare and we'll do something fun. She's gotten really good at putt-putt. I'll see if she wants to go there. Be home when you can because she'll miss you."

"Tell her how much her mama loves her."

"I will. Daddy loves Mommy too."

I heard the smile in his voice. Leaving the university, I pointed my way to Main Street.

"Hey, Kat." Alicia waited for me in the hallway when I arrived.

My nerves prickled. My intentions scared me. "What you got?"

"I have the address of the three boys on the Walmart parking lot on July twelfth. There's the fourth guy that moved to Dallas. I have his address too. I called the store and two of the boys are off today. One is at work now."

"Let's start with the two who are off today. It's possible we'll find them at home."

"And then what? They are under no obligation to tell you anything even if one of them saw something."

"Right. Hey, why do you suppose guy number four worked his last day at Walmart the day Sara Beth died and then moved to Dallas?"

"I don't know, but I can guess what you're thinking. I'm telling you, Kat, I can't get into any more trouble or they'll throw me under the jailhouse." She wagged her head. "You always mean well, but heaven help us."

"You could help yourself by telling the judge or your attorney the drugs weren't yours."

"You'll understand when Bailey is older."

"I sincerely hope not."

"Let's talk about whose house we're going to first."

"Let's start with the closest."

"Kat, is there any way you can let this go?"

"Sometimes in the middle of the night I think I can. But I awake each morning reminded if Cindy killed Sara Beth, she shouldn't get away with it."

"I agree. But Katie, have you thought about what this could do to Billy?"

Breathe. Breathe. "A million times, and I don't have everything worked out in my head yet. But what keeps me pushing forward is Billy."

"In what way?"

"Has it crossed your mind that since she didn't want either of her last two kids, if Cindy did kill Sara Beth and gets away with it, Billy could be next."

"Oh, heaven help me. No, I had not thought about that." She frowned, digging a ditch between her eyes.

"Some days I would give anything to be a let-it-go kind of person."

"I knew by the second day I worked here that you would never let go of something you believed in. And I've always respected that. But I worry about you."

I glared at her. "Let's not get into who's worried about whom."

"Okay, okay. The first house is two miles from here. I've entered it in the GPS. The guy who lives there is Lee Simon." She waved the phone. "Hey, I didn't ask you how class went. Have you eaten anything? I could slice some fresh fruit for you before we leave. It'll only take a minute." Her eyes rolled over my body. "You still haven't put on all the weight you lost when Jordan moved out last year."

My friend was jabbering again today. I gave her a quick hug. "Let's go. I'll eat at home. Don't want to be later than necessary."

#

As we drove to the Simon home, ants crawled over my skin. Everywhere. I had no idea what to say. "Father, please help me."

"Didn't you already ask Him?" Alicia sounded incredulous. "Like, before we were in the car headed to the kid's house."

"Shut up."

We pulled into the driveway that Alicia pointed toward.

"You have the screenshot of Cindy. Right?"

"On my phone." She handed it over.

When I took it, my hand tremored. But I climbed from my car, straightened my clothes, checked a purse mirror for lipstick on my teeth, then walked to the door and knocked.

An attractive lady came to the door and smiled. "Hello, how can I help you?" She wore a pretty flowered apron—unlike the flour-sack aprons my grandma and aunts used to wear—and a dab of flour dusted her cheek. I smelled something wonderful from the kitchen.

"Is your son Lee home?"

"Why do you ask? Is something wrong?"

"Oh, no, ma'am." It was time to think of something. I reverted to an old trick. I opened my wallet, flashed my pocket license and said, "I work for the state of Texas." A technical truth—one I had used when Bailey and I were searching for the grave of the man who murdered her mother. Each year the state board renewed my license and sent a purse copy for visiting hospitals and such. "I wanted to ask him a couple questions."

Her smile disappeared. "Is my boy in trouble?"

"No, ma'am. I wanted to ask him if he had seen anything at work on July twelfth."

"Oh. That's the day the baby died at Walmart. He had nothing to do with that."

"No one thinks otherwise. I just wanted to see him for a couple minutes."

"You said you work for the state?"

"Yes, ma'am. But Lee isn't in trouble."

She walked away from the front door and called him. He appeared in a few seconds.

I held out my hand. "Lee?"

He shook it. "Yes, ma'am. My mom said you wanted to ask me questions."

"One, actually." I showed him the picture of Cindy on Alicia's phone. "Lee, did you see this woman on the parking lot of Walmart the day the little girl was left in the car and died?"

"No, ma'am."

"Can you check one more time? I believe you were on the shift gathering carts from the parking lot that day."

"I was on shift then for sure. Everybody remembers that day, but I don't know the lady."

"Okay, that's all I needed. Thank you for your time."

I walked back to my car, then slipped under the steering wheel and drove away. One down.

#

We drove next to the residence of Gary Morris with near identical results. Nothing.

"Katie, have you noticed the time?"

I checked the clock on the dash. How was it almost 5:00? "Oh mercy, we both need to get home."

"I've got to go home, Kat. My kids will be worried."

"Same here."

I drove her to the office to retrieve her car. When she slid safely inside and started her engine, I almost drove away. But she lowered her window and signaled me to stop.

"Hey."

"Once you said Billy could be next, I was all in. Anything you need, I'll be there for you."

"I already knew that." I smiled. "Go home. I love you."

"You too. We'll start again tomorrow."

#

At home I received a chilly reception. Bailey didn't run into my arms. She stayed beside her dad. Jordan frowned at me. "It's 5:15. We were both worried. I called the clinic, and no one was there."

"You could always call my cell."

"I did. Alicia answered and was very vague. You seemed to be at some boy's door."

"She forgot to tell me." She had to be very nervous to forget. "I'm sorry."

"Bailey and I have eaten. We saved a plate for you to microwave when you're ready."

"Yeah, we left you food," Bailey said, without the hint of a smile.

"Did you mean to say yes ma'am?"

"Yes, ma'am, we left you food. Did you mean to come home earlier?"

"I did. And I hurt your feelings. Can you forgive me, sweetheart?"

"Yes, ma'am." She left Jordan's side and hugged me. "But you coulda called, then we woulda not worried."

"I could have. And I'll do better. I promise." I kissed her and wrapped her in my arms.

#

They sat at the table with me while I ate my warmed-over meal.

"It was hot outside, but Daddy and me putt-putted."

"Did you have fun?"

"Yea … yes, ma'am."

Tension hung so low over the table, I could've touched it. Even broken off a piece.

Jordan scowled and clenched his jaws.

I assisted Bailey with her bath.

She checked her list twice to make sure she'd remembered to do everything. But when she bent to gather her towel, she seemed upset still.

I dropped to my knees before her. "Bailey, Mommy loves you more than anyone ... well, you and Daddy." I slipped her pajama top over her head. "I work too hard and long sometimes. But I know God called me to help people." I held her as she stepped into the jammy bottom. "I never mean to worry you."

"You worried Daddy too. Could you ask God to call you not so much?"

I snuggled her, wanting to weep.

"We'll have a long talk when I get to our bedroom."

"Mommy?"

"What, baby girl?"

"Don't hurt his feelin's. When it was 5:00, I felt sad for him. And he didn't eat very much."

"I promise." I would cry as soon as I left her room.

"Call Daddy to help tuck me?"

He knocked on the hallway wall to announce himself and verify time for tucking.

"We're ready, Daddy."

I parked on the side of her bed as always.

Jordan took both her small hands and placed them near his face. "Father, for this child we prayed." He kissed her palms. "Help us always to teach her of your love. Let us never take the miracle of her for granted." He released her right hand and reached for mine. "Katie Girl and I love her without condition—the way you love us. Keep our girl in the palm of your hands, always and forever."

We all felt a little weepy.

Bailey started to pray, but Jordan stopped her. "Sweetheart, since you are afraid of some parts of 'now I lay me,' would you like to pray whatever is in your heart?"

"Yes, sir." She folded her hands a second time. "Dear Lord, thank you for Mommy and Daddy and our nice home. And that I'm the only little girl they need."

I bit the inside of my mouth to keep from laughing. Or crying.

Bailey continued, "God, please don't call my mom as much. Amen."

We tucked covers and placed her starting-to-look-worn bear. Then we both kissed her sweet cheeks and bade her good night.

Walking toward our room, Jordan asked, "What was the last line of Bailey's prayer about?"

"She was asking about me being late and I apologized and told her I thought God called me to help people."

Sadness shadowed his face. "She doesn't understand, and to be honest, neither do I. You never forget to call when you'll be late. Katie, what in the world?" He turned to gaze in my eyes. "You realize some husbands would wonder. But I know you better than to think you're up to anything outside God's will, or mine either."

A sword stabbed through my body and impaled me to the wall. When I could speak, I said, "Jordan, I'm not only faithful in deed, but in my thoughts and dreams. I loved you before I met you. I loved the promise of you, believing God would someday send you."

"I believe that, Kate, but it's lonely without you. I suppose I thought after we adopted Bailey, you would attempt to be here more."

"Jordan, I'm trying. This afternoon I was checking to see if one of the boys who gathered carts from Walmart might have seen something."

"Is there any way you could let this thing go? Let the police do their job and you counsel people?"

"No."

"Why did I guess that? There may be something you haven't thought of."

I felt faint from exhaustion. "What?"

"Billy. What would he do without his mother, such as she is?"

"There may be something you haven't thought of."

"Okay."

"I've gone through this with Alicia today. If Cindy killed Sara Beth—and it wasn't a tragic accident, and she gets away with it—could Billy be next?" I wrung my hands. "Jordan, she didn't want him either."

Jordan paled. "You're right. Never once has that crossed my mind. But I still worry what Billy would do."

"I have been in that house many times. Rob is the only caring person who lives there besides the babies. Baby. He possesses a pure heart. Remember when we purchased Christmas for his kids? Rob called here the next morning. He dripped gratitude. I believe he loved both of his babies." I shrugged. "We spent several hundred dollars, but Cindy let me know our pile of gifts for the kids didn't seem adequate. I do not have a clue what would make Cindy happy or what it would take for her to have a better attitude."

He took me in his arms. "Maybe Cindy is a lost cause, but I couldn't handle something happening to Billy. Do what you need to do, always remembering Bailey is still insecure and your husband needs you too."

"I promise. But Cindy killed Sara Beth. I know it in my knower."

He kissed me sweet and soft.

Sleep overtook me. I had clients first thing in the morning.

Chapter 31

A li called. 7:30. She'd arrived early to catch up on billing.

"Kat, you're probably just getting up, but can you be here at 9:00 instead of 10:00?"

I wanted to stay home and watch Jordan serve breakfast in bed to Bailey. I longed for time to enjoy my family. "Is it important?"

"Would I call if it wasn't? I know you hate morning." She rattled papers in the background. "Rob Martin called and wondered if he could see you today. He didn't sound good. It's his morning to go in later to work, so he has the time at nine, if you can be here."

Rob Martin. Billy's dad. "Yes. I'll throw myself together and see you at 9:00. Thanks for calling. And yes, it's important."

"Duh."

#

Rob Martin, distraught and pale, weighed roughly 145 pounds. A slight man whose hair had thinned since I'd seen him at his house. I'd gone there to pray for him when Cindy mentioned a malignant growth on his back.

Alicia had put him in my office where he waited. She only made that move when someone seemed nervous or tearful or didn't want to be seen at my office. I went to her desk to say hello and pick up his chart, but there wasn't one. He hadn't wanted to fill one out, instead handing over his insurance card and ID.

Alicia pointed at the two items. "That's never happened before, so I didn't know what to do."

"Whatever he did is okay. You did fine."

She shrugged and returned to work.

I hurried down the hall, grabbed a cup each of tea and black coffee, entered my treatment room, and found Rob weeping.

I stuffed tissues into his hands and sat down, placing my warm tea on the table beside my chair and his cup on a second table. I said nothing. Not my usual way to start a session, but I doubted this would be a regular session.

I crossed my legs and leaned forward, setting my chair into motion.

Rob tried to speak but couldn't. Instead he grabbed additional tissues from the box on the sofa beside him. He sobbed then blew his nose.

I could wait.

He lobbed a wad of mangled tissues into the garbage can beside my chair. His jean-clad legs jerked with tension. His work shirt, heavy with sweat, stuck to his small frame. His shirt pocket held three pens and a pencil. He smelled clean, and I sniffed a faint cologne.

I felt as though I sat before a good man. A proud man. His nails were trimmed and groomed. His jeans held a sharp crease.

I had no doubt he'd ironed his clothes himself. I waited.

He gathered strength before meeting my gaze.

I smiled. "Do you want the coffee or prefer something else?"

His mug sat untouched. "I'm a java drinker, but my stomach won't handle nothing that strong today."

"You came to tell me something."

"Yeah, but I swear I don't know how."

I spoke with genuine compassion. "Rob, I'm so sorry about Sara Beth." Fresh grief washed over me and I felt his loss almost as if it were my own. "How are you doing? I stopped by to check on Cindy but haven't seen you since the baby's funeral." I sat my tea aside. "So, tell me ... how are you?"

"Terrible. God help me. I'm doing terrible. Sara Beth was my sweet baby girl. Her voice calls out in the night, but it ain't her." He wept.

I rocked but kept quiet. He had to do this—whatever this was—in his own time. Maybe he came for a safe place to cry. Many clients do.

"Catherine?"

"Yes."

"I'm gonna hate myself for saying this out loud but ..." He pulled more tissues and shredded them into small strips. "I'm losing my mind."

"I doubt it. Grief and loss are terrible things. This is still fresh." I put my palms together and clasped them beneath my chin. "I can't imagine losing a child. It will take time, prayer, and counseling to get through this."

"I do feel loss and grief." He dropped his head. "But that ain't all."

I hesitated before saying, "What else did you come here to say?"

"You'll hate me."

"I won't."

"Well, I'll just say it. I believe my wife left our daughter in the car on purpose." His feet couldn't stay put. He tapped his heels against the floor, causing his knees to jiggle.

"What a load to bear." I waited a minute. "What caused you to think Cindy would do that?"

"Well, I ain't certain. But I can say for sure I don't believe she loved our daughter and I don't think she gives one flip about Billy."

My tongue stuck to the roof of my mouth as if it were thick and glued with peanut butter. Say something, Katie. Anything. "I'm so sad for you, Rob. Whether or not it's true, your suffering is deep and heavy. That alone breaks my heart."

"Aren't you gonna hate me, or at least be mad? Cindy's been your client a long time. I'm sure you think I'm crazy."

"This is what I think. If you believe this for a second, I suggest you chat with the detective who interviewed Cindy. He will listen. He may investigate further or tell you he has ruled the possibility out and is closing the case." I caught his eyes with mine and kept them. "Either way, you'll feel better."

"I can't do that. I wanted to tell you and hoped that would be enough."

"I understand if you can't talk to the police. In that case, I hope telling me has helped." Rob, I cannot tell you I believe she killed Sara Beth too. That's police business. But I'll never let it go until I find out. You have no idea how far I'm willing to go for additional information. Dallas, for sure.

"You're quiet," he whispered.

"Sorry. Sara Beth's death has affected me too. I grieve with you, and Cindy, of course."

"Remember coming to my house when something was bad wrong with my back?"

"Of course, I remember. You couldn't stand."

"You prayed for me that day."

"Yes."

"Could you pray for me today? Now?"

We stood, and I gathered his hands in mine. "Father, Rob is suffering. First, I ask that you walk beside him as he mourns his child. He can somehow navigate this dark period if you will walk through his life. Jesus, wherever you walked, the blind saw, the lepers healed, and the deaf heard. There is no way to make this easy." Rob's fingers shook in mine. "But with you holding his hand, he can survive." Heavy fog hung inside the room. "Rob is a good man. Shine a light on his path. Amen."

He glanced up, his face red and damp. "Have you ever hated someone you loved?"

"For a few minutes."

"If I had real guts, I'd go to the police—for Sara Beth's sake—and tell them what I told you, but I don't have proof, and what if it was a horrible accident?"

I released his hands and gazed into troubled eyes. "If the police concluded she killed Sara Beth, and they had any proof at all, they would be knocking on your door."

"Cindy and I have been together since high school, except for the break we took. I love her, but she's a hard woman who seems attached to nothing. She's ungrateful and has a small heart. I can live with everything except her lack of love for our babies. She doesn't love me, but I'm accustomed to that." He shrugged. "But the babies ..."

"I'll continue to pray for you and your family. If you need to come again, please do."

"Catherine, if a mother could deliberately leave her baby in the car and the baby died ..."

I waited.

"Do you believe she should have to suffer consequences?"

"Yes."

He dropped his head. "Me too." He walked toward the door and I opened it for him.

He hesitated then turned and gazed at me through puppy-dog eyes. With stooped shoulders, he walked away.

I dropped into my chair with trembling hands, a scrambled brain, and darkness hovering close. I would make sure my heartless client paid for her baby's death. Then, I got still for a minute. *God, if I'm wrong, let peace wash over me.* I waited. No peace could I find.

I called Jordan to tell him I would be late but would be home as soon as I could. Alicia and I found the home of Travon Smith, Walmart employee number three.

I knocked at the door. A handsome African American male, about 21, wearing dreadlocks and a huge smile, opened the door. "Hi."

"Travon?"

"Yes, ma'am. Can I help you?"

"I hope so. Were you working at Walmart on July twelfth when the baby was left inside the car in the parking lot?"

"Yeah. That kid died. Freaked me out."

I held up the screenshot of Cindy Thibbodeaux. "Did you see this woman on the parking lot or inside the store that day?"

"Is she the woman who forgot her kid in the car?"

"Do you recognize her?"

"No, ma'am. Never seen her before."

"Thanks for your time." I turned to walk away.

"Ma'am, there is one thing I can tell you that's bothered me."

Surprised, I spun back to Travon. "Okay."

"Terry Richardson was my best friend at work."

"All right."

"He left for lunch a couple minutes after 12:00 that day. He came back at 1:00, but something had changed. He looked sick. I followed him into the bathroom to ask if he felt okay."

"What did he say?"

"He said, 'Man I'm fine, just a sick stomach.'"

"And?"

"And I never saw him after that. I asked in the office, but the manager said he'd moved to Dallas." He squinted. "We had plans to start college together in the fall, right here in Port Arthur."

I melted into the heat and humidity. "Have you talked to him since he moved?"

"No. I tried to call, but the dude done changed his number."

I swallowed around the lump in my throat. "Thanks again for your time. I hope you hear from your friend soon."

I stumbled to the car and told Alicia everything Travon said. I pulled the Beamer into reverse.

#

Back at the office, Alicia asked, "What day?"

"What day what?"

"What day do I cancel all your clients and make airline reservations for Dallas?"

"What makes you think I'm going to Dallas?"

"How do I know it's hot in Texas?"

"Pick the day with the fewest clients next week."

"You never have few client days unless it rains hard. Then people tend to cancel."

"Well, check the weather report. You going with me?"

"I can't leave the county."

"Alicia."

"What?" she asked.

"Sometimes I want to grab you by your stubborn neck and squeeze."

"Kat, I don't want to discuss Kylie."

"Is that right—"

"You want to squeeze my neck?" Her purse slammed against the wall—raining keys, lipstick, and breath mints. "Well, why not? Do it and release me from of my misery. I'm afraid every minute. For myself, my kids, and even for you. You can't run this place and save the whole world alone." Terror filled her eyes, etching deep lines into her face. "Do you think I like any of this? And Katie, most of all, I cannot believe Kylie capable of these horrible decisions."

"Ali, wait. I—"

She'd run out the back door.

I ran after her.

Chapter 32

I got home at a decent time. Thank God.

Bailey and Jordan were discussing what to cook for dinner.

"Let's skip cooking and go out," I said.

"You're in a good mood, Katie Girl. Where do you want to go?"

"I don't know, but I'm ready to celebrate."

"I got something to cel'brate too."

I lifted her into my arms. "And what would that be?"

"Today Daddy took me to your clinic. I seen Miss Angie."

"Well, okay. Did you like her?"

"Yes, ma'am. But that's not the best news."

"What is?" I asked, as Jordan smiled in the background.

"She said you and Daddy were never gonna leave me, never gonna get tired of me, and she said she didn't think y'all would need another little girl, even if her mother died."

My heart soared and broke for her. "Sweetheart, you can go to see Miss Angie anytime you want. And we've tried to assure you we have no plans now to adopt again." I nuzzled her neck, and she snuggled tight.

Jordan asked, "So where shall we go?"

Bailey scrambled from my arms. "At Luby's you can see all the food at once. I can have anything I want."

"Then Luby's it is." Jordan leaned and kissed her.

#

Later, as we showered then dressed for bed, Jordan said, "Perhaps Miss Angie can help Bailey understand there will always be enough food."

"Baby steps," I said, pulling his face to mine.

I eased onto the back-porch swing after Jordon and Bailey slept. Could I really go to Dallas? Could I ever let Sara Beth's death go? Could I be what God called me to be? A professional counselor? Did I try to stick my nose into the wrong place on nothing but a gut feeling? Well, Sara Beth's dad believed Cindy killed her. Was that enough affirmation? He lived with her. I didn't.

I swung, gazing up at the night sky and watching the moon's glow over the golf course. Our house hovered against the eighteenth hole. The cart path provided a place for Jordan to run his five miles early every morning before the golfers needed the path. He didn't mind, having always been an early riser. I peered into the living room through the window without moving from the swing. The digital clock proclaimed 1:16 a.m. A chill burst through my body although the outside thermometer stuck on ninety degrees. What was wrong with me?

God, you understand what is wrong. Help me find proof one way or the other about Cindy and Sara Beth. I stared at His handiwork—stars flung across the sky. Most times contemplation of this spectacle comforted me. Not tonight.

Father, you know the truth. If you would, share it with me in details that are proof positive. I pulled my knees under me against the chill. *And dear Lord, only you can change Alicia's mind about Kylie and Rikki, and the drugs. Alicia would never go near a drug on her own. It would be awful to turn your child over to police officers. But the drugs belonged to Kylie or Rikki or both.* My fingertips rubbed at my tired eyes. *God, make your presence known in both situations.*

I stood, ready to go inside when Jordan—jaw lined with stubble—walked through the backdoor to join me.

"Hey, baby." His face reflected concern.

I plopped my weary body onto the swing again and patted the space beside me, but he opted for the rocking chair facing me.

My eyes surely shone with adoration. "I love you."

"And I you." He pressed his foot against the concrete, rocking. "Is it Cindy and Sara Beth, or Alicia and Kylie and what's-his-name?"

"Both. And it's Rikki. Not that I'm worrying about him. I have compassion, but until he becomes a stand-up guy and steps forward to admit the drugs were his, it's Alicia I'm worried about." I shrugged. "I love Kylie, but right now she is willing to let her own mother—my Alicia—take the punishment for what she and Rikki have done."

Jordan leaned forward. "If you don't sleep, you can't help any of the above. And you were nearing your normal weight until Alicia went to jail. You're bordering skinny again."

"I'm trying. I know how you worry when I'm too small."

"I do."

"Baby, I need to tell you something and this is as good a time as any."

His eyes clouded, but he didn't speak.

"Jordan—"

"Am I about to be sorry I joined you out here?"

"Probably. But I still have to tell you."

"Okay."

"I've shared with you the information the manager of Walmart gave me about the cart guys who worked their shift at the time Sara Beth died."

"Yes. Heaven help us, Katie Girl, what are you about to do?"

"I've found three of the four guys who worked that day, and none of them saw anything."

Jordan almost whispered, "You've told me."

"The fourth young man who worked that shift quit the next day."

He stared me down.

Jordan could do that. "He moved to Dallas."

"That rules him out then, right?"

"Jordan—"

"The bed is calling me, Kate."

"Wait. Please."

He didn't leave his rocker, and his mouth turned down because he knew what I would say next.

"Baby, the third young man I talked to was best friends with the guy who moved to Dallas."

"And?"

I leaned toward my wonderful husband. "Travon, the guy I spoke with last, believes Terry, his friend who's in Dallas, saw something in the parking lot. Something important about why Sara Beth died in that car."

"You, Katie, love of my life, are going to Dallas. Aren't you?"

I wanted to squirm. Or go inside. To explain. Lie. "Yes," dropped from my mouth.

Jordan froze, stuck to his chair.

I wanted to tell him how much I loved him and sit in his lap and snuggle.

It had only been a little over a year since he'd sat in that chair and told me I was killing both of us trying to save all the kids. Had I pushed him over the edge? Had his heart failed him right in front of me? I jumped from the swing.

"Jor—"

He rose and faced me. "You knocked me over like pins in a bowling alley the day I met you. Nothing has changed. You touch me and I'm weak in the knees. You smile and my world is on fire. I thought …"

"What, baby? What did you think?"

"That your world moved too fast. You were in a hurry all the time. So excited to get your practice off the ground and establish yourself as adjunct professor at the university." He looked away then back at me. "I thought my love would be enough to slow you down. All that's happened is you've speeded me up."

I'd felt chilled before. But now I developed into a heat stack. I stared without a word, becoming Lot's salty ol' wife again.

"I love you," he said. "I'm worried about Billy too. Tell me when you make your reservations for Dallas. I'll be here with Bailey." He touched my warm face. "But Katie, I'm worn out."

"Jordan, you said you would never leave me again, ever."

"I won't. I couldn't live without you."

But he didn't smile. Exhaustion sagged his shoulders and creased his face. He walked inside and pulled the door behind himself without glancing back.

Chapter 33

I surprised Alicia by arriving at the clinic early and stood leaning over the sign-in counter.

"Hey, Kat." She smiled. "What are you doing here? I didn't expect you till later. Haven't brewed anything yet, but our morning cup of goodness can be ready in a jiffy."

I winked. "I set both to brew before I walked to your desk."

"Okay. I would have gotten to that."

"Right." I stayed put.

She worried two pencils into a cup holder. "Do you need me to do something specific?"

"Yes. Leave whatever you're doing and come sit it my treatment room with me."

"O. Kay."

"Today's the day, Alicia. We're going to talk."

"About what?"

"Stop it. I'll grab my tea. You fetch your coffee and I'll meet you in my office."

She started to say something, but I tuned her out.

I sat in my chair and she pushed herself back into the comfort of the blue and mulberry sofa facing me.

"What?"

"Ali, we have loved each other for many years."

She picked at her nails and nodded.

"You never told me everything that happened the night of your arrest. The information I got was from Lexie."

"I didn't want to talk about this."

"No joke."

She reached for a tissue, smoothing it across her lap. "I don't know how to start."

"This is what I've learned. The day Officer Giovanni came here for his initial session, you left to take Billy home and everything seemed fine. You came back to the office a different person. Something happened while you were gone ... something that changed you."

"Kylie called on my cell."

"Okay."

"She sounded strange, almost like someone I didn't know. She wept and babbled about a guy named Rikki. I'd suspected she'd been seeing someone, but she never said. She's been different for a while now, but has never sounded ... I don't know ... altered." She pressed the tissue to her brow.

"I'm sorry. But I need you to keep going."

"I know Lexie told you about the police stopping me. I guess I'm crazy, but I opened my purse so the officer could see why I ran the stop sign. I *was* crazy from finding drugs in my home. Me, Kat. Drugs in my home." She wiggled further into the sofa. "He slapped handcuffs on me before I could finish explaining."

"Any amount of crystal meth or cocaine is a felony in Texas. The officer had no choice."

"Kat, I vow to you I was looking for Rikki's apartment. I've never met the boy, but Lexie thought she knew where he lived. I wanted the drugs out of my house and I wanted to find my child and drag her home if I had to. Those drugs Were. Not. Mine."

"I've known that from day one. You need to tell your attorney who they belonged to."

"Throw Kylie under the bus?"

"No. Let her face consequences for her behavior. Isn't that the basic tenet of human behavior? What I do here? You took my classes a hundred years ago. We only have two rules in the entire field of psychology. Remember? One is, over time behavior is consistent. And the second, behavior is sensitive to its consequences."

"I remember."

"Then let Rikki—whoever he is—and Kylie walk out the consequences for their behavior. Let them feel the sting of what they've done."

"And if that's jail time for Kylie?"

"Compared to jail time for you?" I wanted to scream at my friend. "You didn't commit the crime."

"I've told you her father never claimed her."

"Yes. And I'm sorry."

"My other two have my ex, but Kylie only has me."

"Did you teach her better?"

"You know I did."

"Yes."

Alicia's eyes trapped mine.

I noticed dark circles crouching beneath her chocolate eyes.

"I'm losing my mind," she said.

"No, you're not. You're tired and worried sick about Kylie. And the probability of prison time if you don't start talking. And Ali, the truth is the truth. Sometimes—especially concerning our kids—we might wish it wasn't. But if we have anything, let it be truth."

"You're shrinking me."

"Not so much as loving you. But if I'm honest, you could use some shrinking."

"Probably."

"May we look at your future—without the truth?"

"I'd rather not," she barely breathed.

"Well, allow me to be your tour guide for a moment."

She glared at me.

"Years of living in a six foot by eight-foot box with bars over doors and windows—if you have a window. Powdered eggs and yellow mush three times per day. Fifteen minutes a day outside to exercise and then a nice cavity search upon the return to your box. A dirty commode standing against a wall in plain sight where every other convicted felon can watch you do your business. You won't need to worry about clothes. The same orange jumpsuit with a number on it will be fine for every day." I breathed hard. "A large woman will want you for a wife. You are a cute little thing you know."

"Stop it, Kat."

"No, I won't stop. Whatever year you get out, it won't matter who's running for president, because convicted felons are never allowed to vote again."

Alicia jumped up, jerked open the door, then ran into the ladies' room.

She had to hear this from someone. I preferred it not be a warden. I stood outside the bathroom door and kept talking. "Maybe your wife's name will be Beulah. That's a good name for a prison wife, and she will give you more attention than you'll desire. Hey, I'll slip a knife into a cake so you can protect yourself from her. Nah. On second thought, I won't. You see, I don't break the law."

She near 'bout slammed me to the floor as she pushed the door open. "I. Don't. Either."

"Are you sure?"

"What?"

"You are letting the court believe a lie."

"Kat, I haven't lied to anyone."

"I thought I would die when Jordan left me last year. It was over a lie. I never told one, but let him believe a lie about Bailey. Alicia, I wanted to run from it, but it was still a lie. And the price I paid was huge."

She leaned against the door and slid down it.

I dropped to the floor with her and, whether she wanted me to or not, I pulled her into my arms.

She wrapped both arms around my neck.

We sat like that for a spell. She smelled of soap and a light perfume. I rocked her like I rocked Bailey when she was upset.

Finally, when she could talk, she pulled away from me. Like a little girl she said, "I love you."

"You too. That's why we had to do this."

"Yeah."

"Now that's out of the way, we have to talk practical things. I bailed you out of jail. May I escort you to the next appointment with your attorney?"

"I don't have an appointment or attorney."

"Heaven help us. What do you mean?"

"Just the court-appointed dude that was with me at my arraignment. I can't afford a good attorney. And the guy the court appointed won't take or return my calls."

"I have a good attorney. And she can represent you, but tell her the truth." I feasted on my bottom lip. "Will you?"

She refused to answer.

I stood then pulled her up beside me. "I will call my attorney today. She'll represent you well."

"Thanks."

"Alicia, the attorney is on me, and as of today you have a five-dollar-per-hour raise."

"It's not time for quarterly evaluations or raises."

"As of today."

"We'll have to ask the boss." She looked sheepish.

I chuckled.

Chapter 34

A good day to go home early. Bailey had a visit with Miss Angie during my last session, so we would ride home together.

Bailey ran toward me, again climbing me like a tree.

I waved at Angie when she stepped into the hall, coming from the opposite side of the building. "Bailey, did you thank Miss Angie for seeing you today?"

Bailey spun around, still in my arms. "Oh, thank you so much, Miss Angie. You are so nice." She blew a kiss.

Angie caught it midair. "You're welcome, Bailey. I'll see you again real soon."

"Thanks, Angie." I strolled out the backdoor with my baby girl.

"Is it too hot to put the top down?" she asked.

"Not if you want to badly enough."

"I want to real bad."

I pushed the button to lower the top and smiled about a drive that would be merciless.

But how many times does God give you a daughter? So, we arrived home sticking to the seats, but happy.

Jordan met us at the door. "How're my girls?"

"Fine," we said together.

"And how did your session go with Miss Angie?" he asked.

"Good. Daddy, I love her."

"Well, good."

Jordan and I looked at each other and shrugged.

Her daddy studied her. "Why do you love her? Is it because she helps you feel better?"

"And she teaches me real good things about y'all." She scrunched her nose. "And about us."

"You never have to say what happens in your sessions with Miss Angie. But do you want to tell us something?"

"Y'all … and us … we are cafluent." She clapped her hands together.

"We're what?" Jordan and I asked together.

"Cafluent. We have money."

"Affluent?" I didn't know how I felt about Angie talking money with Bailey. I gazed at my husband.

Jordan led us all to the living room.

Bailey's faced clouded. "Oh no. It isn't true, is it?"

I pulled her onto the sofa between us.

"Why is money important to you, sweetheart?" he asked.

Trouble crept into her eyes. "Cuz, don't you get it? Food. If people are cafluent, they can buy food anytime they want to. And never run out."

"Ohhh." My eyes locked with Jordan's.

Together we said, "We're cafluent."

\#

"Kat, the weather channel announced rain all day Friday."

"Well, good morning to you too, Ms. Alicia."

"You said to watch the weather reports."

"I know. I wish I could do everything I feel I'm supposed to do and still be home with my family."

"Understandable. So, do I cancel everyone for Friday and make plane reservations and get a hotel for you in Dallas or not?"

She spoke a bit terse. She was still smarting from the wife-named-Beulah talk. That chat hadn't thrilled me either.

"If you can nab an early flight, I won't need a hotel. I would like it to be a day trip."

"Kat, you're an emotional dynamo and a physical weenie. That would be four flights in one day. One from here to Houston and then from Houston to Dallas and back."

I thought about it for a minute. "I could drive and spend Thursday night in Houston with my parents and catch an early flight from there, then back into Houston late afternoon and drive home."

"You're making a lot of assumptions."

"Okay."

"All I have for you is Terry Richardson's address. I don't have a phone number. You don't know if he'll be home or what you're gonna find in Dallas, Ms. Collier."

I wished that snippet of truth hadn't invited a flock of butterflies into my stomach. But I stood in front of her desk as though I were Mighty Mouse instead of Minnie Mouse. "I have to try."

As always, when she was anxious, she slid her silver cross back and forth.

"That's what I love about you and why I get mad at you."

My brows peaked into little tin roofs. "Well, missy, I know exactly how you feel."

"I'll be fine. Don't worry about me."

"Right. Make the air reservations from Houston."

I started toward my treatment room but thought better of it and turned around. I walked past the sign-in counter and to her desk. "Stand up."

She stood. I wrapped my arms around her tiny frame. "Ali, I don't ever remember a time when we snapped at each other. Ever."

She pulled me closer by lapping her hands around my waist. "Me either, and I hate it."

"Me too. I'm going to believe that you'll do the right thing about your child and just love you."

"That would mean a lot."

"Well, you got it." And though I hurt for her and failed to understand her, I meant it.

#

Mom and Dad pulled me into their arms. The drive from Port Arthur had taken two hours and exhaustion washed over me. It saddened Jordan and Bailey to see me leave. I'd hugged and kissed them and promised to return by late Friday night. I hadn't missed the doubt clouding Jordan's eyes or Bailey's lips tremoring, but I would be home on time.

My body gained strength as I stood in the arms of my parents. No one had better folks. My dad stood tall and handsome. Of the four girls, only I had inherited his height. The thing about myself I most hated as a teenager when I outgrew all the boys but loved at forty. My mom, shorter but beautiful. Her high cheekbones and soft complexion mirrored my face. I loved being in their home. The warmth and love of God dropped a tent over them and their surrounds. I'd lived a sheltered life. Never aware that evil tiptoed throughout society. I oozed gladness and appreciation for the morals they had instilled in my siblings and me. Happy for a spiritual heritage and the understanding I never walked alone.

Dinner smelled sumptuous from the dining table. "Are you hungry, Katie?"

Dad put his hand to my back and guided me toward the table. "Of course, she is."

"Mom, I'm always hungry in your house." I anticipated Alabama food. She did not disappoint. "Oh, Mom, collard greens and butter beans?"

"And," she said, "fried chicken, squash, and cornbread."

I snuggled my chair closer to the table.

Dad caught my hand in his. "Let's pray."

We prayed at my house, but the warmth of their love washed over me whenever my father blessed the food. A thousand childhood memories flooded my brain. The Red Sea parted when either of my parents prayed. I might be a recognized professional in my community but I bowed as a child in their presence.

#

Flying out of Houston, all the uncertainties Alicia had mentioned consumed me. *Lord, help me find Terry Richardson in a timely manner and return home to my family tonight.*

The flight attendant passed beverages and packaged cookies through the cabin. I never liked coffee and couldn't imagine sipping at 5:00 a.m. I accepted the cookies, hoping to calm my tummy. I wanted my husband in the seat beside me and Bailey hopping in hers. I hadn't thought about it before, but I'd bet she'd never flown. *God, take care of my family, please.*

Chapter 35

I'm sure Dallas is a beautiful city, but I could spare no time for sightseeing. I grabbed my navy briefcase from the overhead bin. I felt a little unstable navigating the aisle—everyone pushing, the world in a hurry. Sensible shoes crossed my mind a wee bit late.

"Thank you for flying with us." The uniformed flight attendant didn't even glance up.

"You're welcome," I said anyway.

Thank goodness I had no baggage. I hurried to find a cab. The taxis seemed to notice everyone else first. Finally, an old-looking cab with an older-looking driver stopped for me. I threw my briefcase and purse in the back seat. Mercy, his wheels rolled forward while I jumped in beside my things.

I rattled off the address. Of course. He didn't speak English. I sat through two semesters of Spanish in college. Obviously, I hadn't listened. With wild gestures and all fifteen words I'd remembered from class, he drove toward somewhere.

The heat tortured me inside the car. I didn't remember enough Spanish to ask about air conditioning. Swiping my fingers across my upper lip and blowing upward to fan my bangs didn't do the trick. Sickness took residence in my belly. Was heat the culprit, or did I just miss Jordan?

"Si," the driver said, as he squealed to a stop, jolting me forward against my seatbelt.

O. Kay. I grabbed my slip of paper with Terry Richardson's address—after I found my purse that had skittered across the floorboard. The scribbled address matched the numbers tacked on the doorframe. As I snatched my possessions and paid the driver with a fifty-dollar bill for a twelve-dollar ride, he pulled away with my change before I could ask him to please wait for me.

I pushed my short hair behind my ears, finger-pressed my navy pants and pink blouse, swung my purse over my shoulder, grasped my briefcase securely against my body, then approached the fence surrounding the house. But as I checked if the gate was locked, an angry black pit bull bolted from behind the house, skidded to the front gate, and displayed an intense desire to eat me.

A statue stood in my place. I'd heard few stories about pit bulls with happy endings. My mission to find evidence against Cindy Thibbodeaux crumbled. I could call another cab on my cell, hot-foot it back to the airport, and be home with Jordan and Bailey. But Sara Beth's blue eyes, blond curly hair, and pudgy hands clapping together held me at that gate. No matter how much I wanted to run away, a tiny voice whispered in my ear, "hewwo." My resolve renewed.

Thankfully, a man wearing jeans and two days' beard hurried from the house. Probably wondering what had upset his dog. But I thrilled to see anyone.

He placed his right hand on the dog to calm him. "You need something?"

"I'd hoped to speak with Terry Richardson."

"My nephew? What you want to talk to him about? He in any kind of trouble?" He scratched his head and ran his hand across his stubble. "I told him straight out he couldn't stay here if he got in a scrape. Ain't got no patience with boys and their predicaments."

I rubbed sweaty palms against rubber legs. "No, sir, he's not in any trouble. I'd hoped to ask him a couple of questions about his last job in Port Arthur at Walmart. About something that happened to someone else."

"If it's about that dead kid, I can tell you right now he don't want to discuss it."

"May I see him for a couple minutes? My intention is not to upset him. It wouldn't take longer than five minutes. That is, if you'll let me talk with him."

"He ain't here."

"May I ask where he is?"

He spat in the yard. "Are you a police officer?"

"No, sir, I work for the state but not the police department."

"But my nephew is not in trouble."

"No, sir, not at all."

"Well, he just left. He's working the night shift at the Walmart close to here. They don't close till 10:00 and he told me he intended to down a couple of beers with friends after work." He rubbed his dog's head. "I don't know what to tell ya, ma'am."

"Will he be here in the morning?"

"S'far as I know."

"May I return then?"

"Suit yourself, but don't be coming around too early. I work the night shift myself."

"Yes, sir."

I stumbled away from the fence. When I found a tree to lean against, I pulled my cell from my purse to call a cab. But where did I plan to go? "God, what am I doing here?" I prayed aloud. "I'd believed I needed to come here. I'm not as sure right this minute."

What had my pastor said? "If He brought you to it, He'll bring you through it." It had sounded so comforting parked on a pew with plenty of air conditioning blowing. Leaning against a tree in Dallas with sweat dripping from everywhere, nothing except Jordan sounded comforting. "Did you even bring me to it?"

The pit bull howled.

I hurried further down the block to a different tree. Unless I ran away from what I'd come to find out, the airport wasn't an option. Jordan would never understand and Bailey might cry. *God, I love them so much.* I lifted the phone to my ear and managed to snag a hotel room in an upscale part of town. I needed to feel safe and it would be important when I called Jordan, aware I would upset him. I called another cab.

The Omni felt safe. Not worth the money, but safety seemed paramount.

I lingered on a gorgeous bed with a lush duvet in the hotel and dialed Jordan's number, then kicked off my non-sensible heels.

He answered on the first ring. "You're still in Dallas, aren't you?"

"I love you so much."

"But it's greeting from Dallas. Right?"

"Yes. I don't know what to say except yes."

"Catherine, if I didn't love you so much, I might wring your beautiful neck."

When he called me Catherine that was never a good sign. "Sweetheart, the guy I came to talk with is working the night shift. I hope I can see him in the morning."

"You hope?"

"I have nothing but an address. Alicia found his address but not a phone number. I visited the house today but talked to his uncle."

"I would say I can't believe it, but I can. When you feel strongly about something, it's just like you to run off with half the information you need."

"Please, please, don't be mad."

"Are you in a secure hotel?"

"Yes, the Omni right downtown."

"Thank God. Katie, hold on. Bailey heard the phone ring and wants to talk to you."

He said, "Yes, sweetheart, it's Mommy, and of course you may speak to her."

"Mommy, are you almost home? It's getting dark, and you said you would be home tonight. Did you say hi to Grandma and Grandpa for me?"

"Yes, I told them. They can't wait to see you." I dropped my head into my available hand. "I told them I would bring you for a visit while you're out of school."

"Good. They love me a bunch. So, are you almost here?"

"Bailey, Mommy loves you so much." God help me. "But I'm in a hotel in Dallas and can't come home tonight."

Stark, angry silence hung between us.

Then, "I'm goin' to bed. I was gonna wait up, but just you never mind."

The phone slammed against a table. Normally I might frown at that behavior, but I deserved it and I knew it.

"Katie Girl, I'm glad I know your heart. It's always in the right place, but I miss you and now Bailey is mad. I'll go talk to her, but what am I supposed to say? Mommy left and has broken another promise, but she really didn't mean to?"

Jordan's sadness threatened my breath.

"Kate, do you want me to say, 'I know our time will come, Bailey, but I can't tell you when'?" Jordan said. The snark caught me by surprise.

"I trust you always to say what you think is best." The knot in my throat grew to gourd size. "I wish I was home."

"Me too."

"What did my grandmother say? If wishes were fishes, we'd have us a fry."

"I'll see you tomorrow, sweetheart."

"I love you more than anything on earth."

"Me too, Katie Girl, me too."

I planted myself in front of Terry Richardson's house at 10:00 a.m., wearing hotel gift-shop clothes and makeup, and sensible shoes. I didn't open the gate, but wilted in the Dallas sun. About 10:30 a young clean-cut guy drinking a root beer walked through the front door with the dog firmly in hand. He ambled straight to the gate. "You the lady wanting to ask me some questions?"

"Yes. I'm Catherine Collier and I'll try not to take much of your time."

"Okay. But what do you want?"

"There was an incident at Walmart in Nederland on July twelfth of this year. I checked with the manager and you were working in that store and parking lot the same day."

"I was. Who could forget July twelfth with that kid dying an' all? But I didn't do anything."

"Mr. Richardson—"

"You can call me Terry."

"Thank you, Terry. I know you didn't do anything." I laid my briefcase on the gatepost and pulled my phone from my purse. I flashed Cindy's screenshot. "Did you see this lady inside the store or on the parking lot that day?"

He emptied his cup on the ground. His hands shook as he glanced past my phone. "I don't think so."

"It's really important. Could you take one more look?"

"I moved to my uncle's so no one would ask me that."

With care and no judgement, I said, "So you saw her?"

"I didn't say that."

"A beautiful baby girl died that day. No one can change that. I thought if you saw her, it might help you to tell someone."

"Help me?"

"It was just a thought, but if I saw anything that could help in an investigation, and I knew a child had died, it would haunt me till I told someone." I turned to walk away. "Thanks, Terry."

"Wait," he called out.

I turned. "Yes?"

"I don't know if what I saw is important or not."

"Something bothered you enough to leave Port Arthur the next day."

Terry coughed multiple times. "I saw that lady on the parking lot when I left for lunch at noon, but I didn't think much about it till the news came on that night and a reporter showed a video of her coming from the store screaming. He said the baby was dead."

"Right." I could wait. And pray.

"Well ... uh ... "

"It's okay. Take your time."

"I walked close to her vehicle but she didn't spot me."

"All right."

"She opened the front passenger door. She was in an old van."

I waited, hardly breathing.

"She threw bags of stuff in her car." He stared into his empty soda can.

I remained silent but my brain pedaled fifty miles per hour.

"It was the next thing."

I nodded.

"She did her nose funny. Like how you do when you smell something awful."

"Yes." My body liquified and spilled onto the front walk.

"Then the lady slammed the van door. She pulled tissues from her purse. She gagged at first then hurled into a wad of tissues, then into her purse." He shook his head as though trying to clear it. "I intended to ask her if she was all right. But she took off toward the store stuffing soiled Kleenex inside her purse."

An elephant crawled onto my shoulders. Sara Beth, I'm so sorry.

"I don't know anybody who would walk around with puke in their purse. It made me sick to my stomach the rest of that day, every time I thought about it.

Until I saw the news." His skin blanched. "And ma'am, I have no idea if that's important or not, but after I saw the news—and I have a wild imagination—it crossed my mind the odor could have been her baby. You know, since she died and all." He stubbed his foot at the dirt along the fence line. "What a terrible thing to say. I wouldn't want you to think bad of me. Maybe I watch too many murder mysteries. Sometimes I wonder if it wasn't an accident, and then I think what a horrible person I am for suspecting that."

"I understand. It would be terrible to blame someone for a tragic accident."

"I'm not accusing anyone of anything. I moved so nobody would ask me about any of it. But what do the police think?"

"It's an open case."

"Huh."

"Terry, if anything you saw proved to be important, and this ever went to trial, would you be willing to testify to what you've said to me?"

"Oh, heavens no. I could never do that."

"Even if it became important?"

"No, and I have to go inside."

"Terry," I pulled my card from my pocket. "if you remember anything else or change your mind, would you call the Port Arthur police or my number? It's on the card."

"I never intended to tell anyone. I'm not sure what happened. I spilled my guts."

I shook his hand. "Thanks, Terry. I sure hope you change your mind. But either way, thanks for telling me." I smiled as I died inside.

"Miss Collier," Terry called behind me.

"Yes?" I turned.

"You were right about one thing. I'm relieved I told you. You're easy to talk to."

I smiled at the boy. "Thanks."

My brain went into overdrive. Cindy probably couldn't have smelled a body that soon, but Sara Beth would have soiled her diaper as the heat became overwhelming, and then vomited. Everything inside her would have expelled itself. Perhaps she'd been savable at that point, but it appeared as though Cindy had vomited and hurried away.

Chapter 36

Exhausted, my head pushed into the seatback as the plane propelled itself over Dallas. I'd succeeded in half my mission. I ferreted out Terry Richardson, but he wouldn't testify. My ears still buzzing from takeoff, I decided to leave the rest in God's hands. I would pray Terry changed his mind, but he wouldn't hear from me again. I would tell Steve Giovanni what Terry witnessed, then whatever the district attorney decided, they decided. My body burned with fatigue and disappointment. Cindy had murdered her sweet baby. She smelled her sick and dying child, hurled and walked away.

But God had blessed me with the world's best family. As I flew over Dallas, staring out the window with in-ground swimming pools sparkling like tiny blue dots, I relished the notion I would soon be home and wouldn't be flying away from them again anytime soon.

#

Darkness had fallen over Port Arthur by the time I drove onto my street, then pointed the Beamer up the driveway and walked into my home. Both Jordan and Bailey slept. I allowed my possessions to fall to the carpet and stay, but I walked into Bailey's room, lifted her into my arms, then padded softly into my bedroom and laid her beside Jordan. I slipped into the shower to wash Dallas from my body. I stepped into my softest jammies then snuggled myself between my husband and daughter. Bailey didn't stir but Jordan awakened at my touch.

"Welcome home, Katie Girl. I love you and am so glad you're safe." His kiss fell soft as a butterfly on my lips.

I couldn't hold him close enough. I wanted to crawl inside his skin, yet that would involve seeing myself as he saw me, and I couldn't bear it. I'd disappointed him. I should have figured Dallas wouldn't be a day trip. Why did I make ludicrous promises? "God as my witness, I will do better."

"What did you say, baby?" Jordan's husky voice smacked of sleep.

"I said I love you and goodnight."

He turned on his side and circled Bailey and me with his arm.

The quick trip to Dallas had exhausted me. I fell into a deep sleep with

Jordan's arm across me and Bailey snuggled at my side. That night, like so many others, I harbored the kind of tired that can't be slept off—but I tried.

My eyes shot open as a painful cry announced Bailey, who ran into our bedroom. She must have kicked her dad once too often during the night and he had moved her back to her bed.

Jordan threw himself from the covers as our daughter tackled and body-locked him. "Bailey, what's wrong? Sweetheart, are you awake?" He appeared unable to tell.

"Bailey." I'd crawled across the bed to stand beside them. "Baby, we got you. Sweetheart, Mama and Daddy have you. Bailey!"

But she appeared oblivious to me and kept shouting into Jordan's face.

"Daddy, Mommy is dead. Daddy, she's not coming back."

"She's right here, but Daddy's got you. I promise I've got you." He walked around the room with her, rubbing circles on her back. "Sweetheart, we're all safe."

When I attempted to touch her, Bailey recoiled. Sweat dripped from her little body.

Her voice filled with such terror, she hardly sounded like herself. "But Daddy Josiah killed my first mom and now Mommy is gone too. She musta died. Her plane crashed." She jerked within the circle of Jordan's arms. "She has blood on her too, just like my first mom."

What had I done? I had promised her Dallas would be a day trip. I ran for a cool wet cloth. Jordan soothed her.

"Bailey, please wake up for Daddy. Mommy is not dead. She's right here. She's home. Remember? She came home last night. You slept between us most of the night."

Returning with the damp cloth, I wiped her sweat. "Bailey. I'm here. I'm right here."

She wrapped herself even further around her dad.

I dried her body anyway. I stood there knowing. Knowing Jordan had never failed our child … not even once. Never worked past time to come home. Never late to take her to school nor to retrieve her from after-school care. Never had he promised her anything he hadn't delivered. He had never been too busy to take her putt-putting or to the grocery store. He never failed on Saturday to put on his redneck cap then place my matching one over Bailey's golden hair. She loved to ride around in his pickup, so off they would go.

Now I could only watch as he comforted her. I flipped on the ceiling lights and both table-top lamps, hoping to dispel her fear and help her come full awake. I reached for her again and was rebuffed.

Jordan walked with her through the kitchen and into the living room to his recliner. He rocked her.

I sat on the floor at their feet. Devastated, listening to her sup-sups. I flipped every light switch the front room offered then dropped before them again. I swiped her still-damp body and wept.

Jordan kept rocking and soothing. He never looked at me.

I knew why.

Guilt came in waves. Waves like the powerful ones we'd seen when we'd taken her to the Galveston beach for a picnic last summer. I'd watched them as Jordan held her—while we crossed the ferry—as she threw leftover bread to the seagulls.

Oh, how she'd laughed. But her laughter died tonight.

Jordan said, "Sweetheart, can you get awake enough to realize you've had a dream ... a terrible dream, and look at Mommy? She's right here. Bailey, if you'll just calm down and look, she's right here and she loves you so much."

Her sniffles quieted. She released her arms from Jordan's neck but stayed where she felt safest.

"Bailey, Daddy told you the truth. You've had a frightening dream. Can you look at me? I'm alive and I'm right here."

She blinked, then sat up awake. Finally, she glanced toward me but didn't reach for me. "You were bleeding. I saw you. And you wouldn't come home. You said you would be gone one 'dark time' but it wasn't true. It was two 'dark times.'"

"I'm here now. The blood was in your dream. It wasn't real." Choking on words, I kept talking. "If you'll let Mommy touch you, then you'll be able to know I'm right here. And I came home. I lifted you in my arms while you still slept and placed you in my bed."

"No, you didn't. I woke up in my own bed."

"That's on me," Jordan said, "you kicked non-stop and I couldn't sleep so I took you back in your room. But Mommy did put you in our bed. She missed you so bad. She missed me too."

Bailey's bottom lip quivered. "If she missed us, she knew where we was ... ya know? She knew."

"Bailey, we explained before you joined our family that Mommy's job is different than most and she is not like other counselors. If she was, you wouldn't be our daughter. Katie fell in love with you as she counseled you and then brought you home with her."

She hiccupped. "I know."

"Sometimes it's hard on all three of us," Jordan said, "but if you try hard enough, you'll understand that other children need her help. It's a work she feels God called her to."

"Okay. I'll try. But I want you to love me, and I want to stay here forever."

"Honey, we love you too." Jordan and I talked over each other.

She pushed one tiny hand toward me. "Can I touch you now?" Her sweet green eyes were puffy and red, but she'd stopped crying.

I reached for her with a gentle hand.

She slid from Jordan's lap and tumbled down into my arms. "I love you, Mommy. Don't scare me so much again. Please."

"Baby, I'll try … harder than ever before. I never meant to scare you."

She put her hands at her waist. "Okay. But the next time God calls this house I want to speak to Him. He should call another mama sometimes."

Oh, just like me, Bailey had a mouth hung on her.

Jordan prayed for us. "Father, we thank you for each other. We thank you that the dream has passed and Bailey is feeling better. Lord, there will be other days when one of us is disappointed, yet we are a family—you brought together—who will love, laugh, play, trust, and listen to you and each other."

"Amen," we said together.

Jordan considered Bailey, still in my lap. "If you're okay, little one, we need some sleep. Can you sleep in your room or do you need to bunk with us?" He smiled. "Either way is good with us. I'm up for a few more kicks to my side." He chuckled again.

"Your choice, Bailey," I said.

She put her arms around me. "If I know you're both here and safe, I'll sleep in my room with my bear if you guys can tuck me again."

"We can," we said together.

With Jordan on one side and me on the other, we kissed our girl and pushed ballerina bear beneath her covers.

"Can I pray now?"

"Of course," Jordan said.

"Dear Lord, I thank you for my mom and dad, but you've let calling this house get a little out 'a control. I want my mama home more. Amen." She snuggled down into the covers with bear.

As Jordan and I pushed our weary bodies down the hall, he said, "Katie Girl, we've discussed it but have been remiss in having the gifts-and-callings talk with Bailey."

"Tomorrow. I promise." I raised my hand.

Chapter 37

Elizabeth, Jessica, Joe, and Judy Gibson stayed in counseling with me. I called a friend who specialized in working with kids who'd suffered sexual assault, and she agreed to see Joey and Carla Gibson and Kathy Fontenot. Judy's anger toward Kathy dissipated as she came to see her as a good kid who had been molested by her uncle. Supervised visitation was established between Elizabeth and Kathy until both Kathy's therapist and I agreed it was safe for them to be together.

Judy and her kids gathered in my office.

"You guys okay?"

Judy spoke first. "It has been rocky for us all." She sighed. "With your help and lots of time spent on my knees, we're gonna get past this."

"Good. Jessica?"

"I thought I would never be okay again after I found Elizabeth in the tub with bruises on her body, but if my sister can heal, I can too."

"Okay. It's evident how much you love her and you're right, Elizabeth is doing well. But I want you to do well also."

"I'm getting there." Jessica smiled.

"Good. Joe?"

"I'm working on forgiveness for Kathy. I'm sorry she'd been molested herself. I truly am. But why couldn't she tell someone instead of abusing my sister?"

"It's complicated. I chose not to counsel her, but she's reported being very sorry. Seeing her as a victim—and no telling for how long—will help some. And remember, forgiveness is not for Kathy, it's for you."

Joe studied his lap.

"Unforgiveness will eat you up and cause you to be an angry, unhappy person. I don't want that for you."

He squinted at me. "I don't either. I'll work harder on it."

"All right then."

Elizabeth speared my eyes with hers. "I want my dad and Carla to be okay. They fought a lot in the beginning but are better now. There's no point in him getting another divorce. He really loves her."

"Well, I learned from talking to their counselor he and Carla are both faithful to attend every session. The therapist believes their marriage will survive."

"Good," Elizabeth said, "he told me that too."

#

I called a session between Elizabeth's parents, Judy and Joey. "Judy, do you blame Joey for what happened between the girls?"

Joey bristled. "That's a great question. Do you blame me, Judy?"

She sat in silence.

Joey relaxed his shoulders. "I would understand if you do. I blamed myself until I really began to hear what Catherine and our other counselor kept saying." He coughed. "Judy, I'm sorry. I would do anything to have somehow known."

There in the same treatment room where I'd told Joey the truth, Judy surveyed his grief and felt his sorrow and his innocence of knowledge of wrongdoing. "Joey, we were married for eighteen years. Once I got past my initial anger, I remembered your heart." She reached for his hand. "You love Elizabeth and would never knowingly allow abuse in your home."

"Never. I failed in our marriage and I'm sorry I hurt you, but Judy, these are my kids … our kids, and I would protect them with my life. I didn't know."

She gazed into his eyes. After a protracted pause she said, "I believe you. You've always loved them. We'll get past this."

#

On Elizabeth's next visit, I asked, "How is Kathy doing?"

"She's good. We'll both be glad when we can play alone … without the games though."

"Yes, without the games. You are happy? Has Kathy apologized?"

"Over and over. I'm not sure she knew how bad the games were because of her uncle, but her therapist explained exactly what you told me. I don't believe she will try that again."

"And if she does?"

Elizabeth bristled just like her father. "Don't you worry. I will never let anyone do that to me again. No matter if I love them."

I reached to hug her. "That's my girl."

#

Elizabeth grew toward health and happiness. Her smile spread across her whole face again. She laughed often. We giggled on the swing with our naked toes in the air in front of us.

But Mr. Hubbard had a different story. Lawrence Ray Hubbard had been released from prison on parole for raping a former girlfriend, just as Joey Gibson had said. The authorities picked up Hubbard within two weeks of the discovery of what he'd done to Kathy Fontenot. While he cooled his heels in a local jail, the sexual assault officer explained to Hubbard that the gap between his front teeth had left identifiable scarring on Kathy's left breast and his fingerprints had left DNA on her headboard. He pleaded no contest to the charges of sexual assault.

His no-contest plea for the sexual assault of Kathy Fontenot automatically reinstated the maximum sentencing for the first rape—thirty years to life. Though he was only forty-two at the time of his incarceration, in Hubbard's case, I suspected the life sentence would be shorter than the thirty years. Even Texas prisoners don't like child molesters.

On a good day, I can weep for the small child inside Lawrence Hubbard, just like the small child inside Janis Joplin—Port Arthur's most famous person. Their brokenness—unnoticed by a therapist or another loving, caring person who might have been able to reach them—left their lives spinning forever out of control.

#

I crawled into bed beside Jordan. He rolled over and pulled me into his arms. Together we thanked God for each other and our child.

"Maybe we could do a prison ministry, baby," I whispered.

"Or you could go to sleep, and remember that one plants, and another waters, but only God brings true change."

"What does that mean for me right now?" I yawned.

"Come here, my little waterer, and I'll show you."

I kissed him, losing interest in sleep.

#

Lewis loved the convertible rides we took together. Yet, he didn't want to ride with the top down on sunny days until I slathered him in sunscreen, or he'd stuffed his head inside a large hat he'd smuggled into my office and stowed under the sink.

He continued to see me weekly so we could work on appropriate words to label honest feelings. He learned when he was angry to say "I'm mad," instead of "I'm going to kill myself." He practiced saying, "I need time alone," and, "My feelings are hurt." He mastered, "I don't understand, Mom, why you made this decision. Could you explain it?" All useful communication skills.

"I haven't wet my bed in a long time," he told me. "I don't think I need my medicine anymore."

"I wouldn't count on that, Lewis. If I had suffered as much as you have, I'd swallow it down gratefully every day."

"Why, if I don't need it anymore?"

"How do you know?"

"I told you already. I haven't wet the bed in a long time."

"I can't and won't try to make you take it, but I recommend against stopping your medication."

"Whatever. I feel mad at you right now." He stuck his nose in the air.

I laughed.

#

"Lewis," I said at the beginning of a session, "it's time to congratulate you on your progress, give you a huge hug, and send you on your way, or it's time to talk about how you feel regarding your own skin."

For a minute, he acted as though he didn't understand what I meant.

His mouth opened and closed, and his head cocked to one side. Words stuck in his throat. Then, he let out a long, deep breath. "I don't know how to talk about it. I mean—Don't. Know. How. I have never talked about it to anyone on the face of this earth."

"All right."

We were on the back-porch swing, but he stood and circled for a few minutes, then propped himself in the wicker chair to my right.

He leaned over and picked up the basketball and pushed it around on his lap. "I'm blacker than my mother."

I nodded.

"I'm blacker than Whitney." He rolled the ball.

I leaned forward.

"I'm blacker than my father." He opened his knees and started bouncing the basketball between them. "I'm blacker than anybody in my whole family."

"Okay."

"I'm the blackest person in my class." He stopped the ball and glared at me. "Do you know how many times I've heard, 'Hey, black boy. Yeah you, black boy.'"

"I'm guessing a lot."

"Well, you're guessing right. I can't talk to my mom about it, and I talk to her about everything."

"And?"

"If I tried to talk to her, what would I say?" He was on a roll. "Hey, Mama, I love being your son, but I hate that I'm so black. Not being black, you understand. I want to be black, I just don't want to be this black." He held out both arms.

He had no idea how handsome he was, sitting in that chair. He had excellent muscle tone. Lean and fit with his father's eyes and getting taller by the day. Absolute beauty. I knew not to tell him. Too often therapists miss great opportunities to shut up.

He left the ball in his chair and paced. "Can you honestly tell me," he turned toward me, "you haven't noticed how black I am?"

"I noticed—"

"Well, duh, yeah, you noticed." He held out his arms again for me to survey him. Standing before me wearing jeans, a white T-shirt and Michael Jordan tennis shoes, he was handsome. Ebony. Stunning.

"I observed, but not in a negative way. It's the same as you having dark eyes and clean sneakers."

"You're lying. We were never going to lie to each other. That first day I came here, and I said, 'don't say something if it's not true,' and you just did." He stood in front of the swing staring at me, with his lip quivering.

"Will you sit down for a minute?"

"No, not until you admit it. My mom's gonna kill me if you tell her I called you a liar, but we both know you're making things up." Angry tears gathered in his eyes.

Chapter 38

"You are blacker than your parents. I noticed that you are ..." I thrust out my palms searching for words. "... black*er*." I swallowed hard. "I picked up clues it could be an issue for you."

"Well, duh, yeah." He balanced with feet planted apart and right knee jerking.

"I knew because my students, who are older than you and more comfortable in group settings, have explained there is a ..."

"There is a what?" he barked at me.

"A kind of social-casting system within the black culture, based on depth of skin color."

"I don't know what's a social ... social ... whatever system you just said, but if it means the lighter-skinned you are the better people like you, then they told it straight."

"Can we talk about it?"

"Well, what are we doing now? This is talking, isn't it?" He made an impatient gesture with his hands. "I've been waiting since the day I got here to talk about this. I figured we would talk about it a long time ago." He searched around the yard and worked the knee-jerking motion. "I'm really honest-to-god glad I don't pee my bed anymore, don't get me wrong. That peeing thing was awful. Every night, and I do mean every night, before I go to sleep, I say, 'God, oh dear God, thank you that I don't pee my bed anymore.' But, man, how long would I have to come here before you would recognize I'm the blackest boy you've ever seen?"

I did an emergency serial search of every black person I had ever met. My brain turned colorblind. I wouldn't lie. Man, what was that dude's name in *The Green Mile?* "Coffee, John Coffee, like the drink only spelled different." How did he spell coffee? He was black as onyx. As my mind kept searching, I wanted to stand up in front of Lewis and scream, "I love black people," like Tom Cruise did in *Jerry Maguire*, but I didn't. I sat and looked at him and wanted to cry. I didn't do that either.

"Aren't you going to stand up and scream, I love black people?" Lewis asked.

Oh, mercy, faces do break out in words. "I love black people." I screamed before I could even get to my feet. But once there I threw my arms out in grand style and screamed again, "I love black people."

But instead of a wonderful breakthrough where Lewis screamed with me, he dropped to the chair and wept. He cried hard, putting his face down and pulling his elbows up around his ears. He grasped the back binding around the neck of his T-shirt with both hands.

I dropped beside him. I tried to comfort him, but he shrugged me away.

I waited beside him, silent and miserable. I was glad he cried though. I didn't tell him that either.

When he finally glanced up, his T-shirt wasn't all white and clean anymore. He had pulled the tail from his belted jeans and used it as a handkerchief when he'd started to gulp.

"I know what you're gonna say," Lewis said.

Oh, thank God. I nodded yes as though I did. But my face was lying. I didn't have a clue what to say.

"*Jerry Maguire* is your favorite old movie," he said in a sing-song voice. "Oprah is your favorite person in the whole world." He sniffled. "Denzel is your favorite actor. O. J. is innocent and LeBron James is your favorite basketball player." He peered at me through huge eyes, blinking.

"O. J. Simpson killed two people in cold blood, and I don't watch basketball."

"You've never been the blackest person in your school," he said.

"I have not."

"You can't help me with this."

"I can, if you want me to. I have been among the poorest in my school."

"Who cares about being the poorest?"

"The poorest in the class."

"You don't look poorest. I look blackest." He pointed at his chest. "I don't want to talk to anybody driving a car like yours about being poor."

"'I've come a long way, baby, but Whoopi Goldberg isn't the only person, 'from the projects.'" I waited for inspiration to continue. I needed to say the right thing, but my brain hurt. "23-B Rosedale Courts, Tuscaloosa, Alabama. Federal housing. And my home."

He snubbed, his shoulders jerking with every sound, but he listened.

"The first Halloween after we moved to Rosedale Courts, I heard Suzanne, the most popular kid at school, ask Sarah, another popular kid, if she planned to trick-or-treat at Rosedale Courts." I looked at the top of Lewis's head. "Before I could speak up and say, 'Hey, that's where I live,' Sarah turned her nose up with disgust and said, 'Oh, mercy no, the houses may be close together, but those people are so poor they don't have anything good to give.'"

"What did you say?"

"Nothing, but my face burned. I went home and asked my mom if it was true. Were we poor?" I smiled. "My mom is wise. She said, 'We get to decide that for ourselves, Catherine.'"

"What does that mean?"

"Well, I'm glad you asked. She meant life is what we decide it is, not what other people may try to decide for us." I stopped to see if he was with me.

He nodded and looked like he was hanging.

"We didn't have much money, but we had everything else that counted. We loved each other. We loved God and church and working hard and doing things right."

"Were you ever popular at school?" He stood again and moved back to the swing beside me.

"Not really. My teachers singled me out as intelligent and I had a few good friends. But no, never popular. I was tall and skinny. I towered over my girlfriends and didn't have a boyfriend at school."

"My mom thinks you're pretty. I think you're okay. Tall is good."

"I appreciate the compliments from you and your mom, but I'm no longer fourteen, looking for a date to the ninth-grade dance. And you're not fourteen barely reaching my chin and willing to take me."

Lewis knit his brows, needing to say something.

"What?"

"I wanted you to be black. When my mom said she was bringing me here, I didn't want to come. But if my mom had to bring me, I wanted you to be black. I wanted you to be real black ... charcoal. I wanted you to take one look at me and know exactly how I felt."

I shrugged. "I can be proud that I am tall. I can work hard, get an education and make a lot of money, but I can't be black. I can know what it's like to hurt and be different, but I will never be black. I figured out why I hated cold food and started liking it, but I'm white."

Lewis repositioned, scooting his back against the chains so we could face each other. "You knew the first day, didn't you?"

I slid to the other end and pulled my feet in under me. "That a major part of your pain came from being blacker than you wanted to be? Yes, I knew."

"It was like you were looking a hole right through me," Lewis said. "I wasn't just shaky and jumpy because the swing hit the back of my legs. That created problems, my stomach used to hurt all the time, but it was much more. I have never looked at anybody except my mom and felt like she could see my soul. But you could." He took a deep breath and shook his head back and forth. "It's a strange experience when a person can see your soul. It can make a kid jumpy."

"You are a good person."

"Why didn't we talk about it then?" He slammed his hands down on his lap. "Why didn't you let me off the hook and just talk about it?"

The squirrels that all disappeared when I was shouting about loving black people played up and down tree trunks again. The humidity smothered. "Is that a real question?"

"Yeah. You knew I hurt and all."

"Look at me." I reached for his hand. "Are you gonna sit here and tell me we could have had this conversation without building a relationship? That I could have looked at you the first day and said, 'Hi, my name is Ms. Catherine. So how do you feel about being real, real black?'"

He started to bob his head yes but thought better of it and looked pitiful.

"Therapists can't say everything they feel without emotional permission from the client. I talked about many similarities between us. Why do you think I told you the first or second session I had been in therapy? I rarely tell a client. Not that I care if they know, but it isn't always relevant. I sent you a loud message that my not liking cold food was analogous to your not liking the sun. There were reasons. You weren't ready to talk about it, but you had a reason."

"I waited for this talk," he said honestly.

"Lewis, I waited for this talk too. Some clients leave therapy because therapists say too little. They use little trite phrases like, 'How do you feel about that?' and 'Tell me more,' but many more clients run away from therapy because therapists say too much too fast. If you had run away, you would not have your medication."

"Oh man, I could still be wetting my bed. Please tell me I will never wet my bed again."

"If you take your medicine, you won't wet the bed. Also, given enough time, your body may learn new habits and eventually you might not need the medicine."

He shook his head rapidly back and forth. "I don't intend to find out. I need my medicine."

"Lewis, back to the first sessions for a minute. You gave me every sign I needed to know what stirred inside your head and heart. I checked them out gingerly. Some people do talk about huge issues right up front." I reached to pick up a small rock. "You put up emotional stop signs every time I made a move. I respected that. You are a wonderful young man with lots of pride and I will always honor that. It was up to you to decide if we ever had this talk."

"Thank you."

"Lewis, kids at school don't pick on you because you are dark."

He jerked his head up and the top half of his body bristled. "Oh, yes, they do."

"They don't." I held up my hand to signal him to let me speak. "They pick on you because they can. They pick on you because you let them." I held up my hand again. "They pick on you because you have given them emotional permission to do so."

"I have not."

"Excuse me, but yes you have. You've bought what the kids at school have been selling."

Confusion crowded his eyes.

"An emotional purchase," I said. "They have sold you a bill of goods. Lewis is real black and real weak. He is a wuss and threatens to kill himself." I reached over to lift his chin. "Lewis, making the offer was about them, buying into it was about you."

"How do I change it?"

"By treating that whole pile of junk about blacker is lesser like the cold-greasy-fried-chicken issue that it is and refusing to let it hold power over you another day."

"Can you start teaching me how to do that today?"

"I can start today."

#

I became relentless with Lewis. At that point we only had ten days before school started. Allison brought him to my office, or I picked him up every one of those days including Saturday and Sunday after church.

Bailey came with me on the weekend and played on her tablet in the office.

Lewis and I role-played. We swaggered. We strutted. We entered rooms over and over until he learned to possess the room with his entrance. He watched old reruns of *The Cosby Show* to see how Theo walked and talked with pride and sophistication.

I called him "black boy" to give him practice handling it. I watched him go from wincing to strutting. He felt angry in the beginning and told me, "he hated my guts." I laughed and reminded him he loved my guts. A couple times out of frustration he called me a "tall skinny poor gal from the projects who gets sick in restaurants."

I laughed again and said, "I am a statuesque babe who drives my Beamer home to the golf course where dinner is waiting to be shared with my man who thinks I'm perfect."

I watched pride wash over him. I witnessed the rebirth of a young man filled with a sense of self-worth. Not arrogance. Allison and Michael's son wasn't arrogant. He decided, however, he wouldn't suffer at the hands of mean-spirited kids any longer.

"I have something else to say."

"Okay."

"My dad moved back in."

Sometimes I loved my job.

Chapter 39

I met with Steve Giovanni early in my office. 8:30 again. "I have information on Cindy Thibbodeaux I want to share. It is less than I wish it was, but more than I had."

"Really?" He sipped warm coffee.

"I went to Walmart to visit the manager."

"And you did that because …?"

"I wanted to find the names of guys who worked on July twelfth as baggers and then gathered carts during the slow hours."

"And you thought we wouldn't think of that?"

"No. I knew you would cover it. But I also figured you wouldn't give those names to me."

"No, I wouldn't have." His brows raised. "Katie, did you obtain those names somehow?"

"Yes."

"How?"

"I never said."

"You're too cute."

"Trust me. I obtained those names in confidence."

Steve coughed. "What did you do once you had the names?"

"I visited the three boys who still live here, showed each a picture of Cindy, and asked if they remembered seeing her in the store or parking lot on July twelfth."

"What makes you think you had the right to question any of those boys?"

"Sara Beth is dead, and one of those boys might have seen something … anything that would help us find the whole truth. I let Cindy leave the clinic with her when I knew in my heart she didn't seem able to care for her." I latched onto Steve with my gaze. "I owe it to that baby to find out what caused her death."

"You're being pretty hard on yourself."

"I feel hard on myself. I could have taken Sara Beth home with me."

"And how could you have realistically done that?"

"Cindy is stubborn, but if I'd told her I would call Family Services if she didn't let me have Sara Beth for the night, she would have let me take her."

"Katie, did you really believe she would kill Sara Beth?"

"No. Dear Lord, no."

"Then no part of this could be your fault. Katie, did the boys give you any information?"

"None of the boys here had seen her. They all remembered the incident."

"What do you mean 'none of the boys here?'"

"There were four young men working during the time Cindy's van was parked at Walmart. One guy working that day went to lunch at noon, quit his job the next morning, and moved to Dallas the day after that."

"How do you know?"

"One fellow I talked to here in Port Arthur is Travon Smith, and he was worried about his friend, Terry Richardson … a co-worker who moved suddenly and had changed his phone number." I folded my hands in my lap then wrung them together. "Travon thought if anyone knew something, it would be Terry."

Steve squirmed on the sofa. "I questioned Travon Smith, and he never mentioned Terry Richardson."

I did my best to look totally innocent. "Maybe he doesn't like cops."

"Well, I don't get it. What did you say to get him to talk to you?"

"I'm not certain. I asked him a few questions and then listened."

Steve scratched his head. His black eyes seemed to rotate ideas in his head. "I guess I'll have to get permission from the department and fly to Dallas."

I sat quiet as a whisper.

"Katie?"

"I've been to Dallas and have talked to Terry Richardson."

"What?"

"I've already been."

He speared my eyes with his. "And what did he say?"

"That he went to lunch at noon straight up and when I showed Cindy's picture to him, he recognized her."

"What else?"

"He saw her when she threw packages into the front seat."

"Anything else?"

"She made a face like she smelled something awful, then vomited into her purse."

"Will he testify to this?"

"He said he wouldn't."

Steve moved to the edge of the sofa. "Then how come he told you?"

I smiled. "I'm easy to talk to."

"Well, I'll be headed to Dallas."

"Give him a little time."

"Why?"

"I believe he will call me."

"Because ..."

"A gut feeling."

"That's good. But I have to check this out."

I raised my brows. "And if he won't talk?"

"He'll talk."

"Okay." But I didn't think so.

Steve stepped through my office door as Alicia climbed the three steps. His eyes appreciated her. Not ogled, but still. He nodded and stumbled over his feet.

She stepped into the hallway. "Morning."

I poked my head from the treatment room. "Ali, good morning. I need to chat with you before you start working."

"Okay." She took tentative steps into my room.

"I've called my attorney. She will represent you." I smiled. "We have an appointment this afternoon at 5:30."

"We?"

"Yes. I won't say anything but I won't let you go alone."

"Katie, I've made up my mind and you can't change it."

"I told you I won't say anything and I won't." I shrugged. "What you're doing is breaking my heart, but all I can do is love you through it."

"I'm glad you're going with me then." We stared at each other. Raw naked fear filled Alicia's eyes.

I felt as though she looked at a mirror image in mine.

#

We'd already worked a long day then walked toward the car at 5:00. We were tired and our hearts heavy.

While walking, I asked, "You okay?"

She opened the door, slid into my car, and latched her seatbelt. "Nervous is all."

Latching my own, I peered over at her. "She's a great attorney and easy to talk to. You'll be fine when we get there."

"Okay. I hope so."

I reached for her hand and found icy fingers. "Ali ... I ... I love you."

"I love you too."

I sat for a moment without starting the car. "Alicia—"

"Yeah, I agree. Let's pray together before we go."

We'd known each other for a long time.

"Father," I prayed, "My Alicia has found herself in an unexpected crisis. I don't know anything to do except love her and obtain counsel for her. But you can work this out for her good."

She leaned in and I put my arms around her. "I've said and done everything I know to say to my friend and your servant. Guide her from here. Let her feel your presence as she speaks to the attorney. Lord, give the attorney wisdom and guidance. Amen."

She prayed soft, teary words. I could barely hear her. "Father, don't let me puke up or pass out. I know you understand. God, you sacrificed your son to save the world, now I must save my daughter. Strengthen me as I proceed. Amen."

God, knock some sense into her head. Amen.

I pushed start and my car rolled itself toward Beaumont.

#

We waited our turn. "Did you tell Kylie you were coming here?"

"No. Just Lexie. I called her from the office to tell her I would be late and why."

"How is Lexie doing?"

"Fine. She thinks I should turn Kylie in."

I didn't say a word for fear of saying too much.

"I've thought about it night and day. I would if I could. I can't bring myself to say Kylie and Rikki owned the drugs."

"And what does Kylie have to say about all this?"

"I don't really know. Kylie has been avoiding me. She's been staying with my mom since the whole incident, and when I try to see Kylie she conveniently disappears. I didn't want to freak my mother out, so Mom knows nothing about the drugs or my arrest."

"I'd like to get my hands on that girl."

"In that case, I'm glad Kylie's out of reach."

"Sorry. I'm just worried about you." I squeezed her still-icy fingers. Being Bailey's mom and having a mouth hung on me too, I pressed my lips together.

A secretary called Alicia's name.

We stood.

"Ms. Washington will see you now."

Delores Washington smiled at Alicia and introduced herself before turning to me. "Catherine, nice to see you."

I shook hands with Delores.

"Have a seat, ladies." She gestured to a couple chairs facing her desk. "Ms. Green, I'd like you to tell me why you need an attorney."

Alicia blanched but sat still without speaking.

I leaned toward her. "Alicia, you must tell Ms. Washington why you need her help."

"Well." Her lips trembled. "A cop pulled me over and I had drugs in my purse."

"How did the officer become aware drugs were in your purse?" Delores asked in hushed tones.

"Because I opened my purse and showed him."

"You what?"

Silence.

"Okay, how did you obtain the drugs?"

"I found them behind …"

Delores watched her closely. "Yes, ma'am?"

I wanted to scream the answer.

"If I tell you, do you have to tell the judge?"

"Ms. Green, I can only tell the judge what you want told." She frowned. "But what kind of drugs and in what quantity? Please say it was a small amount of marijuana."

Alicia looked like an abandoned puppy. She shook all over.

"Uhh … no, ma'am … it was white powder and some little rock-like things with a small mirror and a straw."

Delores studied for a moment. "You didn't finish saying where you obtained the drugs." She tapped a pencil on a pad. "Behind … what?"

"Behind a baseboard in my daughter's room."

"Keep talking."

"Kylie is my daughter. She is a great kid. She has a bad boyfriend named Rikki. I don't know his last name." She grimaced at me.

My breath caught in my throat. I couldn't fathom what I was hearing.

She continued. "The drugs are his, though."

"How did Rikki's drugs end up in your purse?"

Alicia told her. Thank God once she started talking, she told Delores Washington the whole story. Kylie and the changes in her behavior, Rikki and his reputation, finding the drugs behind Kylie's baseboard, putting them in her purse, trying to find Rikki's house, opening her purse to show the policeman why she'd been upset enough to drive through a stop sign, her arrest and arraignment … everything.

Chapter 40

Alicia reached for me, and I clamped my hand to hers.

Delores peered at her. "You have quite a story."

"I'm afraid so."

"And you don't want me to tell the judge anything you just told me?"

"I don't," Ali whispered.

"You're willing to go to prison—and you will go to prison because any amount of cocaine or crystal meth is a felony in the state of Texas—while your daughter and her boyfriend walk free."

"Yes, ma'am."

"I understand you want your daughter safe, but you realize I have to obtain information from you to put a defense together. And you also must understand I totally recommend against what you are doing one hundred percent."

"Yes, ma'am."

"Ms. Green, show me some fight. Sitting there quietly saying 'yes, ma'am' will land you in federal prison. I'm good. Very good. But I must have something besides 'yes, ma'am' to work with. Give me ... no, give yourself a break."

Tears glinted in Alicia's eyes. "Katie, I need to go."

"Go where? Delores Washington is the best attorney between Houston and Lake Charles."

Alicia glanced at Delores. "Thank you very much, but I intend to plead guilty."

Delores leaned forward. "Guilty to a felony? Do you honestly believe some judge will say, 'Well, that's okay, Ms. Green, I know you love your daughter so you can go now?'"

She cried. "No, the judge will put me in prison and ... and ... I'll have a wife named Beu ... lah."

"What?"

I peeked at Delores and shook my head. "Nothing."

"Ms. Green, please stay. I don't believe you have any realistic understanding of what will happen if you persist in your notion of pleading guilty. It's awful to be put in prison when you're guilty, but when you're not ... "

"I guess I'll be finding out."

Loud voices sounded outside Delores's office. Loud enough for her to stand. "I'm so sorry. I have no idea what's going on, but let me find out." She bolted from behind her desk and toward the noise.

The same secretary who had announced us opened the door looking nonplused. "Ms. Washington, I told these girls ..."

Lexie hurried in behind the flustered secretary dragging Kylie by her arm.

Alicia stood, hurried toward her daughters and pulled them into her arms. "Lexie, Kylie, what are you doing here? How did you find me?"

Lexie faced her mom. "You told me where you were going, and I googled the address."

Kylie seemed absorbed in her shoestrings.

I hadn't seen either of the girls since this whole mess started. I nodded at Lexie—Alicia's blond-haired daughter, then took Kylie by the arm.

She tried to twist loose but found that I could hold on tight when I needed to. She stood with rounded shoulders and her brown mop of hair hung in her face.

"Kylie, look at me."

She wouldn't.

Anger pushed its way into my throat. "Kylie, the only reason you won't look up is because if you do, you'll have to see what you and your stubbornness have done to your mother." I dropped her arm and put my hands on her shoulders. "Your mom has always been small, but she's fading away. Her eyes are those of an old woman. I haven't heard her laugh in months." I shook Kylie ever so gently. "I said look at your mother."

Alicia wilted like petunias in August.

Lexie pushed Kylie toward her mother.

Delores Washington waited in silence. But hope lit her eyes.

I prayed to the only one who could help us.

Kylie stumbled toward Alicia from Lexie's push. But once in front of her mom, she glanced up.

Maybe she hadn't really noticed her mother in recent months. Because when she stared eyeball to eyeball with her, she fractured into tiny pieces.

She wept for ten full minutes before she could speak. "Mama ... Mama, I'm so sorry. I don't know what I was thinking."

Lexie stared at Kylie. "You weren't thinking."

Alicia pushed her daughter's hair from around her face. "I love you, Kylie."

Kylie's eyes puffed and reddened. "Still?"

"Always."

"Shall we all take a seat?" Delores sat behind her desk.

Mother and weeping daughter sat in chairs facing the attorney.

Lexie and I seated ourselves on a pink silk sofa along the wall to Delores's right.

"Kylie, I'm Delores Washington, your mom's attorney. Before you came in your mom was busy talking her way into a ten-to-fifteen-year stint in federal prison due to possession of felonious drugs. Do you have something to say that might change that?"

"Oh, Mom, you were really going to prison?"

Lexie addressed Kylie from the sofa. "I told you that."

"I didn't really be … lieve you," Kylie shot back to Lexie through a very shaky voice.

Lexie closed her eyes, shaking her head.

"Girls, you can fight at home." Delores looked at each sister. "What we all need right now is for you, Kylie, to tell me exactly where the drugs came from, whose they are, how they got behind your baseboard, and anything else."

Alicia grasped her hand.

Lexie grabbed mine.

"Yes, ma'am." Kylie stared at her mom's attorney. "Rikki is … was my boyfriend. The drugs were his."

"Just his?" Delores combed Kylie's eyes with a laser.

"Yes, ma'am. I promise."

"It doesn't matter what you promise. It matters what I can prove."

"I can prove it with help from my friends at school."

"How?"

"Rikki does drugs and flashes them around at school. He has a few customers there too." Kylie leaned her head onto Alicia's shoulder. "My friends caught him trying to persuade me to do drugs with him. They also heard me say no to cocaine and meth. I believe some of them will testify against him."

Delores scratched something on a legal pad. "That would put him at risk for possession and trafficking. And what drugs have you done with him?"

"Marijuana."

Alicia turned and Kylie's head slipped from her shoulder. "Is that the truth, Kylie?" She pulled her child's face between her hands. "You've been different. You scared me so much, I was afraid it might be harder stuff."

Delores worked her pen against the pad. "Kylie, do not speak one word that's not true in this office. I'll find the truth, anyway." Tap tap tap. "And if you lie, I'll be mad. You don't want an attorney mad at you … believe me, missy."

Tears dripped down Kylie's face. "Mom, since I'd never done any drugs before, I got pretty messed up on weed a few times. But If Ms. Washington can help us, I'll never as long as I live smoke that crap again." She looked at Delores. "I didn't like it. I hate feeling out of control. I wanted Rikki to like me."

"What is Rikki's last name?"

"Anderson."

"How did Mr. Anderson's drugs find their way behind the baseboard in your bedroom?"

Kylie wiped her face. "He was over one night and got the drugs from his backpack. He offered them to me again. I said no." She chewed her nails like a child. "He was pouring cocaine on a little mirror when we heard mom come home. The zipper on his backpack stuck and he couldn't get it open." Regret soaked her words. "Mom knocked on the door and Rikki jerked the baseboard loose and shoved them behind. I told him he would have to take them the next day, but I guess mom found them first."

Delores seemed to weigh Kylie's words. "Unless you've smoked a lot of weed, you know the authorities arrested your mother for possession, she spent the night in jail, and was arraigned the next morning. She would still be there had Ms. Collier not bailed her out."

Kylie crumbled in her chair. "Mama, I'm so sorry. I was scared and didn't know what to do, but that wasn't your fault."

Alicia gathered her fatherless daughter in her arms. "It'll be okay, baby." Pulling a couple tissues from her purse she wiped her nose then sopped her little girl's face with the other. "We'll get through this. Just answer all Ms. Washington's questions honestly."

"I'll do anything, Mom. I just want to come back home and I want my normal life again." Kylie looked at Delores. "Ma'am, I'll tell you the truth about everything. I already have, but I'll give more detail or whatever you need."

Delores made a few notes on her pad. "Thank you, Kylie." She smiled. "That's enough for today. I'll contact the prosecutor from the DA's office and tell him there's new evidence and see where we go from there." She laid her pen on the pad. "It's possible he'll take the new evidence to the DA and the best-case scenario would be the DA decides not to take the case to court. But DA's are just people. Let's hope he's in a good mood."

"That would be wonderful," Alicia breathed.

"Ms. Green, we may still have a problem."

"What?"

"You had the drugs in your possession. Do you believe you're the first person who's said, 'These drugs were not mine'?"

"They were Rikki's," Kylie practically screamed.

"I believe you. Now we must prove it."

"My friends will testify the drugs were his, and don't forget he sold some at school."

"I hope so. But you wouldn't be the first surprised little girl if you find your friends have all been struck with amnesia." She winced. "I'll call the prosecutor first thing tomorrow. I'll get back to you all as soon as I know anything." She stood and shook hands.

Lexie and I walked toward the desk and Delores shook our hands as well.

"It's nice to see you again, Catherine."

"You too, and I know you'll give this your best shot." I hugged her.

"You can count on it, my friend."

We all left the room a little bedraggled.

Chapter 41

I sat in the driveway in front of my house. The minute I hit the garage door opener, Bailey would come running. Pulling myself together before greeting my family was paramount. Alicia could still be in trouble even though Kylie miraculously came forward for her mom. Waiting for Alicia to feel ready to face an attorney had been a mistake. Though I hated doing it, I should have pushed harder. By allowing weeks to pass, her case had already entered the system. We church girls didn't understand DA's and systems, nor how fast they worked when we wanted them not to hurry.

I had found Terry Richardson but he wouldn't testify. "Sara Beth, I promise you I am trying to prove your death wasn't an accident." But my family didn't deserve to catch all that on my face when I came home. Bailey's nightmare the evening I arrived home from Dallas broke my heart and the fault belonged to me.

I lowered all my car windows, hoping the neighbors weren't watching. Arms flailing, I pushed ghosts—the ones living in my head and inside my vehicle— outside of my car.

Reenergized, I glanced in the mirror then brushed my hair and refreshed my lipstick. I pushed the button.

Sure enough, Bailey came into the garage and pasted herself against the door to provide room for me to park the car.

She grinned all across her face.

I had insured improvements to my schedule since her nightmare, but this long day had ended with the attorney. I had explained why I would be late, but I hadn't shared Alicia might be in trouble. A seven-year-old didn't need that, and she loved her Li'sha very much.

I opened the car door. "Hey, turkey-lurkey. Don't you look cute today?"

She twirled. "Thanks. This is one of my best spinners." Bailey loved dresses that flared out when she twirled.

We walked inside the house arm-in-arm. "Mama, I'm glad we talked about the gift-and-call thing."

"Me too. God doesn't call people on the phone. A calling is a feeling you have that grips you and won't let go. A feeling that stays and never grows cold, to do a certain thing. And it can't be slept off, prayed off, or forgotten about. You must walk out your calling to be happy or fulfilled."

"I know. You told me already."

I tousled her hair. "You're right. Why are you glad we had the talk?"

"I figured out what gift I have."

"Okay."

"I think I have the gift to love the kids you bring home. Ms. Angie helped me understand you and Daddy help lots of kids, but I'm your girl no matter what." She beamed. "Others will visit here maybe one 'dark time' or two 'dark times' but you will probably take them home."

"You amaze me, child." I felt overwhelmed by her words. "Did you tell your dad about your gift?"

"Yes, ma'am. He said he couldn't wait for you to hear this. Then he said, 'I think God is really proud of you—just like I am.'"

We trekked inside. She tugged at my hand. "I'm sorry I wasn't nice to Elizabeth at first."

"Sweetheart, you more than made up for it. I love my baby girl."

Jordan had again filled my bathtub, laid my towels and robe on side of the tub. We'd had dinner and Bailey had been fed, bathed, devotioned, and tucked.

I stepped into the bubbles while he pulled an antique stool beside the tub to share his day and learn about mine. "What are Alicia's chances for getting the charges dropped?"

"It all depends on what the DA tells Delores when she meets with him." I lowered my body further into the water. "Other than that, it's a wait and see. And there's God."

He reached over to touch my face. "Speaking of God, what do you think of that daughter of ours and her deciding He gave her the gift of loving broken children?"

"I think we are the most blessed parents ever. She already has a heart for God." I laid my head on the bathtub pillow. "And, Jordan, to think we … you and I … have the gift of being the parents who taught her. The only background she knew before us was people who professed to love God but hated each other." I sat up. "It makes me crazy what a devout Christian her stepmother claimed to be while she openly despised Bailey. Who could hate the child who fills our hearts and this house with joy and laughter?"

"I don't know. But one thing I do know, she's a keeper."

I stood from the tub and Jordan dried my body with a fluffy towel. I reached for my robe, but he touched my hand to stop me.

"Do we really need the robe?"

"No."

He took my hand and led me from the bathroom.

#

I heard the first whisper of fall as I left the house for work. Trees turning color but leaves already tumbling toward the ground. In southeast Texas, turning leaves don't stay put long enough to photograph. But we have wonderful magnolia trees with their shiny green leaves that bloom with large, fragrant white blossoms. The state tree for Texas is the pecan tree, but any southerner ... and I am one ... will declare the magnolia to be the bell of the ball. I breathed in the promise of pumpkins, fall mums, the hope of lovely days, and cooler temperatures.

And my little girl had started third grade. She grew too rapidly.

Steve Giovanni interrupted my thoughts about trees and Bailey. He called my cell as I drove toward the clinic.

"Hey, Steve, what you got?"

"Katie, I returned from Dallas late last night."

"Terry Richardson?"

"Yep."

"And?"

He sighed. "And nothing. He wouldn't admit he even saw Cindy Thibbodeaux on July twelve. I could tell he had something, but he didn't want to talk."

"I'm sorry. Believe me, he saw her."

"I know. I could always subpoena him but until we have real evidence— such as his testimony—we don't have enough to go to court. So, no reason for a subpoena."

His frustration was palpable. And mine. "You and I both have done everything there was to do."

"That statement must taste like rusty nails." He chuckled. "I didn't think you ever gave up."

"I don't, but for now all we can do is leave it in higher and larger hands."

"I wish I could experience your certainty about God."

"You can."

"One day, I hope."

"Count on it."

"Well, I admit we need a miracle to move forward for Sara Beth."

"Catch you later. And Steve, we'll get a miracle."

#

Just as I ended the call from Steve, Alicia phoned.

"Katie, are you almost here?"

I heard tears in her voice. "Yes. Two minutes."

"Okay, hurry." Click.

I arrived, flew up the back steps, then into the hallway. No waiting clients yet. Alicia bolted from her chair when she spotted me.

Coming around her desk she walked straight into my arms.

I hugged her. "Ali, what's going on? Is there bad news from Delores?"

"No. But that lady knew what she was talking about."

I pushed back so I could examine her face. "Concerning?"

"You won't believe it. I don't believe it."

"Try me."

"Not one kid at school will testify for Kylie or against Rikki."

She stepped back and pushed her cross back and forth on its chain. "What will we do? What on earth will Kylie do? Kat, I'm not talking about casual friends, I'm talking about best friends that started kindergarten with her."

"Delores knows most everything there is about what happens in situations like Kylie's. She spoke to us from lots of experience." I bit at my lip. "I'm sad but not surprised."

"Well, Kylie is. Her friends—or I guess I should say kids from school who stood and watched Rikki doing drugs right in front of their faces—say they're not sure what they witnessed. Some of them are his customers. Customers with amnesia."

"They are scared they have culpability too."

"Kat, really, what am I going to do?"

"I'm not sure right this minute, but God is sure. He has watched this nightmare play out from the beginning. I believe there will be a happy ending, I just don't know how it will happen yet." I squeezed her hand. "And Kylie will survive as a better person. What if in the end this mess keeps Kylie out of more serious crimes than marijuana?"

"I have to trust that." She sniffed. "Kat, remember when I was your student years ago?"

"Yes, ma'am, I do."

"Remember when I knocked on your office door at the university and ended up giving my heart to God sitting right in the chair beside your desk?"

I smiled. "Of course, I remember."

"I ... well ... I'm just glad, that's all."

"Me too."

"You stood in front of our class talking about Freud, Pavlov, and the guy who first talked about schedules of reinforcement."

"B. F. Skinner."

"Yeah. Him. But Kat, it didn't matter who or what you talked about, you were just different. While I learned about Freud's stages of development, I learned something more important."

"Yeah?"

"Yeah. I learned you had something I didn't have. And I wanted it." She smiled as she dried a tear. "And I'm so glad I have God in my life now. Thank you, Kat."

"My greatest pleasure. But all I did was point the way."

"I know. But that's all I needed."

"And from your decision to accept Christ, faith came. And right now, we use our combined faith to believe there is an answer for Kylie and for you." I chucked her chin. "Just wait, you'll see."

Chapter 42

Excitement animated Lewis's voice. "You'll never guess what."

We were walking toward Dairy Queen. "Try me."

"I have …" he held out both hands in a ta-da pose, "… not will have, not gonna have, but have two hundred and sixteen dollars in my wallet."

I grinned and nodded at Lewis, arching my brows with mock surprise. "Get outta here."

Sometimes I loved my job.

#

After he celebrated his money, Lewis dropped his head and seemed quiet for a child who had been thrilled five minutes before.

"What's wrong?"

"Nothing."

"Remember, we pledged to tell only the truth to each other."

"I didn't listen to you about the medicine."

"Okay."

"I stopped taking it."

"All right."

"I guess you can figure out what happened?"

"Did you wet your bed, sweetheart?"

"Not the first night but by the third night."

"It took a few days for the medicine to clear out of your body."

"That's what my mom said."

"So, what did you decide about taking your meds in the future?"

"I'm not waiting for the future, I'm already taking them again."

"That's wise." I lifted his face with the back of my hand. "It's okay, Lewis. You needed to learn the value of your medication for yourself."

"I'll tell you one thing for sure." He held his shoulders high. "Sometimes I might forget to brush my teeth, or even forget clean underwear. But I will always remember my medicine."

I hugged him.

#

I couldn't sleep. A quick trip to the bathroom settled my bladder, but my brain remained in high gear. My covers tangled into knots. The kitchen called my name, but a snack and cup of warm milk did nothing. Bailey slept snug in her bed. I felt as though I anticipated something, but didn't know what.

The bedside phone rang. The clock heralded 1:00 a.m.

"Hello."

"Ms. Collier?"

A young man sounded nervous. "Yes, this is Catherine Collier. May I help you?"

"This is Terry Richardson. I hope it's okay to call. I know it's late."

"No, no. It's fine." It's fine. It's fine. It's wonderful.

"Do you remember me?"

He had no idea. "Of course, I remember you, sweetheart. I came to Dallas to speak with you."

"Yes, ma'am. I can call at a better time if you want."

"Oh no. This is a perfect time. I couldn't sleep."

"I probably shouldn't have called."

"Terry, you called to say something … and I want to hear it."

"A cop came to see me."

"Okay."

"About the same thing you came here to talk about." He coughed. "You know the baby who died and all."

"Did you talk to him?"

"He pushed too hard."

"He probably takes his job seriously."

"I guess."

Silence.

I waited.

"Been thinkin' 'bout that baby."

"Have you?" Me too. Me too. Come on, Terry. Don't push, Katie.

"I sure hate about that little girl."

"Me too."

"You didn't know her personal, did you?"

"As it happens, I did."

"Oh, no."

"Her death was tragic to many."

"She a relative or something?"

"No."

"I kept your card. Well, I threw it away several times, but I always rescued it."

"What made you hang on to it?"

"Because of what I told you I saw."

"All right."

"If they did hold a trial, and I decided to testify, do you think what I saw would be important?"

My chest became an inferno. Flames licked my vocal chords. "I do."

"I can't sleep without dreaming of the baby."

"That has to weigh heavy on you." I laid my hand on my drumming heart. "Sometimes ... well ... it has been my experience that when something is eating at you—something that won't let go or allow you to sleep—talking to the right person can bring relief."

"You mentioned something like that when you stood at my fence. Your business card says you're a counselor.

"Yes."

"I've been so miserable I think I'm ready."

Easy. Go easy. "To do what, Terry?"

"If you really believe testifying to what I saw could make a difference, I'll do it."

"I really believe it."

"Okay. Then I will."

"Are you positive you won't change your mind?"

"Man, I gotta sleep sometime. I gotta make the night monsters go away. I'm positive."

"First thing tomorrow when I speak to the detective working the case and tell him you're willing to testify, the Port Arthur police department will contact you. Can you handle that?"

"I called you this late because I have to get this off my chest. Moving didn't fix anything. Yes, ma'am, I can handle it."

"Terry, I can never thank you enough. And you can call here any time, day or night."

"Ms. Collier, for the first time since July twelfth, I feel sleepy. And don't worry. Once I make up my mind, I'm a sure thing."

"Good night, Terry. Have a wonderful rest."

"You too. Good night."

I lay there, grateful yet infinitely sad. What about Billy? What about his dad? What about Cindy? But there had been a precious baby girl. One who'd fluttered her baby lashes and called me K.T. Rob Martin's voice rang through my mind. "Katie, do you believe if a mother kills her own child, she should be held accountable for it?"

"Yes."

#

At first light I called Steve. I told him Terry Richardson had called and would testify.

"Well, Ms. Thang, how did you manage that?"

"I didn't. Just answered my phone."

"I went all the way to Dallas and tried everything to get that kid to talk." He groaned.

"Be grateful he called."

"I am."

I opened the fridge and chose a can of Diet coke. "What will happen now?"

"I'll talk this morning to the DA. I believe with Terry being willing to take the stand the DA will find probable cause to issue a warrant to search Ms. Thibodeaux's house." He paused a long minute. "I'd like one more piece of corroborating evidence, but we'll take what we have."

"Steve, when Terry testifies, Sara Beth's father will fold."

"How do you know?"

"I just know."

Chapter 43

Steve called my office at 5:00.

"What you got?"

"Can I come over?"

"Yes. I thought clients were back-to-back till 6:00, but I'm finished now. Jordan won't be expecting me before 6:15. I'll wait for you."

I passed the phone to Alicia. She reached limp-handed for it, shoving it back into the saddle. Depression spilled from her eyes and drooped her shoulders.

"You okay?"

"I could say yes, but it would be a lie."

She needed to hear from Delores. Like Anne Murray, she "sure could use a little good news today."

"I know. And there's always truth between us."

"We finished early. Go home and rest."

She eyed the phone.

"Delores has your home number."

"There's also telepathy between us." She smiled with still-rounded shoulders. "I will go if you don't mind. You coming?"

"Not yet. Steve is dropping by for a few."

"Steve?" she asked.

"Yes. Scoot. Circles are growing beneath your eyes."

Pollyanna appeared where Worried Wanda had stood. "Steve Giovanni?"

"The only Steve in my circle."

"I remember there's filing I need to finish." She twinkled. "And I'd dumped the leftover mud. He'll want it fresh."

"Mud?"

"Yeah, we were chatting and Steve said cops call coffee mud."

"Oh, he did, did he?"

Her cheeks pinked.

"And what further have you two chatted about?" I cocked my brow. "And why are you talking cop?"

"I'm not. But don't you think Steve's good-looking and all?"

"And all? You sound like a school girl crushing on a football player."

She stuttered. "No. I just wanted to make fresh mu … coffee."

Before the pot dripped, Steve walked through the clinic door.

That was Ali's clue to make herself scarce, but she forgot to leave. She posed in the hall and looked him over. She left the brew to rain into the pot then locked the front door behind him. I beckoned him toward my room but he slowed to say hello to her.

The air charged between them. I'd never known Alicia to show interest in a man since her divorce. Happiness bubbled in my thoughts. It was past time something good walked into my friend's life. I think he just had.

Trudging away from Ali reluctantly, Steve stopped at the counter, removed the carafe and pushed a mug under the flow.

I smiled and speared my finger though the curled hoop of a mug and filled it with Red Zinger. "Do you always hurry your coffee?" I laughed.

"At the department there never seems to be enough to go around, so we've learned shortcuts."

"Okay. What's on your mind?" Other than Alicia.

"I was at the DA's office by 9:00. He listened to what Terry Richardson said to you, then he called him and took his preliminary statement over the phone. Terry came through big time."

"Have you searched Cindy's house yet?"

"Yes, my partner and I pulled into her driveway right after lunch."

"And? Did you find anything that could lend credibility to your case?"

"We found nothing."

"Oh."

"You're not hearing me, Katie. We found *nothing*."

"I must be tired. Help me out here."

"Let's play out a scenario." He scooted forward on the sofa and I could feel his excitement.

"Let's do."

"Have you counseled with other clients who've lost children?"

"Unfortunately, yes."

"Have you listened to them describe what they did to preserve memories or even visited their homes to lend comfort?"

"Both."

"What did you see?"

"Some set up shrines to their children—not sure that was healthy—gathering everything their child had ever loved and put it on display. Framed school pictures from pre-K to the last grade attended." Memories cloistered my brain.

I started to glisten. "Some more conservative, but always the child's favorite stuffed animal or skateboard and framed pictures of the family's vacations and Christmases. Most kept the child's room exactly as it stood when last occupied."

"We. Found. Nothing."

I dropped my face into my cupped hands. "Nothing proving Sara Beth had ever lived there."

"That's it. Nothing kept. No tiny pink outfit worn home from the hospital. We opened the closet and drawers where Cindy reported having kept Sara Beth's belongings. Empty or full of her older daughter's clothes." Steve sipped his coffee. "We checked under beds attempting to find a forgotten toy. It appeared as though someone wanted even her memory gone. A clean slate."

The reality of his words left me speechless.

"The only clean spots in Cindy's house were places we should have found signs of Sara Beth."

"I'm accustomed to her housekeeping. My papa would have called her sloven."

"It's a circumstantial case. However, when enough circumstances coalesce, they can be the foundation for the best cases."

"Well, she did puke in her purse."

"Yeah, but what would your papa say? She was sloven." He slid further into the sofa. "I'm thinking of another issue."

"What?"

"Parking near the school where Rikki Anderson and Kylie attend school and check out the situation."

"You think you might see him doing something illegal—like selling drugs?"

"I won't know unless I try."

"True."

#

When Steve left—after lingering and laughing at Ali's desk, I drove toward Cindy's house.

She still had not called.

As I motored into her driveway, she tiptoed down her front steps.

Frown lines marked her face.

I lowered my window.

She leaned against my car.

"How are you, Cindy?"

"Better than you might think. I'm sad, but life goes on."

Faster for some than others. "I'd still expected to hear from you."

"Katie, I meant to call. But life got in the way. And I'm in a hurry so I have to leave."

"Okay." I started to back up but then stopped before Cindy reached her car. "Oh, Cindy."

"Yeah."

"Nice purse."

"Yeah. My old one finally fell apart."

"Oh." A dark sickness bubbled in my belly. I couldn't wait to get home. Sometimes I hated my job.

#

After dinner we played Sorry with Bailey. The little turkey beat me. She showed proficiency with board games and progressed in every school subject. Our smart, beautiful baby girl—growing up too fast.

We put her to bed with ballerina bear. Curled on her bedside, the desire to linger filled me. I touched her face over and over, tracing the outline of her cheekbones.

Jordan noticed the extra time I sat with her. "Katie, everything all right?"

"No. I mean yes."

Bailey watched me. "You seem worried."

"I left work a little sad today."

She brightened. "Do you need to bring a child here for me to love?"

"Not now, baby. But it means a lot that you asked."

#

After an extra fifteen minutes with Bailey, Jordan and I left her room.

He pulled me close when we reached the living room. "It's Sara Beth, isn't it?"

I stayed in his arms and told him everything Steve had shared with me.

"If she's guilty, and my heart says she is, somehow it's still sad that she's thrown her whole life away. It's heartbreaking. No matter what happens there will be no winners." I snuggled deeper into the arms of my solid rock. "Everybody loses."

Jordan poured both of us a glass of chilled wine. "You hardly ever drink, but this is as good a time as any."

"Thanks."

Walking to our suite, I set my glass on the bathroom vanity and hopped into a quick shower. I retrieved my stemmed-crystal and slid onto the bed with my husband.

We fluffed our pillows so we could sit in bed, sip our wine, and watch the 10:00 news.

The news anchor spoke. "We bring you our top news story tonight. Cindy Thibbodeaux was arrested today and charged with the murder of her three-year-old child." The news channel displayed a picture of her. "She left her small daughter in a van during the hottest part of summer in July, and the child died from heat exposure. Mrs. Thibbodeaux has always maintained her innocence, but the DA has received new evidence he believes will prove a willful act—not a tragic accident. Stay tuned for updates." The newscaster swiveled toward his co-anchor. "What inflammatory tweets has President Trump sent today?" She shrugged and laughed. "Well, as it turns out ..."

My brain turned to Swiss cheese.

Jordan pulled me inside the circle of his arms again. "You had to expect this arrest would happen."

"I did. But now it's so real. And how does Sara Beth's death belong in the same verbal paragraph with Donald Trump's tweets?"

"It's just a job for news anchors. They can't dwell on every story."

"It sounded so cold."

He touched my face. "I agree. It did."

"Jordan, nothing can ever happen to Bailey. Promise me."

"Sweetheart, I don't know more hands-on parents than we are. We watch her every minute she's with us and have run background checks on every after-school program she's ever attended." His arms circled tighter. "Katie, I didn't tell you this, but I had our attorney run additional checks on her ballet teacher and her gymnastics instructor."

He checked to see if his information soothed me.

It did.

"Oh, and after all we've heard about coaches, when our baby reaches high school, we'll know all about him before she sets foot on campus."

"I love you. You think of everything." Placing my glass on the table, I hugged him, slipped under the cover, and rolled over.

I'd been handed information about Cindy and Sara Beth I had worked hard to obtain. Yet I wept into my pillow.

#

The next morning I sat in front of my computer and typed: Texas Penal Code. If Cindy's jury found her guilty, she would face capital murder. A few years back Texas added a statute to its penal code relating to the murder of children under six. In such cases the perpetrator would face capital murder—resulting in a sentence of life without the possibility of parole. Furthermore, if the jury pushed hard enough a panel of four judges would decide if the offender would be put to death by lethal injection.

That information was hard to stomach before my first cup of hot tea.

#

I needed to see my daughter. Jordan usually awakened her with breakfast in bed but I wanted to wake her that morning.

"Of course. I'll fix her tray while you do that."

I thanked him and moved toward her room, crawling under the covers with her as I had so often when Jordan had moved out of the house last year, leaving just the two of us. I snuggled her and sniffed the sweetness of her.

She didn't wake for a few minutes, which was fine with me. I held her as she slept.

She opened her eyes and peered at me. "Mama, are you okay?"

"Absolutely. Why do you ask?"

"You seemed worried last night. You kept kissing me. And Daddy usually wakes me with breakfast." She squeezed my hand. "It's okay though. You can wake me anytime you want."

"I wanted to talk to you about something."

"Okay. What?"

"That I love you more than anyone except your dad."

"I know. I love you and Daddy more than anyone too."

"But today I want to make sure you understand we would never let anything happen to you." I brushed hair from her face. "We have been intentional not to leave you with anyone—not even your teachers—without confirming they are good people."

"Mama, I like all my teachers. They're good people."

"Believe me, your dad and I know for certain." Jordan trekked toward us.

"Are my girls ready for me?"

"Yes."

"Oh, yes sir, for sure."

He set the tray on her bedside table so he could hug and kiss her.

She reached for him with the same love and trust as she had me. We must always deserve that trust. *And Father, please watch her when we cannot.*

Chapter 44

October arrived with intermittent cooler days. Many warm days would still visit Port Arthur. As jury selection ended and Cindy's trial started, Bailey's birthday sneaked near. She'd been born the week of Halloween on the twenty-seventh.

Bailey and I sat at the table making party plans. Jordan had left to run an errand.

"What games do you want to play? The evening news is predicting the arrival of cooler weather by the end of the month, so the party could happen outside on the deck."

"Yes, ma'am. Our deck is huge. I can invite lots of people." She bounced in her chair. "Oh, if it's on the deck we can bob for apples without making a mess inside."

"Yes, we'll absolutely bob for apples."

"And pin the tail on the donkey?"

"Yes."

"Could Daddy play the guitar and teach everyone Jumbo the Elephant?"

"Ask him. I'm sure he will."

We heard Jordan's truck nose into the garage.

She ran to the door.

"Just the girl I wanted to see," Jordan said. "You can help me bring some things in the house."

I watched as they trudged inside. Bailey's arms were laden with two large pots of mums—one red and one golden yellow.

"Set those on the hearth," Jordan directed, "and we'll grab the other things."

"Okay, Daddy."

Jordan had always loved the fall season. When he and Bailey had retrieved everything from his truck, we owned eight pumpkins and six pots of mums in various colors. I helped arrange them in glorious clusters around the fireplace hearth and mantel, and in the center of the kitchen table. Bailey and I pulled fall-colored foil wrapping around the pots and tied huge raffia bows. Like her dad, Bailey was infatuated with October.

"I've never seen so many punkins and pretty flowers."

I cocked my head sideways. "Get used to it. Your dad loves autumn."

"Who's Autumn?"

I explained while Jordan laughed. He loved autumn and Bailey, and he loved me.

#

Bailey reveled in her party. The deck held everything she had asked about. But we also rented a blow-up castle filled with balls for the kids to navigate and toss at each other. We hired a magician who performed all the best tricks. The caterers provided an ice-cream bar, allowing the kids to concoct their own sundaes. Each happy child left encumbered by a bag filled with surprises.

How often does God hand one a child?

Jordan and I lay in bed later that night, exhausted and happy.

He pulled me into his arms. "Do you think she liked it?"

I laughed. "It happened to be the best birthday bash ever."

"The enormity of her party," he said, "made me wonder what in the world we'll do for her wedding." He chuckled. "We didn't give her a celebration last year. I feel bad about that."

"Baby, you didn't live here last October, and no matter how much I loved Bailey, there was no party in me. I kept myself busy losing weight and grieving."

He took a deep breath. "You'll never have to face that again."

"I know."

"You're quiet." He looked at me. "You're usually all chatty after an event. Are you thinking about Cindy and her family?"

"Yes. Cindy should have to pay for taking Sara Beth's life, but even as unlikable as she can be, I don't have to be happy about it."

"I hardly know her, and it makes me sad. My heart breaks for you, Katie Girl. And for Billy."

"It's Billy I'm most concerned about."

Jordan fell asleep while I hugged him and worried. Alicia's situation hadn't been resolved either. *Father, we need a miracle.*

My thoughts drifted between the two people with serious situations. Alicia, whom I loved, and Cindy … not so much. I would feel sorry for her, for what her future held, and then I would see Sara Beth kiss Mickey's hand or clap hers together after snapping a puzzle into place.

Cindy had said, "I think she's stupid."

God, your will be done.

#

I walked into the office Monday morning. Alicia almost ran me over.

"Well." I held her in my arms. "This is either terrible or fantastic news."

"Oh, Kat. You won't believe it, you just will not believe it."

"Let's grab something to drink, then have a seat in my office and tell me what ya got."

"Okay. But you don't have a lot of time to listen."

"Ali, if someone has to wait ten minutes it won't wreck their day."

"You're correct."

Her hands quivered, so I filled both our mugs and walked behind her into my treatment room. Her face gave away nothing.

"Delores Washington called."

Something vacuumed my lungs. I spent more awake time with Ali than anyone else on earth, including Jordan and Bailey. She could not go to prison for something she Did. Not. Do.

"What did she say?"

"First I have to tell you what Steve did."

"Do tell."

"For the past two school days he staked out Rikki's school. Thursday turned up nothing. However, Friday Steve peered through binoculars as Rikki strolled into the school yard after lunch with a couple friends. Steve observed the exchange of a small packet from Rikki to a second student. Steve leapt from his vehicle, found the drugs and arrested both guys on the spot. The one student for possession, but he charged Rikki with possession and trafficking."

A parade started in my head. Bells, whistles, the whole shebang. "Then what?"

"Steve took both boys downtown, booked them, and they're cooling their heels in the county jail."

"Has Rikki confessed to anything?"

"No, but Steve caught him red-handed."

"Did Delores tell you this?"

"No. Steve phoned me at home last night."

"Oh, he did? Now what would make him think to call you at your house? And wonder why he didn't call me?"

"I told him I'd tell you."

"Interesting."

"Well, you know."

A grin spread across my face. "Yes, I do know."

Color crept up her neck.

"What did Delores say?" I asked.

"Oh, Steve called her too. Based on the information he relayed, she has a solid case against Rikki Anderson."

"Give me the bottom line."

"According to Ms. Washington, the DA charged Rikki with possession and trafficking of illegal substances. It was marijuana he sold at school but when his home was searched the detectives found cocaine. A felony." She grimaced. "He'll go to prison."

"And the charges against you?"

"I'll still have to face the judge, but Ms. Washington expects with a first offense, a clean record, and great character witnesses, I should be okay. She anticipates the judge dropping charges."

I left my chair and knelt before her. "This is the miracle I have been storming heaven over. Let's offer a gratitude prayer." I sniffed. "Father, we have asked, and you have answered." I flashed back to a picture in my mother's entryway. Jesus standing outside a door knocking. "Your Word says we don't have because we don't ask. Alicia and I have bombarded you asking that the truth be revealed." I stopped to wipe snot and tears. "Father, we both know Steve didn't just happen upon Rikki selling drugs. The timing was yours. For this miracle, that neither of us could ever have earned, you freely gave as a gift. And we thank you. Words are insufficient, yet we offer up our voices in praise for your mercy and grace."

She sat in silence.

"Do you want to pray?"

She cried so hard she couldn't.

She ultimately looked up and whispered, "God, what she said."

I held her and laughed. "Joy comes in the morning."

"Oh, yes."

"Did Delores say anything else?"

"That she's happy for me."

"We are thankful for this godsent miracle. However, I want you to promise if anything even resembling this should happen again, you'll call me before you touch the problem." I squeezed her hands. "Jordan and I will come up with a plan that requires a cool head. He's a great problem solver."

"I'm grateful. Kat, how do we get your money back?"

"I imagine after you stand before the judge, and Delores is correct about charges against you being dropped, his office will provide paperwork. He should give us a copy we can fetch to the bail bondswoman. She should return the money."

I heard Olivia and Ron enter the building.

"Okay missy, we must go to work."

"Oh, mercy, I didn't mean to talk this long."

I released her hands and stood. "I prayed too long and hard for this miracle not to hear every detail."

Ali skipped and danced all around my office. "Father, I love it when you show up, but I like it even better when you show out."

I watched her waltz out my door, singing a little ditty as she traveled to her desk. "God, you have saved me. I'm not going to prison. You are gracious. I'm so unworthy. You did it anyway. I praise your name."

Nothing could top that. I hurried to the ladies' room. Clients waited. I slapped on additional makeup and combed my hair. A quick glance in the mirror proclaimed I should have started from scratch. But I had no time for a do-over. I reapplied the sponge, but it was pitiful. All day I wore a patch job.

Chapter 45

Thanksgiving season swept its way to our house. The days turned cool enough for a sweater. Angie, Olivia, Ron, and Lauren proved to be invaluable at the clinic. Alicia switched on praise music as she worked and fell smack dab in love with Steve Giovanni. With Terry Richardson's witness, and the testimony of her husband, Rob, Cindy had been found guilty of murder and sentenced to life with no parole.

I appreciated that she wouldn't have to die. She'd sadly gotten what she'd wanted—a life without a child to bother her ever again. And Rikki Anderson had stood before a judge for a bench trial. The judge sentenced him to seven years in federal prison.

Lewis Davis had a sixth-grade dance. He grinned all over—entering my office with the confidence of Theo Huxtable—when he reported the girl had asked him. Of course, he brought pictures. Both looked beautiful and happy.

#

Billy's sadness tied me in knots.

"My mama is goin' somewheres for a very long time."

"I know."

"How'd 'ya know?"

"I talked to your dad."

"He's bin cryin'."

"Yes. He's heartbroken."

"I won't have no mama till she gits back. How long ya' think she's gonna be gone?"

"A long time, sweetheart."

"How 'bout could ya be my mama till she gits back?"

"Your dad loves you very much and would be sad if you left. He's already sad about your mom and we can't make him sadder." I pulled him onto my lap on my living room sofa.

"I don't understand where Sara Beth is."

"Did you ask your dad?"

"Yeah, but he jus' walks around in the backyard."

I kissed his cheek. "Sara Beth is dead, Billy."

He turned in my lap, face to face. "I had a dog once that died. He never comed back."

"Sara Beth won't be back either. I'm so sorry."

"She's a good sister."

"Yes, she was a wonderful sister."

"Ever'body's leavin'."

"Not your dad. And I've asked him if you may come to my house for dinner two nights a week, and he said yes."

He put his arms around my neck. "I glad. Who's gunna keep me when he works?"

"I asked him that. First of all, you'll also come see me at the clinic two days instead of one, and he's hired your favorite neighbor to care for you till he gets home each day."

"Miss Smith?"

"That's right. Mrs. Smith. She's excited to care for you." I patted his shoulder. "She says you're at her house a lot, anyway."

"Yeah. She bakes cookies and ever'thing."

"You'll be okay. I'll be checking on you often."

"A lot?"

I grinned. "Yes, a lot."

I drove him home to his father, with my heart in my throat.

Bailey placed flatware beside the plates. "Are we still going to Grandma's house for Thanksgiving?"

"Absolutely. She's anxious to see you."

"Me too. I haven't seen her for a long time."

"I know. Two weeks without Grandma is a long spell."

She grinned. "Well, I love her a whole bunch."

"She loves you more."

"No. I love her more."

I winked at my daughter. I set additional candles at the table and lit every one. Tapers, short fat ones, and votive cups. The pumpkins cast an orange glow as the light reflected their sheen.

Jordan walked through the door. "For months you have worried too often. Tonight, you and the table look as if you have something to celebrate. I know you're relieved about Alicia being cleared."

"Yes."

"Anything else?"

Bailey glanced up waiting for my answer.

"I'll tell you after dinner. Both of you remain seated after you've eaten. I have a surprise."

Dinner lasted an eternity.

When our plates sat empty, I stood and retrieved my purse.

Bailey stared at me. "Hey. Where you going?"

"The surprise is in my purse."

"Okay then. Will I like it?"

Jordan stayed put, watching me.

I returned to the table and opened my handbag. "This has been a difficult year. I wanted us to do something special together."

They both nodded.

I pulled gift-wrapped flat envelopes from my purse. "I have one too." They stared at me. "So, open them already."

They tore at paper and ribbon.

Jordan looked up after scrutinizing the contents of his envelope. "Katie Girl, is this for real?"

I bobbed my head.

Bailey scrunched her face. "I don't know what mine is."

Jordan stood and wrapped his arms around my shoulder while grinning at her. "Little one, it appears your mom has purchased tickets for the three of us for Hawaii." He read further. "Looks like it's two full weeks."

"My job is hard on all of us. You both deserve this and so do I. We'll leave the week after Christmas."

Jordan sat down. "Katie, you have never left your clients for two weeks. Ever. Can we count on this for sure?"

"You bet. Alicia will be here and she has help now. And she won't be lonely. Angie, Olivia, and Ron are all good therapists. I have a supervision meeting with the two interns each week. They're ready. And Angie has built herself quite a practice."

His brows shaped into question marks.

"Mama, I never been on an airplane before. Is it scary?"

"You'll sit between your dad and me."

"I won't be scared then."

Jordan's eyes glued to mine. "Is there anything that could stop this trip from happening?"

"I need to make sure I'm feeling well enough to go."

He reached for my hand. "Are you ill?"

"Not at all. I went to my OB-GYN a month ago. Other than the obvious, I don't know how this happened. We're pregnant."

CPSIA information can be obtained
at www.ICGtesting.com
Printed in the USA
LVHW090516071019
633380LV00001B/1/P

9 781946 016874